Fear and Yoga

in

New Jersey

Also by Debra Galant

Rattled

DEBRA GALANT

Fear and Yoga

in

New Jersey

ST. MARTIN'S PRESS 🜄 NEW YORK

This is a work of fiction. All of the characters, organizations, and events portrayed in this novel are either products of the author's imagination or are used fictitiously.

www.stmartins.com

Library of Congress Cataloging-in-Publication Data

Galant, Debra.
    Fear and yoga in New Jersey / Debra Galant.—1st ed.
        p.   cm.
    ISBN-13: 978-0-312-36725-1
    ISBN-10: 0-312-36725-2
    1. Hatha yoga—Fiction. 2. New Jersey—Fiction. 3. Domestic fiction. I. Title.

PS3607.A385F43   2008
813'.6—dc22
                                                              2007043633

First Edition: March 2008

10 9 8 7 6 5 4 3 2 1

For my parents, Ray and Shirley,
who bought me my first typewriter
and praised the things that came out of it.

Acknowledgments

Thanks first and foremost to Dori Weintraub at St. Martin's Press, every author's dream editor and publicist, and to Lisa Bankoff at ICM, for putting us together. Also to Holly West at St. Martin's and Tina Dubois Wexler at ICM for all the things they do, big and small.

For meteorological help, thanks to Ken LaPenta and Bruce Carmichael. Everything I got right about the weather is because of them. All the mistakes are my own.

For the much-needed time and respite, thanks to the Virginia Center for Creative Arts, the Geraldine R. Dodge Foundation, and the Kripalu Center for Yoga and Health. And special thanks to Liz George, my business partner at Baristanet, for giving her blessing to all my absences.

For friends who help in all kinds of ways, whether it's supplying advice, cookies, or Adirondack chairs: Liza Dawson,

Pam Satran, Dot Frank, Sue Kasdon, Jessica Sporn, Fran Liscio, Susan Borofsky, Nicky Mesiah, and John Mutter. Thanks to Margot Sage-El and Lillian Trujillo, booksellers extraordinaire, for service above and beyond.

And to the residents of my home and heart, Warren, Margot, and Noah, thank you for allowing me to live inside my laptop—and, even more, for occasionally pulling me away.

You can safely assume that you've created God in your own image when it turns out that God hates all the same people you do.

—Anne Lamott

Fear and Yoga

in

New Jersey

Friday

Nina was in the middle of yoga nidra with her nine o'clock intermediate class when Debby Jacobs from the ten-thirty beginners ran in. Interrupting yoga nidra, as everyone knew, was a major breach of yoga etiquette. Even a beginner should know better. Nina closed her eyes and allowed herself a deep, long exhalation before deciding how to handle the intrusion. Ginseng candles were lit, Gaelic flute music floated up from the speakers of a portable CD player, and all seven members of the class lay flat on their backs as they imitated corpses. If there was one thing that distinguished Nina's classes from the dozens of other yoga classes available locally, it was the hard-wrought serenity achieved during yoga nidra—the practice of complete relaxation—which took up the last five minutes of each class. Nina was strict about no giggling or whispering—even in the classes filled with writers, who never wanted to shut up, ever. It was a time of rest and regeneration. But there she was, Debby Jacobs, bringing all her Russell terrier energy into the studio and positively gyrating with excitement.

Nina placed a silencing finger on her lips. Already Anita Banschek had popped open a curious eye.

In an exaggerated pretense of civility, or else her interpretation of Marcel Marceau imitating a burglar, Debby tiptoed over. "I really didn't want to interrupt," she said. "I knew you'd be mad. But"—she lowered her voice and made the universal gesture for waves, or a snake, maybe—"there's a flood in the waiting room."

It had been barely three weeks since Nina moved into her new yoga studio, in the swankest part of town, where brick crosswalks set in a herringbone pattern provided safe pedestrian passage for the blond wives and children of the rich men who took off for New York every morning on the 5:58, the 6:27, and the 7:03 to move massive amounts of other people's money around.

The shopping district was in one of the older Essex County towns, where, with the exception of a few gaucheries like Dunkin' Donuts, things looked pretty much as they had for decades: parking meters, alleyways between Tudoresque buildings, a movie theater whose old-fashioned marquee was protected by a historic preservation commission, and street planters carefully tended by a committee of shopkeepers. The timeless effect was reinforced by a towering verdigris-edged public clock, the old-fashioned analog kind with hands that swept around in a circle as they counted off the dull suburban hours, paid for by a local jeweler in business for three generations and now part of the township's official logo.

The commerce, in this part of town anyway, tended toward goods and services that pampered and cosseted. Except for the contents of one hardware store (specializing in brass house numbers and Ralph Lauren paints) and one deli, there was nothing for sale that anyone could possibly consider a necessity. If, on the other hand, you were looking for candlesticks in the shape of fez-wearing monkeys and were willing to pay $183, you'd come to the right place. But for the occasional thirtyish male with shaved head and tiny glasses tapping away on a screenplay in Starbucks, the district might be a sorority composed of women twenty-five and up. The younger ones jogged after infants perched in special aerodynamically designed chariots. Women a bit older held the tiny peanut butter–smeared hands of toddlers who had known only toys made of wood and natural fibers. Women in their thirties or forties, wearing impossibly small jeans and talking on cell phones, darted into hair salons and therapist offices, running hard to accomplish whatever they could before three o'clock, when they turned into taxi services for lacrosse-playing, karate-chopping, Irish step-dancing, back-talking offspring. Women old enough to have grown children emerged from expensive German cars, bearing shopping bags almost always destined for return.

This wasn't Nina's milieu, not exactly, though it was comfortable enough. It did make her a bit self-conscious of her peasant ancestry, of the fact that her hair was black and coarse and puffed up at the slightest hint of humidity and that, no matter how much yoga she did, her body tended toward the zaftig. In fact, the neighborhood was kind of a WASP version of the Long Island town where she'd grown up—although she liked to think she'd outgrown all that and arrived at a more enlightened place. She'd been raised in Princess territory, bred to marry a dentist like her father, and had been bestowed with a Bloomingdale's card, her very own name embossed and capitalized across the bottom, at her sweet sixteen party—equipment for honing the shopping skills critical to the Long Island Jewish matriarchy to which she was supposed to aspire.

Alas, those aspirations were dashed in twelve short weeks during her sophomore year at Brandeis, when she took a life-altering women's studies class. It all started with Anna Mae Babcock, a pioneer woman who'd lost two children to whooping cough in the summer of 1817, whose diary was assigned as an example of the rare primary source that recorded "her-story" rather than "history." Nina had known, of course, about the tragically high rate of child mortality, but she'd assumed that there hadn't been too much grief, because such deaths were so common. Anna Mae's diary put an end to that misconception. Then she read stories of Chilean women whose husbands had been taken in the middle of the night by the henchmen of Augusto Pinochet. As Nina read of their terror and their bravery, their fearless demands for answers as they sought their husbands' remains, Nina began to see her own life for the silly two-dimensional cartoon that it was.

When she came home that year for winter break, Nina was determined to interview her *bubbe* about the pogroms in Russia. But Nina's mother dismissed the idea with a wave of the hand. "Who wants to remember all that?" she said. "Please, she gets agitated." Later, when Nina saw her mother's cleaning woman, a Guatemalan named Feliz, down on her knees scrubbing the kitchen floor, she tried to liberate her on the spot. "You don't have to clean rich people's houses just because you're of color!" Nina said. "You should go back to school, get a degree." But Feliz's command of English was marginal. "You want colors done? Laundry?" she asked, running upstairs to Nina's hamper to put in a dark wash.

Nina shopped for new clothes during that break, haunting thrift shops and adopting a new uniform of long skirts, gauze blouses, man-style work boots. She stopped wearing gold, which broke her mother's heart, preferring instead chunky jewelry made of silver and turquoise. After college, she moved to a Brooklyn neighborhood her parents found menacing, worked at jobs they considered dead-end, and decorated her rooms with a series of parental castoffs that otherwise would have gone to Feliz.

The migration from Brooklyn to New Jersey, a few years after marrying Michael, wasn't so unusual. It was a well-established route, trod by many earlier pioneers, so she was reassured that there would be organic food co-ops and used book stores when she got there. It helped that the town was a shade-dappled place with fine wraparound porches and old-fashioned rose-covered trellises, much sought after by filmmakers and people who made TV commercials, and unlike the suburb she grew up in, her adopted town had black people. The integration of the public schools was almost as much a matter of civic pride as the fact that there were six Thai restaurants in town. True, she wasn't the renegade she'd been in her twenties, but she prided herself on being a good citizen of Mother Earth. She drove a Prius, recycled religiously, eschewed synthetics, shopped organic, drank bottled water, and bought all her stationery from third-world countries.

And she taught yoga. What could be more vital in today's stressed-out world? She'd started when Adam went to full-day kindergarten, and had made a lovely studio in the attic of her house. But it was cramped; she could have only three students at a time; heating and air-conditioning were problematic. Nina had decided last spring, after a consultation with a highly regarded tarot reader, to expand her business and she'd been looking for space on the grittier end of town, or what her *bubbe* would have called the *schvatze* neighborhood, where the hair-braiding joints and check-cashing establishments were, but which had recently attracted an upscale French restaurant that had gotten a good review in the Jersey section of the *New York Times*.

But this space, her new studio in the posh end of town, had opened up quite unexpectedly and was just too good to pass up. It had last been occupied by a ballet teacher, now facing child-endangerment charges, who'd had to vacate rather suddenly after it came out that she'd slapped some of her young students. The landlord, wanting to put the scandal quickly behind him, let Nina pick up the lease at a bargain price. It was a lovely space, with tall floor-to-ceiling north-facing windows, which infused the second-story room with a serene light. As a former ballet studio, the space had floors that were already gleaming, a polyurethaned light oak, and the wall opposite the windows was fully mirrored, adding to the sense of openness and light, and allowing her students to see how their poses actually looked.

It took almost nothing for Nina to convert the space, just a small outlay for yoga mats, pillows, and blankets. She'd also put a nice sisal rug over the ugly linoleum floor in the waiting room to add some warmth, picked up a Tibetan fabric wall hanging, and found some simple chairs in a birch veneer from Ikea. The final touch, the one thing she'd hoped to provide the enchanting entrance to her studio, was the chakra meditation fountain, which she'd ordered over the Internet and which, she supposed correctly, was causing the flood.

Michael Summer took his pink slip, which actually wasn't pink at all but a regular white 8½×11 inch piece of paper, creased it down the middle, folded each side into a nice flap, folded it again to create wing tips for additional lift, and touched the pointy little nose with pride of craftsmanship. Then he walked out onto the control tower's weather observation deck and launched the plane in the general direction of the tarmac.

Just an hour ago, he'd been on autopilot, driving down the Parkway with his windows down because it was unseasonably warm and the air-conditioning in the ten-year-old Honda was still broken, then rolling them up as he passed the fried chicken joints and liquor stores of Irvington. The four blocks of ghetto were part of his route because the highway engineers had been too stupid or cheap to build an actual eastbound exit ramp from the Parkway to I-78. Thirty minutes ago, he'd typed his user name and password into the system and discovered, three times, that it was no longer providing him entry into the airline's dispatch system. Twenty minutes ago, he'd called his supervisor to find out what the hell was going on, and just a minute ago, he'd been handed the piece of paper informing him that his job had been outsourced. To the frigging Philippines.

Apparently anybody, anywhere in the world with a working Internet connection and who knew how to read a synoptic chart, could do Michael's job: letting the pilots and air dispatchers know whether it was safe to put planes into the air above Newark.

The paper airline sailed effortlessly for about thirty feet, after which it spun several times and nose-dived onto a black tar roof. The crash destroyed the plane's fuselage but still the breeze picked it up and carried it onto the ground. Michael watched as it rolled and bounced toward the runway like a paper tumbleweed, and then stared out for a long while after it disappeared. It was the first time he'd made a paper airplane since he was a kid.

He turned to the process of clearing his desk. A lackey from the airline had already brought him a corrugated box to pack everything in. There was a pictogram on the box showing a person putting items from a desk into a box and waving goodbye. Amazing. They actually manufactured packing crates just for downsizing. People were employed in some factory somewhere at this very moment making boxes expressly designed to cart off other people's careers. Strange, and strange, too, that he should be packing already, just minutes after being told his job had been eliminated. He'd expected two weeks' notice. Wasn't that the American way? Two weeks' vacation, two weeks' notice? But apparently, the last thing anybody at an airport wanted in this age of terrorism and office shootings was a soon-to-be-terminated employee hanging around with an airport ID and a fat grudge. He was told to be out before lunch, although his compensation package, of course, would run for several months.

There wasn't much to put in the box. A photograph of Nina and Adam on vacation in Cape Cod, his prize nineteenth-century nautical barometer, some swag he'd picked up at weather conventions—key chains and mouse pads advertising various online weather services. Everything else, everything he used to ply his trade, was online, on the computers. Michael remembered what his father had said, all those years ago, when he'd been deciding between joining the merchant marines and enrolling in the atmospheric sciences program at Penn State. "You always have a job with a career in meteorology, son. No matter what happens in this world, there'll always be weather."

His father was half right. There would always be weather. Only now, like everything else, it could be outsourced. He thought about calling Nina, but he didn't want to interrupt her day. To be honest, he really didn't want to tell her at all. She was already anxious about money, more so since she'd started paying rent on her new yoga studio. No, after he was packed, he'd just go home. Nina could wait until dinner to find out.

Michael stopped at the door and put his box down for a minute, looking back at all the guys with their headsets and their computer monitors, all busy in the process of landing and launching planes, and took a second to freeze the image before he walked out. Charlie Kavorski, Ed Halloran, Jack Knutson, guys he'd known for years. He'd taken phone messages from their wives, listened to their vacation stories, given them cigars when Adam was born. He couldn't believe this was it, his last time in the control tower.

Charlie Kavorski looked up from his monitor and flicked

Michael a tiny salute. Michael saluted back, then bent down for his box and left.

"Continue with your yoga nidra. I'll be right back," Nina said to the class, before allowing Debby Jacobs to lead her into the waiting room. Debby's step had a little premature victory in it, as if she were an eight-year-old who'd just pulled her mother away from the stove to tattletale on a misbehaving sibling. Flood? Nina was sure Debby was making a big deal out of nothing. Someone had probably spilled a cup of tea.

Yet, sure enough, when Nina entered the waiting room, she found her ten-thirty beginners all perched on top of chairs, looking as if they'd just smashed through a roof and were awaiting rescue from a hurricane. "There!" Debby said, vindicated, jutting her chin in the direction of the gushing fountain.

There was already an inch of water on the floor, rising quickly, and Nina saw that it was almost to the level of the electric outlet she'd plugged the fountain into. Worse yet, she was in charge. In a jumble, the situation presented itself to her brain: Water! Electricity! She knew they shouldn't mix, but she didn't have time to puzzle the situation out. Reaching down to unplug the cord seemed foolhardly. And yet if she didn't . . .

Nina grabbed the cord and instantly felt an unholy tingling, as if she'd just been struck by a giant tuning fork. A split second later she was up on a chair herself, with the rest of the class, looking down as the plug thrashed, sizzled, and sputtered in the puddle below.

So this is how it was to end. She was going to die, along with her entire ten-thirty beginners class, electrocuted by a meditation fountain.

Breathe, Nina told herself. Breathing was the simple admonition she always relied on in a crisis, and yet strangely, at this moment, it didn't seem to help. Still, she couldn't afford to fall apart. She was the teacher, the guru. And, more ominously, the proprietor. The one who would get sued. Or prosecuted? Nina quickly scanned the room. They were still all there, on the chairs, more wide-eyed than ever, but alive. Thank God for small miracles.

But now, ridiculously, she was stuck atop an Ikea chair, looking down at the lethal brew, knowing that at any moment her intermediate students could get up from yoga nidra or more beginning students could waltz in. Nina calculated the distance between her chair and the studio door, and planned a Tarzan-style leap. Yes, she could do it. She could leap off the chair, push open the door, and land, safe and dry, in the studio. And then what? She didn't know, but something would come to her.

"I'll be back," she yelled to the troops before her jump. "Stay out of the water."

Nina executed her leap, throwing her weight against the door, then tumbling back into the studio with a leaden thump. Several of the corpses lifted their lazy heads, but Nina (ever the yoga teacher) signaled them to continue resting. She longed to join them herself, to pull up a mat and lie down, not to be the one in charge of this emergency. Instead, she grabbed a blanket off Sue Kasdon, who was always complaining about hot flashes anyway, ran back out to the waiting room, and threw it onto the floor. The water slowly bubbled up through the blanket's natural fibers, drawing patterns in little continents, which grew and connected to each other until the whole blanket was one sopping mess. She stood there, allowing the blanket to do its job, and when she was convinced that the electric cord had stopped writhing, Nina picked up the fountain and dragged its dribbling hulk down the hall to the ladies' room. It was a very bad sign that her new chakra meditation fountain, purchased to consecrate her new studio, had caused a nearly lethal flood. What, she wondered, had she done to aggravate the universe?

It was the day before Lisa Epstein's bat mitzvah, and the cafeteria of Central Junior High School was positively thrumming with anticipation. The girls were talking about how much they would dress up, the boys about how much they could dress down. Mara Peebles and Jenna Heller had appointments for manicures and pedicures right after school, but Lisa easily topped that, announcing that local cosmetics mogul Bobbi Brown herself was coming to Lisa's house at seven-thirty Saturday morning to personally apply her bat mitzvah day makeup. A few unpopular kids, on the wrong side of the social divide, moved peas around with their forks, hoping no one would notice their silence. Being on the guest list for Lisa Epstein's bat mitzvah was crucial, this being the first big social event of the fall, way bigger than the back-to-school hoedown organized by the parent–teacher association to welcome the new seventh-graders, bigger even than the first school dance, planned for Halloween. It wasn't that anybody relished waking up early on Saturday to sit for hours in synagogue; it was the party Saturday night that mattered. And it all mattered because of who Lisa Epstein was, Central Junior High's answer to Paris Hilton.

Lisa was big. *Big* meaning tall, *big* meaning popular, *big* meaning developed. And big because it was rumored, and probably true, that Lisa's father worked as a lawyer for Joey "the Undertaker" DeFilippo, who was now, despite Mr. Epstein's best efforts, in the middle of a twelve-year stint in Leavenworth. DeFilippo was reputedly the most important Mafia figure in Essex County and supposedly the inspiration for TV's Tony Soprano. It was widely believed that mob money had paid for the Epstein family's Costco-proportioned house and pool, as well as the horse that Lisa boarded at the stables in West Orange. Lisa, of course, did nothing to dispel such rumors. It was, in fact, a Lisa Epstein legend that when the assistant principal took away her cell phone in sixth grade, she'd fixed him with a defiant stare and said, "You know, I could have you killed." She'd come to school with a new, tinier cell phone the next day, and the assistant principal, over the summer, accepted an assignment as a wrestling coach and gym teacher at a high school in Morris County.

Lisa's bat mitzvah invitations had been colossal, almost the size of the things Adam's parents called record albums. There was $1.82 in postage on each one, and when you opened the envelope, gold-colored confetti exploded out like July Fourth fireworks. Luckily, Adam had made the cut. One of the monster invitations had shown up in his mail, and the confetti had spilled all over the living room floor. So, of course, had Adam's best friend, Philip, who stood seven inches taller than Adam and who, because of his height, affected the bearing of someone much older and more sophisticated. Philip's pedigree also included being the son of a former foreign diplomat (now at the UN) who had lived in Paris, Geneva, and Moscow. So it was hardly surprising that Philip was now explaining, for the benefit of those poor benighted eighth-graders whose parents had not served as foreign diplomats, what exactly did and did not constitute black tie.

Philip also spoke with authority because he was Jewish, 100 percent. Adam, on the other hand, was only half Jewish, and his mother was anything but proud of her heritage. Nina Gettleman acted as if being Jewish were something to outgrow, like Long Island, or a speech impediment. When she saw Lisa Epstein's big lavender invitation and the residue of glitter it had deposited over the living room floor, she'd shaken her head in disgust and announced to Adam that thirty-six dollars was all she planned to write a check for. Lavish bar and bat mitzvahs, Adam knew, set his mother's teeth on edge. Which was just part of the reason why, after she'd married a non-Jewish husband and had a child, she'd joined them up to be members of the local Unitarian Church.

"And if you want to rent a tuxedo, you're going to have to do it with your own money."

Adam, who didn't like to dress up even in a suit, had no interest in renting a tux for Lisa Epstein's bat mitzvah. In fact, he'd been wondering whether he could wear a baseball cap in the synagogue, rather than a yarmulke. Now he was discovering that Philip not only planned to wear a tux to the nighttime party at the Mountain Edge Chalet, but he *owned* one.

"No baseball cap," Philip said. "And I'll lend you the tux I outgrew in fourth grade."

Suddenly, to Adam's relief, the conversation lurched in a much more interesting direction. How much money, Chris Atalier asked, did people think Lisa Epstein would get?

"No way," said Philip. "Asa Samuelson got eight thou, and his parents don't live in a mansion. Think about it. These mob guys, they give out envelopes filled with fifty-dollar bills at regular old birthday parties. Don't you watch *The Sopranos*? And there's all her rich relatives, too. Twelve thou. Minimum. And I wouldn't be surprised to hear twenty."

Chocolate milk spurted from Adam's mouth. "What?"

"Oh, believe it, my friend," Philip said, handing him a napkin.

"And how much are you, you know, are your parents, um, giving her?"

"Oh, a hundred. That's standard."

Adam gulped. That was sixty-four dollars more than his mother planned to give, and he couldn't exactly take a check written by his mom and cram extra cash into the envelope. What a racket, he thought, having a party and then charging people to come.

It was three o'clock, and all her classes were over for the day. The floor in Nina's waiting room was finally dry, but a big blister of water damage had bubbled up and stared accusingly like a linoleum cyclops. Great, just great. What would it cost to fix that? And then there was that big klutz, Charlotte Hendricks, who'd dashed into the ten-thirty beginners class ten minutes late and gone flying when she hit the slick floor, landing smack on her tailbone. Nina had apologized profusely—she felt terrible, just terrible, as if she was personally responsible for Charlotte's pain—even though anyone with a grain of sense wouldn't try to sprint late into a yoga class. For ten full minutes, Charlotte had whimpered pitifully on the floor, preventing anyone else from getting any yoga done, before she wobbled to her feet and limped out. Nina had a feeling she hadn't heard the last about Charlotte's fall.

And now it was time for her to go home, to tear Adam away from the computer and make him start homework, to figure out dinner, and to try to salvage the blanket she'd sacrificed to mopping up the floor. But that could wait. First Nina was going to treat herself to a good old-fashioned Nina Gettleman–caliber session of yoga nidra.

Nina rummaged through a bin of CDs until she found her favorite, the Imperial Tiger Eunuch Chorus, then she lay down flat on her mat, adjusting herself into a perfect corpse pose. She closed her eyes, allowing the music to gently pull her into quiet oblivion. She felt her breath and her spine both beginning to lengthen, the tension melt from her neck. She visualized her body as taffy, being stretched. . . .

And then a light tap on the door. Nina fought to keep her eyes closed, feeling certain that it was just a student back to retrieve a watch or a sweater from the growing lost-and-found pile in the corner of the studio. Whoever it was would surely peek in, see that Nina was resting, and quietly depart. When she heard the knock again, it was hard to repress her annoyance. Was there no rest for the weary?

"Come in," she said with an exaggerated sigh.

Nina opened her eyes, half-expecting Debby Jacobs to be standing at her threshold, eager to announce a brand-new disaster. But the woman at the door wasn't Debby Jacobs or any recent yoga student. In fact, she was no one Nina recognized at all. Her visitor looked exotic, vaguely Oriental—or wait, Asian, that was the proper term these days—with short black hair and almond-colored skin. Actually, Nina thought, Asian crossed with something. The young woman wore a long batik skirt in blue-and-white and a plain white tank top, and carried herself with an air of becalmed poise.

"My name's Coriander," she said. "Mind if I join you?"

Without waiting for Nina to answer, Coriander walked over to the pile of yoga mats, found one, and laid it out next to hers. She assumed the corpse pose expertly. Not, of course, that it was very hard.

"Coriander, like the herb?" Nina said. She felt stupid for addressing the woman so politely. Stupid and outmaneuvered. This complete stranger had waltzed in, pulled out a mat, and lay down next to her as if she owned the place. Nina ought to sit up and demand she leave. Or at least state her business. But she was too tired for a confrontation, and this Coriander, whoever she was, couldn't have weighed ninety pounds dripping wet. She certainly wasn't a threat.

"Spice, actually. It's the seed form of cilantro."

"Well, I guess it's better than Fennel," Nina quipped.

"Actually, that's my sister's name. Anyway, you're probably wondering why I'm here. I work on the first floor, right below you. The water, earlier today—?"

Now Nina did sit up. Here it was, the other shoe she'd been waiting to drop. Her stupid flood had ruined this lady's office, or studio, whatever it was down below. And now Nina would have to pay for that, too.

"Oh, I'm sorry! Really. I don't know why that happened."

"I do," Coriander said.

"You do?"

"Oh, yes. I practice feng shui. And I do a little aura work, too."

Any mention of auras always put Nina on edge. It was

15

probably all hocus-pocus, but what if it wasn't? Nina had a secret fear that people who called themselves aura readers might actually be able to search inside her and detect a whiff of something fetid, something corrupt or damaged at her core, which no amount aromatherapy or positive thinking could mask. At root, Nina was afraid she'd be discovered as a fake—she was afraid, deeply and privately, that she was a fake—not the Prius-driving, aluminum-recycling vegetarian she really was, but a forty-six-year-old Jewish American Princess.

"You've got some definite issues with the previous tenant, you know, the ballet teacher?" Coriander said. "Her energy still permeates your space."

"Oh," Nina said, relieved. So it wasn't Nina who was tainted, but the ballet teacher. Of course. Why hadn't Nina realized it herself? In addition to getting the rental bargain of the century, Nina had also acquired some bad, um, energy in the deal.

"It does?" she squeaked.

"Oh, certainly. And that's certainly what caused your fountain to overflow today. That, and, you put it against the wrong wall. But I can help."

"You can?" Nina said.

"Absolutely."

Nina lay back down on her mat and exhaled deeply. There was something special about this Coriander character, something vastly reassuring. "I hope you'll stay for yoga nidra," Nina said. What uncanny luck that her fountain had flooded on a feng shui practitioner! Nina felt infused by a warm glow. Coriander was here. She would fix the bad energy in Nina's studio, and everything would be okay again.

Adam was surprised, when he got home from school, to find his father's car in the driveway and his dad sitting at the computer in the sunroom, playing *The Sims*.

"What's going on?" he said, throwing his backpack down.

"I can't get Scottster to take out the trash. There are flies buzzing around the kitchen. And the guy keeps urinating right where he's standing. Right in the middle of the living room."

Adam leaned in to look at the screen. "You haven't built them a bathroom, Dad." He grabbed the mouse and paused the game so he could do some construction in Scottster's house, starting with a bathroom. "What I meant was, why are you home?"

"Oh," Michael said. "I was outsourced."

"Which means?"

"Downsized."

Outsourced? Downsized? Adam had heard these words on the radio, but never paid attention. "Fired?"

"That's about the size of it."

"Oh." Adam pulled a chair over and sat down. He flicked through a few *Sims* screens and saw that his father had really made a mess of things. Not only were there flies in the kitchen and puddles of urine all over the place, but all the indicators—mood, hygiene, money, health—were screaming bright red. He also realized it probably wasn't the best time to ask if they could give more than thirty-six dollars to Lisa Epstein.

"Are we poor?" Adam asked.

"Not yet." Michael shrugged, acting as if losing his job was no worse than the Yankees being down a run. "So, show me. How does this Sims stuff work?"

Adam manipulated the digital family on the screen. Trash was taken out, puddles cleaned. He turned on the boom box in the family's kitchen, and the characters started dancing, which raised their mood indicators up a few notches. If only real life were this simple. Then Adam pointed Scottster toward the curb and had him bring in the newspaper. He clicked on the button that said, "Look for a job."

Scottster, the *Sims* father, bent his head and folded back the paper.

A balloon appeared: SCOTTSTER IS TOO DEPRESSED TO LOOK FOR A JOB.

Nina felt a spring in her step as she walked to her car. Feng shui, that had to be the answer. How could she not have thought of it herself? Of course the slap-happy ballet teacher had left bad energy in Nina's new studio! Why else was the rent so cheap? And what was she doing buying a meditation fountain and just plugging it into any old wall outlet? She needed to make a bagua chart, like Coriander said, and concentrate her efforts on the wealth corner. She needed to attract chi, the life force. The art of channeling wind and water, that's what Coriander called it. In retrospect, it was all so obvious. Well, Nina rationalized, if the fountain disaster had introduced her to Coriander, then perhaps it was all for the best.

Nina rolled down the windows to enjoy the breeze, then tuned to WFUV, which just happened to be playing "Carey," one of her favorite Joni Mitchell songs. The traffic lights all turned green as she approached, as if synchronized for her personal convenience. She started planning dinner, and it didn't seem like a chore at all, but play. Did they have any wine? She'd put on music while she puttered in the kitchen, not *All Things Considered*. Why did she always torture herself with all the death and despair, the suicide bombings, plane crashes, earthquakes and hurricanes? The news destroyed chi; music attracted it. Why hadn't she figured this out before now?

Nina drove onto Berkeley Place, noticing its special loveliness this time of year, with the leaves just starting to turn, and felt beneficent. She wouldn't nag Adam about homework, look at bills, get bogged down in e-mail. There was half a bottle of chardonnay in the fridge, but maybe she'd pull out some red, something good—maybe that bottle of Châteauneuf-du-Pape they'd brought home from France back in the early nineties. They'd never celebrated her move to the new studio. Why not?

Then she noticed Michael's Honda in the driveway. A disharmonious note. It was just four, way too early for Michael to be home.

When Nina opened the door, she heard the annoying garble talk from one of the computer games Adam liked to play coming from the sunroom. Usually, it was just the noise of the game that irritated her, but it struck her now, after the magical ride home with the breeze and the beauty of the fall landscape beginning to reveal itself through her windshield, not just as an annoyance but as a crime against nature. Or, at the very least, against leisure. Why, on a beautiful day, was a thirteen-year-old boy sitting in front of a computer? He should be outside, in the fresh air, riding his bike, shooting hoops, skimming stones in a creek, flirting with girls, anything! She'd known this, of course, when Adam was little, and she'd worried about him sitting too close to the television set with all its low-level radiation, or whatever it was that the television sets emitted. But she'd given in. Or no, to be perfectly honest, she'd acquiesced. Adam's time in front of the television, or the Game Boy, or the computer—whatever—had become time for *her,* a gift that she'd accepted (she now saw) at Adam's expense.

Sims, that was the name of the game Adam was playing, she remembered as she set her bag down in the kitchen. As if a simulated world, constructed of animated little characters walking across screens, was in any way a substitute for the real one.

Nina walked into the sunroom, prepared to give a little speech, but stopped short. Because it wasn't just Adam playing *The Sims;* it was Michael and Adam sitting together.

The two of them were so clearly delighted, laughing uproariously at whatever it was that was happening on the screen, that they didn't even seem to notice she was standing there. She folded her arms across her chest and waited. Suddenly, the little sermon that she had improvised about fresh air and computers flew out of her head, replaced by a single, much more urgent, question: What was Michael doing home at this hour?

Adam noticed her first and elbowed his father to get his attention. Michael looked up, an expression of surprise on his face, as if Nina's appearance at home at four-thirty in the afternoon was the thing that was unusual.

"Nina," Michael said. He looked at Adam, then at the computer, then up at Nina. "Nina," he started again. He had something to tell her, but it flew off every time he opened his mouth, like a nervous starling.

Adam supplied the crucial information. "Outsourced," he said.

"Outsourced? As in . . ."

"Fired. Laid off. Out of a job."

"Axed," Michael contributed.

"Canned."

"Made redundant."

Nina felt the floor drop out from under her, security vanish, as her men played Ping-Pong with synonyms for what was clearly a disaster. And she'd thought the flood was bad! She'd heard about it from time to time, in hushed voices at the playground or the A&P. These were the ghost stories of the modern age, what wives talked about when they wanted to scare each other: husbands laid off in midcareer, unpaid mortgages, families that couldn't afford soccer cleats. They could hardly cover the bills as it was, with Michael's regular paycheck. And now, with the rent she was paying on the yoga studio . . .

"Hey, Dad, did you actually get a pink slip?"

"Yep," Michael said. "But it wasn't pink." He was studying Nina's face.

"Can I see it?"

"Sorry. I made it into a paper airplane and flew it away."

Nina felt unsteady. Had it just been a few moments ago that all the traffic lights yielded for her, the radio brought forth her favorite songs, the breeze and the scenery conspired to create perfect happiness? The world changed in the blink of an eye. That's what her mother always said, usually when someone's husband keeled over with a heart attack, but it applied here, too.

"I think I need some wine," Nina said, walking into the kitchen. It would be the chardonnay after all.

Saturday

Michael woke up early, much earlier than he usually did on a Saturday morning, and with a start. He'd had one of those falling-forward dreams, where it feels like your face is just about to hit the ground, only you're lying on your back and the ground is up. He checked the clock, not even eight, then looked over at Nina, whose back was still rising and falling in the steady mechanism of rest. He envied her slumber. What was the point of a Saturday morning if you couldn't sleep late? Then it hit him with a thud, just as the ground had hit his face in the dream. He was unemployed. Saturday equaled Sunday equaled any day of the week. What did it matter anymore if he slept late? He could sleep late tomorrow, or the next day.

He got out of bed and walked over to the window. Altostratus clouds, portending rain. His mood matched.

Michael walked downstairs to make coffee, and as he waited for the machine to gurgle and deliver up his morning dose of attention, inspiration struck. Pancakes. Hadn't he done that every Saturday, or almost every Saturday, when Adam was little? When had that little tradition disappeared? When Adam started sleeping late, or years before? He couldn't remember.

Yes, Michael decided, it would very nice to make pancakes for his family. That was a small advantage of being unemployed, the silver lining on the altostratus cloud, so to speak. He had time for pancakes, time for simple pleasures he'd long given up in the interest of his weekend to-do list, time to do nice things for Nina and Adam. Michael found himself whistling as he grabbed *The Joy of Cooking* from the kitchen book rack and ran his finger down the *p*'s in the index, searching for the basic pancake recipe. He was almost happy. He just had to remember to stay positive.

Shit. She'd overslept. She was getting a late start and would spend the rest of the day either catching up or getting in her own way. And Saturdays were the days she could least afford to get in her own way. Saturdays were a tough day in the yoga business.

Nina's Saturday classes were filled with lean hardened women with $250 haircuts and body-hugging, color-coordinated Lycra outfits, who took the train into the city every day and whose weekends ran on the same clocklike efficiency as their weeks.

There was no interaction among the Saturdays. They picked up their mats, laid them out with architectural precision, and assumed the lotus pose, eyes squeezed tight and palms turned up—as if Zen could be achieved by the same standards of hard work and concentration that made mergers happen. Frankly, they put out an impatient vibe, these mistresses of the universe, making Nina worry that if she didn't deliver value, they'd drop her like an underperforming stock. She wondered if they'd notice the water stain on the floor in the waiting room, and the way it had bubbled up like an angry zit. It was important to keep up appearances. The Saturdays had money and tolerated nothing second rate. They wanted spa-quality surroundings, and if Nina didn't provide it, there were dozens of yoga instructors in town who could.

Nina needed to be centered on Saturdays, on top of her game. She had a ritual of waking up early, going upstairs to her old studio to meditate, then leaving early enough to stop by Starbucks for a grande latte and taking her time with it before the Saturdays arrived.

It was important for Nina to connect with her god space (*god* with a small *g*, of course). Her upstairs studio had a large window, hanging plants in macramé holders, and a pine table that showcased expensive candles, smooth rocks, and seashells from walks on Cape Cod. A womb for a grown woman was how Nina liked to think of it, and she advised all her students to create a similar womb in their own homes, where they, too, could surround themselves with little totems they loved and meditate without interruption from toddlers or telephones.

But today, even her god space couldn't settle her. Nina had monkey mind, thoughts chasing each other like sex-crazed chimps. Why had Michael lost his job? What would they do now? What about health insurance? How much would it cost to fix the floor in the studio? Nina's heart was speeding up, not slowing down; her breaths were shallow; she cursed herself for mangling this simplest discipline. Nina wasn't meditating; she was having an anxiety attack. And if she didn't start meditating in the next five minutes, she was going to have to skip it, or else skip Starbucks.

Downstairs, the telephone rang. Normally, she would have tuned it out completely. Now it bugged her. Who was on the phone? She heard heavy footsteps trudging from the kitchen to the second-floor landing. "Nina!" came Michael's voice. "Your mom!"

Nina resented the interruption, resented Michael for shouting up to her when he should have known better. She should just stay, ignore it. . . . But today, well, the last thing she wanted was for Michael to let it slip that he was out of work, and then to have Belle Gettleman get hysterical. Her mother had always had a thing about "good providers"—which husbands were and which weren't—and Nina couldn't bear to have Michael examined under that particular microscope. And she didn't want Belle starting again about how Michael ought to be doing weather on the television. Nina sprang up—sprang as fast as someone in full lotus can, that is—and ran downstairs, grabbing the cordless from Michael.

"Sweetheart," said Belle, canasta queen of Delray Beach, mother of three, judger of the universe. "You sound out of breath."

"I just ran downstairs," Nina said.

"You're supposed to be out of breath when you run upstairs."

This was typical; in the relationship between Nina and her mother, there was nothing too small to escape scrutiny. "So what's up, Mom?" Nina tapped her fingers on the nightstand. The simple rhythm of a Saturday, that was all she asked. To get up on time, meditate, and make it to Starbucks before class. Was this too much to ask? Apparently.

"You're up early."

"If you thought I'd be sleeping, why did you call?"

"I have to have a reason for calling? I can't even chat with my little girl?"

Here it came: the guilt trip. Belle never got to talk to Nina. Belle never got to visit with Nina. Belle never got to go shopping with Nina. Nina was the cold lump in the center of Belle Gettleman's universe, the one package of frozen peas that Belle's charm couldn't thaw.

"Mom," she sighed. "I have class in twenty minutes."

"Okay, okay. Here's why I called. Daddy and I were think-ing about coming up for Thanksgiving. And we were wonder-ing if Michael could use his airline discount to get us tickets."

Nina thought about what to say. It was going to be pretty hard to get an airline discount when Michael wasn't working for an airline. Would he even have a new job by the end of No-vember? And, if not, could she endure four days of her mother's hand-wringing and helpful suggestions? And Thanksgiving, of all holidays, the annual holocaust of the turkey! Belle had never accepted that they were vegetarian, and she made it her business to tear out articles from magazines, whether they were in doctors' waiting rooms or not, that proved vegetari-anism was the reason Adam was so short.

"Nina?"

"Sure, Mom, I'll get right on it. All right?"

She hung up, started looking for her yoga bag and her yellow pullover. It was never easy to find anything in the bedroom, be-tween the books and heaps of clothes that occupied every sur-face. And whenever she was running late, whatever she needed seemed to disappear into a hamper or under the bed.

"We're not going to tell Mom about your job, okay?" she said to Michael, who had been sitting on the bed, reading *The Atlantic* since handing over the phone. "And, by the way, to-night's the potluck supper."

"Potluck supper?"

"I told you weeks ago. At the church. A fall get-together." They'd joined the Unitarian Church after they'd had Adam, which seemed like a rational thing to do. It had none of that creepy Jesus-on-a-stick stuff and, appealingly, none of the an-cient neuroses handed down from generation to generation by *her* ancestors. The Unitarians believed simply in what was right and good, in social justice, in taking care of the earth. What a religion should be. She and Michael had agreed, years ago, that it would be good to raise Adam *something*. But in truth, they were actually lapsed Unitarians. They showed up for folk song gatherings and rummage sales, but tended to sleep in on Sunday mornings. Not that it made any difference to anyone at the Unitarian Church.

"Sorry, hon," Michael said. "I've got a poker game."

She didn't even want to start with Michael about the poker game. Why he'd risk their money, which would be tight now that he'd been downsized, and hang out with a bunch of guys when they could be having some nice family time. Or the fact that he always came home after poker smelling like cigars. She was running late already.

Nina went by Adam's room and swung the door open. "Potluck tonight!" she chimed, trying to inject extra brightness into her voice. She expected to find Adam still asleep, but there he was, actually awake and dressed, wearing khakis and a green herringbone sport coat and trying to put on a tie.

"Oh, sorry, Mom," Adam said. "I've got Lisa Epstein's bat mitzvah tonight. The party, I mean. The service is actually— Can you give me a ride to the synagogue?"

"Fuck," Nina said. So she'd be going to the Unitarian Church's family potluck alone. And if she gave Adam a lift, there went Starbucks.

And then, from downstairs, came the smell of something burning.

"Michael!" she yelled.

"Oh." He put his magazine down, looking befuddled, as if cooking had been a distant activity, something he'd done, perhaps, in a former life. "My pancakes. I forgot."

They rushed downstairs, where a dark gray cloud billowed over the stove and the smoke alarm bleated its earsplitting refrain. Michael rushed to turn off the burner and inspect the damage. Luckily, the flame hadn't leapt up the wall. There were just three black pancakes and a scorched Teflon pan, smelling up the kitchen like burnt tires. Still, Nina had to wonder: a flood one day, a fire the next. Was the universe trying to tell her something?

"Come on," she said to Adam. "Get in the car. You need me to write a check? For the girl? Lisa?"

"No, it's okay," Adam said. "I got money out of my piggy bank."

Adam's mom pulled up to the synagogue and gave him just enough time to jump out before she sped off. When he went inside, the lobby was deserted, which meant unfortunately that he was late. Now he'd have to walk in while the rabbi was talking, and everybody would look at him, including Lisa Epstein and probably some key capos in the New Jersey mob. It wouldn't be so bad if he were at the Unitarian Church, but entering a synagogue was like visiting a foreign country. They spoke a whole different language, for starters, and the prayer books read from back to front. Adam stared at the basket of lavender yarmulkes, took one, and then puzzled over the bobby pins that had been provided. Was he supposed to use one? What about those scarf things with the fringes that were hanging on the rack? And more important, where should he sit? In the back, where he might be able to slip in unobtrusively? Or on the side near the front, where all the kids sat at Max Applebaum's bar mitzvah last spring?

He was saved from these decisions by the sudden appearance of Philip, who strolled out of the sanctuary as jauntily as if it were a school dance. Philip high-fived him and nudged him in the direction of the men's room. "Shouldn't we go in?" Adam asked, gesturing toward the sanctuary.

"Are you kidding?" Philip said, nodding at Mara Peebles, who was leading a posse of girls into the ladies' room. "Lisa would be out here now if she could get away with it."

Michael had unscrewed the blaring smoke detector and now, with Nina and Adam gone, was trying to clean up the mess.

He turned on the ceiling fan, opened the back door, and put the frying pan in the sink. When he turned on the faucet, the water hit the bottom of the pan in an angry sizzle, sending up a new accusatory eruption of smoke. Even more than the wail of the smoke alarm, this served as a reprimand, reminded him of the danger he'd inadvertently subjected his family to. He left the skillet to soak.

And then, like the sun breaking through an overcast sky, the thought came to him. Why not start again? Make more pancakes? True, he'd imagined making them for Nina and Adam and neither of them was home, but there was still plenty of batter left, and what was the point of letting a little fire—not really a fire, even, just a little smoke—set him back? He got out another frying pan, greased it, and turned on the radio.

Scott Simon was interviewing an old blues guitar player from Kansas City. You could tell by the guy's voice that he was missing teeth, almost like he had no teeth whatsoever. It was funny, Michael thought, how an old toothless man, someone who'd certainly be taken as bum if he were hanging out at the Port Authority, was a blues legend, and how this radio show, beaming out to households all across the United States at this very moment, recognized this fact. Then Elvis Mitchell held forth about a sexy thriller, starring what's-her-name, that beautiful actress who won an Academy Award in—Oh who could keep track of these things? Michael was terrible at crap like this. At the bottom of the hour, the news headlines came on, and they mentioned a tropical storm heading for Florida.

He wondered, momentarily, if he should get on the National Weather Service database and check it out, then call his in-laws down in Florida. Maybe that was why his mother-in-law had called this morning; with the fire, he'd never gotten around to asking. Nina's parents hadn't been thrilled when they found out what Michael did for a living. A weatherman? Like Willard Scott? No, not like Willard Scott, Nina had said.

Willard Scott is an actor. Michael is a *scientist*. He could picture Max turning to Belle as soon as Michael and Nina had left, that first night he'd had dinner with his future in-laws. A weatherman? How much do you think a weatherman makes? But ever since they'd moved to Florida, they'd discovered that having a meteorologist for a son-in-law was a handy perk, especially during hurricane season.

No, he decided. If Belle wanted information about the storm, she'd call back. She wasn't shy, that was for sure. And they were still calling it a tropical storm, anyway—not a hurricane.

The pancakes came out round, fluffy, and uniform (it was always nice when one could get consistent results), and Michael was just kneeling on the floor of the pantry, looking for the maple syrup his sister had sent down from Vermont last year, when the doorbell rang. Annoyed, he got up. There was nothing like getting interrupted just as you were about to eat. Before going to answer the front door, he double-checked that the stove was off.

Standing on the porch were two well-dressed black women, both wearing raincoats that hit below the knee, smiling at him as if he was their favorite nephew and had just come back from the war. Everything about them, from the radiance of their smiles to their shoes and stockings, was oddly out of date. He felt like he was looking at a movie about civil rights protestors, in the South, in the 1960s. Maybe they were cleaning women, looking for work? Then he remembered: Jehovah's Witnesses. These were the people who marched around the neighborhood, often but not always on Saturdays, handing out magazines and reminding people about the Lord.

He was glad Nina wasn't home, because if God forbid the Jehovah's Witnesses interrupted *her* morning, he'd hear about it for hours. But he was as glad as much for these nice ladies. Everyone hated the Jehovah's Witnesses; he knew that. But for Nina, who hated religious proselytizing of all sorts, hated TV evangelicals, Lubavitchers, Moonies, even the Salvation Army guy who stood outside Kmart at Christmastime ringing his little bell, the Witnesses were the worst of all. Michael pictured Nina's face twisting into lemon-sucking indignation, pictured her closing the door right on these nice ladies, who stood there so politely. . . .

"We wondered if you had a minute—"

"Come in," he heard himself say. He was aware of smiling, and his smile seemed sincere, not fake. Was he really happy that the Jehovah's Witnesses were visiting? Was he just responding in kind to their display of human openness? Or deep down, was his politeness a secret rebellion against Nina? Michael opened the door and stood back a few feet, giving them room to step inside. "Please"—he started walking toward the kitchen—"follow me." He walked a few steps and then turned around, to see if they were following. They weren't. They were standing right inside the front door, looking at each other anxiously.

If someone had asked him that very moment why he was inviting them in, he would have said it was because he was just about to eat the pancakes, which had been only a bottle of syrup away. He wanted to be polite, but he wanted to eat his pancakes, too. Isn't that what you'd do if a friend showed up in the middle of breakfast? Invite him in, sit down, offer food? But he suspected that he was actually responding to something else, some internal light that kept shining through their faces. It just seemed right. These women, in those uncomfortable-looking hard street shoes, must be on their feet for hours at a time. And he had a whole stack of pancakes fresh and fluffy. Why shouldn't they deliver their spiel in the comfort of his kitchen, sitting down?

"Please," he insisted.

Taking short, cautious steps, the women followed him into the kitchen, which he suddenly saw through their eyes. There was the burnt frying pan, crowning a full sink of dirty dishes.

There was the Saturday paper, stretched over the kitchen table as if spread out for a party of second-graders and a tub of finger paints. Adam's backpack was on the floor next to the sliding doors, and Michael's box from the office was next to that, and there were a bunch of paper grocery bags, from the last Kings shopping trip, which nobody had yet bothered to fold up and put into recycling. And of course, the smell of burnt pancakes. Somehow he was sure that both these women had tidy kitchens, with little ruffle curtains and matching seat cushions, and a picture of Jesus, his head tilted angelically to the side. Suddenly, the stack of pancakes didn't seem quite such an enticement.

But if the kitchen looked as disreputable as a methamphetamine factory, the Witnesses kept it to themselves. "Mmm-mmm," said one of the women. "Fresh pancakes."

"Did your wife make them?" said the other.

Michael snorted. "Nina make carbs?" The women stood there without changing expressions.

"Oh, where are my manners?" Michael said. "Please sit down."

He pulled out two more plates from the cabinet, then two forks from the silverware drawer, checking to make sure there wasn't anything gummy or crusty on them. "I can't find the syrup," he said. "But my son and I like pancakes with jam. Or I could get out the powdered sugar?" He glanced up at the chrome clock, which Nina had picked up from a diner that had gone out of business. It was barely ten-thirty. It would be hours before Nina came home. The pancakes, and the Jehovah's Witnesses, would be long gone.

Michael listened to their spiel, glad that his mouth was full and he didn't have to say anything, took their magazines, and accepted praise for his pancakes for fifteen minutes or so before finally ushering them out. It made him feel broad-minded, treating these women likes real people instead of pests to be disposed of as quickly as possible, even if he knew it was a little eccentric to have invited them into the house. He also knew he wouldn't be mentioning anything about it to Nina.

Joey "the Undertaker" DeFilippo may have been in Leavenworth, but his patronage was unmistakable at Lisa Epstein's bat mitzvah. For one thing, it was because of Joey, who among other things owned a limousine fleet, that Adam, Philip, and all Lisa's other friends got to ride up the hill to the Mountain Edge Chalet in white stretch limos rather than rented school buses, as was the custom. The guy who drove the limo that Adam rode in had black hair puffed into a pompadour, which he combed obsessively while waiting for the children to load in. Before turning on the ignition, he lit a cigar, oblivious of local social mores against secondhand smoke. Frank Sinatra was playing on the radio, and though the kids exchanged mocking glances, as if finding themselves inside an episode of *The Sopranos,* they were far too intimated to ask the driver to change the station.

Halfway up the hill, when Philip took out a bag he'd set on the floor next to him, the driver stiffened, as if expecting Philip to pull out a semiautomatic. *Don't,* Adam tried communicating telepathically to Philip. *Don't make any sudden moves.* He'd seen *The Godfather.* Half the time it was some misunderstanding that resulted in a bloodbath. Wouldn't it just be perfect, he thought, to get rubbed out on the way to a bat mitzvah party? Adam imagined his mother looking vindicated, as if she'd always predicted that something dire would happen as a result of a bat mitzvah and now it had.

But Philip was oblivious to the driver's nerves, and to Adam's nonverbal warnings. What he pulled out of the bag was made of black fabric and somewhat rumpled. He held it up: a small tuxedo. "For you, pal," he said.

The tuxedo looked like a miniature version of what a grown man would wear—or perhaps one of the Munchkins in *The Wizard of Oz*. But Adam could tell at a glance it was the perfect size. He was the second-shortest boy in eighth grade, standing just half an inch taller than the shortest, Tyler Wyatt.

"I don't want to wear a tux," Adam said.

Philip ignored him. He reached into the bag again—Adam saw the driver again study the rearview mirror—and brought out a bright red cummerbund and bow tie.

"You don't want to embarrass yourself," Philip said. He looked at Adam, then glanced significantly at the watchful eyes in the rearview mirror. "Or offend anyone. Besides, girls love a man in a tux."

The Mountain Edge Chalet was made of giant stones ("Where's the moat?" Adam said, getting out of the limo) and the doors to each of the separate ballrooms—all three of which were being used for Lisa and Lisa alone—were ten, maybe twelve feet high and made of thick, heavy wood, like the kind in real castles. There was a hallway filled with so many tropical plants that it felt a little like a jungle, and at the far end an indoor swimming pool, which Adam was certain he'd seen in a movie. The pool was decorated with white statues of Greek or Roman gods—Adam wasn't sure which—the walls covered with mosaic tiles, and the water itself was the most vivid turquoise Adam had ever seen. The air was hot and thick, as it usually is around indoor pools, and some of the girls were in bathing suits, sitting on the side, their legs stretched out, their feet and ankles dipping into the water. He tried to remember if it said anywhere on the invitation to bring a bathing suit and wondered if maybe Philip had some old trunks in his bag as well.

Standing at the end of the pool, wearing headsets with little microphones, were two guys with bulging forearms, wearing black T-shirts and surveying the pool like Secret Service men. Philip leaned over to Adam. "Mountain Edge Chalet charges three hundred dollars per person for one of these things," he whispered. "And requires one chaperone for every ten kids."

"These guys are chaperones?" Adam said. "They look like trained assassins."

"Come on," Philip said. "Ready for your costume change?" Indeed, with the exception of the bodyguards, every Y chromosome in the place was wearing a tux. Adam reluctantly allowed his friend to lead him into the men's room, then stood there as Philip fussed over him like a British valet, expertly fastening cuff links and tying the red bow tie in place. When the cummerbund was finally tightened, Adam felt if he'd been stuffed into a cardboard tube.

Adam looked at himself in the mirror and frowned. "I look like an idiot."

"You look like class itself," Philip said, opening the men's room door. "Come out and wow the ladies."

And indeed, wow the ladies he did. They clamored over him, hugged him, adopted him as their pet. Lisa Epstein, who barely acknowledged Adam's existence at school, insisted that he sit on her lap. During "Coke–Pepsi–Seven Up," the girls fought over who would be his partner. Lisa naturally got her way, being the girl of the hour, and when they locked arms, back to back, everybody laughed because she was so tall and he was so short, and Adam felt ridiculous. True, it was demeaning to be fussed over for looking like a penguin Beanie Baby, but attention was attention, he had to admit, especially when it came from Lisa Epstein.

All the elements of the standard supersize twenty-first-century American bat mitzvah party were played out one by one, only bigger, more elaborate, and infinitely more expensive than any Adam had ever seen, like a bat mitzvah on steroids. And because of Mr. Epstein's line of work, there seemed to be a few Italian wedding customs thrown in as well. The cocktail party, with little pigs in blankets and endless trays of raw oysters and sushi, went on for almost two hours. The table assignments were written in gold on the bottom of snow globes, one for each guest, with the Mountain Edge Chalet encased in glass and looking like a miniature version of Cinderella's castle at Disney World.

The DJ had a team of ten assistants to teach dance steps and hand out all the toys and to tend the dry ice machine, which sent out billows of smoke, tinted lavender by special gel lights. There was a giant screen at the back of the ballroom, where live cameras projected pictures of guests dancing the Macarena or sitting at tables and trying to talk—almost like TV coverage of a political convention. A magician walked from ballroom to ballroom, dealing cards as fast as some crazed *Saturday Night Live* samurai chef. A photographer with a whole wardrobe of old-fashioned costumes took sepia-toned pictures of guests dressed as saloon hussies, Confederate soldiers, and nineteenth-century robber barons. In the hallway, two caricaturists were set up with sketchbooks, and stilt-walkers and unicyclists made the rounds continuously, lending a European festival air.

Lisa's cake was the size of a small aircraft carrier. And, Lisa being Lisa, there weren't just thirteen candles to be lit at the candle-lighting ceremony, but eighteen. *"Chai,"* Lisa explained. "There's just too many people I have to thank." Candle eighteen was for Uncle Joey—"who unfortunately can't join us because of his prior commitment at a bed-and-breakfast in Pennsylvania," Lisa said, and everyone laughed. She lit Uncle Joey's candle herself, a small tear rolling down her cheek as she did.

"Cripes," said Philip. "She should try out for the school play."

The only thing that seemed to be missing was a theme. People expected something large, like the *Titanic,* or ironic, like *The Sopranos,* and no one would have been surprised if a giant animatronic King Kong had stomped in, picked Lisa up, and dangled her, mock screaming, from a ballroom chandelier. Then somebody mentioned that the theme, appropriately enough, was "castle."

And somebody else more specifically identified it as San Simeon, though Adam hadn't heard of that.

The DJ had been promising a special surprise all evening, and although Philip continued to speculate about Hollywood-style special effects, Adam thought it might be a musical guest of national stature. He'd heard of a bat mitzvah where Christina Aguilera performed. Anything seemed possible.

At last, the moment came. The party was already going on six hours. There'd been two long extended horas, and Lisa, her parents, her little brother, and half of the New Jersey mob had all been hoisted on chairs. Candle lighting was over, cake served, the cappuccino bar was shutting down, and quiet began to descend. The DJ put on "Wind Beneath My Wings," disappeared momentarily into a back room, and returned pushing a Federal Express box large enough to contain a flat-screen TV—although you could tell that whatever it contained was light.

He reached down, cut open the container, and released thirty thousand monarch butterflies.

Four hundred and fifty people gasped. The effect was stunning. The monarchs, lit by the ever-changing reflections of a disco ball, fluttered through the room like live fairy dust, transforming the dome-ceilinged ballroom into a gigantic snow globe.

But a few seconds later, one of the butterflies nose-dived into the lacquered head of Lisa Epstein's grandmother, who screamed and pulled at her hair as if she'd just been ambushed by a bat. Grandma Epstein fled the dance floor, cursing in Yiddish, followed by Lisa Epstein's mother, who tried to calm the old woman—while friends and neighbors kept coming up to bid good night and thank her for a lovely time.

Lisa, apparently mortified, rushed out in the opposite direction, toward the ladies' lounge, followed by thirty-five of her closest friends, all of them wearing white socks over their pantyhose and no shoes. They looked like anguished bridesmaids chasing a forlorn bride, or perhaps anguished bridesmaids in a fairy tale in which the floor had been enchanted to make them slip and slide at every step.

Clearly this was not the effect that the bat mitzvah girl or her parents had intended.

"I don't think the butterflies followed the script," Philip said.

Then they noticed a strange thing. Butterflies had started to land on Adam. Two, three, a dozen, and suddenly hundreds, it seemed, were all perched on Adam's red cummerbund. Dozens more had alighted on his matching bow tie.

"What the fuck?" Adam said.

"My mom always said that butterflies were attracted to bright colors."

Adam squirmed. The butterflies didn't gross him out or anything, but they were starting to tickle. "I wonder if they leave presents," he said, flicking one off his tie.

"Don't." Philip shook his head. "Think about it. God has given you a gift. You want the monarchs on you when the girls come back from the ladies' room, don't you?"

It pained Adam that Philip was always right. He was right about being able to hang out in the men's room during the bat mitzvah ceremony. He was right about the tux. And he was right now, too. Adam leaned back against the wall, going for a look of Humphrey Bogart nonchalance as the butterflies collected on him in ever greater numbers, and pretended not to watch the door that Lisa and her friends would have to come through when they returned from the ladies' room.

It was just a minor freak of nature, Adam knew. And yet, what was the parting of the Red Sea but a minor freak of nature? As the girls ran toward him, giddy over the butterflies, and even the adults turned toward him with growing curiosity, Adam began to wonder. Not only had he made the cut and been invited to Lisa Epstein's bat mitzvah, but he'd been doted on the whole evening. He'd been chosen first in Coke–Pepsi–Seven Up. Now he'd been chosen by the butterflies. Could the message be any clearer? Despite his mother's best efforts to eradicate all vestiges of Judaism from his life, he was one of the Chosen People. The butterflies were an interesting fluke, yes, and a useful girl magnet. But maybe, quite probably even, they were even more. A sign.

Elliott Nash hosted his Saturday-night poker games only once every two or three months, but no matter how long it had been since you'd played last, it was easy to remember the rituals. The guys arrived, threw a few dollars in a cigar box, and took out an equivalent amount of poker chips. This paid for the pizza that Elliott always ordered from Vito's, greasy and laden with pepperoni, which arrived midway through the second or third hand. Beer was kept in the refrigerator, soft drinks in a cooler out back, and potato chips and tortilla chips, eaten straight from the bag, wound up in small pieces crushed into the carpet.

Elliott, conveniently divorced, kept a green-felt poker table in his dining room because, other than poker games, he didn't entertain. There were usually five or six guys, dressed like slobs, and before the first deal, Elliott made his standard announcement: cell phone calls from wives, girlfriends, babysitters, or children would result in an automatic penalty, a red chip for a first offense, blue for a second. The only other rule was that there were no rules. Profanity, political incorrectness, burping, and farting, even, were allowed. After pizza, the cigars came out, and usually someone would pull out a joint, too, and the bluish smoke grew thicker as the evening wore on. When the poker players got home, most of their wives would insist that they take a shower and put their clothes in the hamper before getting into bed. At least Nina did. But during the game, they were grown men playing at being little boys playing at being grown men, and there were no wives around to cramp anyone's style.

Michael had looked foward to the game all week, although he hadn't mentioned it to Nina until today, but when he got there, he felt strangely shy, on the edge of things, unable to participate in the kidding around. It was, of course, still sinking in about his job, the indignity of it, the brand-new pit of fear he'd felt on waking up early this morning. You had to worry, with property taxes of fourteen thousand, a three hundred-thousand-dollar mortgage, and a kid just five years away from college. He looked around the table and realized that, though he recognized all the faces, he still didn't know most of their names. They were just poker guys. You'd see them at the pool or at some restaurant, and you'd nod and smile, and your wife would stand there awkwardly, waiting for an introduction that was not forthcoming. Nina, who saw every social situation as an opportunity to get a lowdown on pediatricians or contractors, was always amazed that Michael could spend a whole evening out with the guys and not come home with any useful intelligence whatsoever. All they did was tell jokes, Michael explained. She found it hard to believe.

But tonight, Michael was having trouble even following the jokes. Jeff Berger, who was wearing a LIFE IS GOOD baseball cap, had just delivered a punch line—" 'I don't know,' the Invisible Man said. 'But my ass sure is sore.' "—and everybody was laughing except for Michael, who hadn't heard the setup.

"What's the matter?" Paul Goodson said. "Wonder Woman your sister or something?"

"No, he's busy counting the cards."

"Yeah," said Elliott. "Look at that big pile of chips in front of him."

It was true; Michael had won three out of the last five hands. One game of Texas Hold 'Em, one game of five-card draw, another of seven-card stud. Dumb luck: the cards were just turning up.

"Is something the matter?" Brad Ellison said. "For a winner, you're awful quiet."

Michael didn't want to bring the party down. This was poker, not *Oprah*. People were there to have fun. He waved them off.

"Nothing." He shrugged.

"Vee have vays of making you talk."

"Yeah. Who's got the hot bamboo sticks?"

Okay, Michael thought. It was no big deal. He was laid off, like thousands of other men. No shame. Why act like he'd just contracted the clap? "Well," he finally confessed. "I did lose my job yesterday." Michael looked around the table as faces fell and wished he'd just kept his mouth shut.

"I guess I won't be flying Aeronautica anymore," Jeff said. "How are they going to know whether it's okay to fly? By reading the newspaper?"

"Meteorologists in the Philippines, believe it or not. I've been outsourced."

"Ouch," Paul said. "I remember when that happened to me."

"Me too," said Jeff. "The first time? Or the second time?"

So, Michael wasn't the first guy in the room to lose his job. "How long did it take you to find new jobs?" he heard himself ask. He knew it was hard to find work if you were over forty, and he was already dreading the idea of typing up a new résumé.

"I haven't."

"Me either."

"Join the club," said one of the guys Michael knew by face only, a bald guy who always wore a baseball cap. "Half the guys in this room are out of work."

Heads nodded.

"Yeah," said Elliott. "And now it's time for your out-of-work initiation ceremony."

He disappeared into the kitchen and came back a few minutes later with a plastic juice pitcher and a six-pack of beer. He emptied one bottle after another, until there were sixty-four ounces of beer in the pitcher.

"Your choice," he said. "The beer, all at one time. Or that big pile of chips"—Elliott pointed to Michael's winnings—"into the middle."

Jeff started beating his fist on the table. "Drink! Drink! Drink! Drink!" The others joined the chant. "Drink! Drink!" Michael brought the juice container up to his mouth. Shit, Michael thought. Nina would smell this a mile away. But halfway through the sixty-four ounces, Michael noticed, the pain began to recede. So that's what his life had come to: unemployed, playing poker in the burbs, and partaking in some fraternity-boy idea of an initiation ceremony. He burped. Jeff was right, he thought, just before passing out. Life is good.

The red oilcloth on the tables had been scrubbed and folded and stored in the stainless steel drawers of the Unitarian kitchen for so many years that its creases had hardened into permanence. Nina couldn't help thinking about all the sponges that had traversed these cloths, sponges that inevitably harbored more bacteria than soap, and made a mental note not to eat anything that physically touched the surface. One table had a sign labeled MEAT, the other VEGETARIAN. Nina set her fruit ambrosia on the vegetarian table and searched the room for familiar faces. Beanstalk men with infants strapped to their backs or torsos talked to women dressed in L.L. Bean, while toddlers tumbled wildly on the small raised platform that, on other occasions, hosted flea market displays and flower communions. Everybody was familiar, even to the point of stereotype, but there was nobody Nina knew. All seemed to bask in the glow of family and friends, except Nina.

"Oh, you'll want to put that in the kitchen with the rest of the desserts."

Nina looked down and saw a white-haired woman, four

foot ten at best, carrying a clipboard, which she scrutinized through reading glasses perched low on her nose and secured with a tortoiseshell chain.

"Oh, but no," Nina corrected. "It's not meant as a dessert. It's a side dish."

"Your last name?"

"Gettleman, I mean Summer. Gettleman-Summer. Why?"

"Hmmm. Well, *G*'s are supposed to be bringing main dishes, but *S*'s are supposed to bring desserts. Let me see, which name did you sign up under?" The woman squinted through her glasses at the list on her clipboard.

Nina knew her name wouldn't be on it. She hadn't filled out any forms or called any RSVP numbers. That was one of the charms of the Unitarian Church, wasn't it, along with the guitar playing and the peace protests and the fact that blue jeans were practically obligatory? This officious little biddy was getting on Nina's nerves—even if she was somebody's grandmother. Letters assigned to dishes, checking people off lists. What happened to just showing up with a covered dish? Nina had spied a spinach lasagna when she'd put down her ambrosia, and could feel her stomach rumbling. How could she get past the potluck Gestapo and start filling her plate?

A middle-aged woman with blond stylishly cut hair suddenly appeared like a Unitarian fairy godmother. "Go right ahead, dear," she said, draping a protective arm around Nina's shoulder and shepherding her toward the food. She leaned in and whispered conspiratorially: "Tales of the Chronically Overorganized. New member. Good intentions, but a tad overbearing. Here, have a plate."

It was Styrofoam and would sit in a landfill for hundreds of years, but Nina, at that moment, was so grateful to her rescuer, she skipped the lecture. "Oh, thank God," she said, approaching the table.

"If you believe in God." The woman laughed. "I'm Genevieve Harris, by the way."

"Nina Gettleman."

"The yoga teacher?"

"Yes." Nina felt flattered. She was always flattered when strangers had heard of her. She hoped her reputation would spread by word of mouth, without the need for expensive advertising. It was so important to fill up her classes now that she had rent payments and Michael was out of work. Had she brought her new business cards? Certainly she hadn't left them at home, had she?

"Do you do yoga?" Nina asked. She felt a small pang of panic. Was she supposed to know Genevieve Harris?

"Oh, no. I've never done yoga. I just know one of your students." Genevieve indicated a row of seats next to the wall, where Nina recognized Charlotte Hendricks, the one who'd slipped so spectacularly after yesterday's flood. A cane leaned up against Charlotte's seat.

"Oh," said Nina.

Charlotte looked up. She patted her cane, just in case Nina had somehow missed it, and glared. Nina tried a cheerful little wave, but Charlotte did not reciprocate.

Nina turned around to thank Genevieve Harris, but she'd already left to rescue the next person arriving with a covered dish; then she continued her forlorn search for an acquaintance or friend. Everyone looked nice, as Unitarians always did, but Nina might have been in a Unitarian meeting hall in Westchester or California. Charlotte Hendricks remained the only person she knew personally. Had it been that long since she'd been to church? She could hear her mother's voice inside her head. *See? You should have joined a nice Reform shul.* To which she answered, internally: *If this were a Reform shul, I'd have to be dressed up and they'd have figured out some way to charge me a hundred dollars.*

She ate her spinach lasagna standing up, distracting herself briefly at a bulletin board with notices for a drumming circle and an ongoing gay/lesbian/transgender film festival. Finally, the visit to Charlotte Hendricks could be put off no longer. Nina tossed her Styrofoam plate into a trash can, shaking her head at the ecological wastefulness, then crossed over to her damaged student.

"Charlotte," Nina said, touching Charlotte's knee in a gesture of concern. "How are you doing?"

Charlotte cringed, as if Nina's hand were covered with oozing lesions. "I'm in pain," she said stiffly.

"Can I get you anything? A plate? Some wine?"

"Morphine?"

"Oh, I don't have any. That is—"

"Just kidding. I've been living on Percocet since the MRI."

Nina gulped. "MRI?"

"I find out the results on Monday or Tuesday. Meanwhile, I'm spending just about all my time in bed with the heating pad."

"Oh, Charlotte," Nina said. "I feel so responsible."

Charlotte looked away. Clearly she felt Nina was responsible, too, but didn't want to get into questions of culpability at a Unitarian potluck supper.

"I thought the floor was completely dry," Nina pleaded. "I really did."

"So did I," Charlotte said. "So did I."

THREE

Sunday

It was the one morning of the week that Nina didn't have to set an alarm—no Sunday yoga classes, the real diehards took Falun Gong at the Y or did tai chi in the park—yet she'd woken up early and couldn't fall back asleep. Michael was a huge presence in the bed, snoring, his breath redolent of half-digested beer. When Nina took her morning pee, she discovered Michael's clothes from the night before all over the bathroom floor, still reeking of cigar smoke. Annoyed, she opened a window to air the bathroom out.

But when she went downstairs and discovered the burnt frying pan from Saturday still charred black and in the sink, her irritation began to deepen. She'd ignored the mess yesterday afternoon, when she was whipping together her fruit ambrosia for the potluck. Then, when she'd come home from the potluck, she'd glanced quickly at the kitchen and decided to leave it as a test. Did she really think Michael was going to come home from poker and do dishes? No. But maybe that was the point. Maybe she was really waiting for him *not* to do it, so she could feel the victory of righteous indignation.

No, not just indignation. Fury. She was mad. Yes, mad. The humiliations of the night before came back to her. Showing up at the potluck alone, like somebody without a family. At least Adam had a good reason for not being there; he'd been invited to that bat mitzvah back in August. But what was Michael's excuse? A poker game, ahead of community, ahead of family? And now he was laid out upstairs like a beached whale.

Nina picked up the scrubber and squeezed some liquid soap into it, then proceeded to attack the bottom of the frying pan. That was disturbing, too, that Michael had gotten so distracted by one telephone call that he'd left pancakes on the stove and almost caused a fire. Now that he was going to be around during the day, and she would be at work, did she have to worry about him burning the house down? She let the frying pan clang noisily against on the side of the sink, hoping to disturb his sleep.

It was, she noticed on the margins of her anger, a beautiful October day. Though she had no idea what to do with it. Something as a family would be nice for a change. A family dinner at the very least. For now she was satisfied stomping around the kitchen, clearing clutter and clanging pots. Then she noticed the damn pantry moths. God's punishment for eating organic whole grains. She'd have to go to the hardware store and get the moth traps again.

She went back upstairs, slipped on jeans and a T-shirt, and grabbed her bag. Why was it that when she wasn't in a hurry to go anywhere, she could find everything? Michael's Honda was parked behind her Prius, but there was no point in moving cars around. She got in the Honda and backed out.

But a funny thing happened on the way to the hardware

store. The car zipped right past and found its way meandering through a series of back roads, all the way to the Mall at Short Hills.

Michael felt half-dead when he woke up. He leaned on his elbow to check the clock, his head wobbling like a sack of potatoes, and stared at the time: 10:37. He rubbed the dry, burning sockets that housed his vision and stared at the time again. Yes, it really was 10:37. Michael hadn't slept this late since . . . He couldn't remember the last time he'd slept this late. The inside of his mouth was as dry and rough as an old wool sweater, and he felt an overwhelming craving for orange juice. Then he belched, releasing a noxious effluvium of stomach acid and stale beer, and suddenly understood which circle of hell he'd woken up in, the one where they sent people with beer hangovers.

Thank God Nina wasn't in the bed. Or was she? Michael rubbed his eyes once more and checked. No, Nina wasn't in the bed. But she was somewhere. Probably sitting tight-lipped in the living room or the kitchen, reading the paper, waiting for him to come downstairs so she could pounce on him. Michael knew he needed orange juice, knew he needed to go downstairs to get it, but he dreaded the price he would have to pay. He got up, crossed into the bathroom, saw his cigar smoke–infused clothes from the night before scattered across the bathroom floor, and shook his head. Oh yes, he would pay for this. He took his piss and then splashed cold water on his face. Cold water, a gift from the gods. Good morning.

But when Michael brushed his teeth and went downstairs, he didn't find Nina. She wasn't in the living room reading the paper, or sitting in the kitchen with a bowl of yogurt. He walked into the sunroom to see if she was checking e-mail, but that was empty, too. Michael went back in the kitchen, pulled out a half-gallon container of orange juice, and put the carton to his lips. It tasted awful at first—he should have waited to brush his teeth—but he imagined millions of little molecules of vitamin C rushing around his bloodstream and repairing all the alcohol damage, and finished the juice in one long swig.

When he walked outside to get the Sunday paper, he was surprised to see the Honda gone. It wasn't like Nina to leave without saying anything.

Adam dreamt. In the dream, thousands of butterflies had grabbed hold of him, lifted him up, and were flying him across the sky. He passed Lisa Epstein, who was being held aloft on a chair, listening to an iPod, and he went higher, higher—over mountains, valleys, patchwork-patterned farmland. In the distance, there was a city, and from the city rose gold domes, and as he flew over the city he saw a great wall made of huge stones, like the Mountain Edge Chalet, where men in black bobbed back and forth, strangely, like little penguins.

The butterflies dropped him onto a huge throne made of solid gold. All around him were gold coins, and in front of him was an enormous television. The television was tuned to a porn channel, and first he saw naked pubescent girls, thin and small breasted, on hands and knees, balanced on each other to form a pyramid of flesh. The girl on top then swelled into a full-grown woman, with pendulant breasts, and she climbed down off the pyramid onto his lap, straddling him, and pushing her breasts against his face, wrapping her arms around his back. He woke with a start when he realized it was Lisa Epstein, dressed only in a prayer shawl, and was horrified to discover that the front of his boxers was wet and sticky.

She'd started out in Macy's, where everything was on sale, and she picked up a new blue jeans jacket, very cute, just thirty-four dollars. From there, she went to Hold Everything, where she found some jute boxes she could use in the studio, to hold something or other—yoga ties, maybe. Eventually, she found her way to the New Age music section in Borders, wanting to pick up something new for her classes—tax deductible, of course.

On the way to the checkout counter, she noticed the career section of the bookstore and stopped, wondering if she should pick something up for Michael. It was only Sunday, but he hadn't talked at all yet about what he was planning to do next. Maybe he could use a little nudge. There were books on midlife career change, alternative careers, résumé building, dressing for success, interviewing for success, visualizing success, even *Success for Dummies*. Somehow, though, she didn't think any of these books would have much to say to a weatherman. What was he going to do at this stage of his life, become a mortgage broker? No, Michael had one skill, predicting the weather, and he'd pretty much have to take whatever he could find. If there was anyone in the family who could use success tips, it was Nina. She had the potential to grow her business, hire extra teachers, add spa services, open satellite studios in other towns. It looked like she might have to. . . .

Nina suddenly realized she was famished. She'd left the house without so much as a sip of coffee. She stopped at Mrs. Fields and was waiting in line, trying to decide between macadamia nut and peanut butter, when she noticed that all the people in front of her seemed sleek, elegant, well-dressed, rich. Women wore twin sets and tassled loafers. Pearls, even, on a Sunday.

Pearls before swine.

Nina felt like a slob; she'd just pulled on the first thing she'd found. When she left the house, she'd just intended to go to the local hardware store and buy moth traps. Now, she realized, she wasn't up to the mall's standards. Everything about the Mall at Short Hills intimidated. Every store window was minimalist, every customer-rumpled sweater restored to catalog perfection in microseconds; you couldn't find a belt for less than seventy-eight dollars. Even a child, a little girl of about six, holding her mother's hand in the cookie line, looked impossibly sophisticated. The girl's blond hair was pulled back by a plain white stretch hairband, and Nina could have sworn it looked like her hair had been professionally highlighted. Was that possible? Nina glanced at the mother and realized the child was practically a clone. The same highlights, the same cheerleader nose, the same high cheekbones, the same ice-blue eyes.

It wasn't bad enough that there were Stepford wives, Nina thought, now there were Stepford children.

When the child and her mother got up to the counter, Nina watched carefully, prepared to find whatever they did contemptible. The mother would be haughty. The little girl would vacillate between three different cookies, and the mother would let everyone in line behind her wait. Nina was already irritated at the little girl's greed and the mother's obsequiousness, and neither had even opened their mouth. And then something strange happened. The mother looked down at her daughter and rapidly moved her fingers. The girl repeated finger motions, smiled, then stepped up on her tiptoes and ordered two chocolate chip cookies. The mother got out her wallet and paid.

American Sign Language, Nina realized. The mother was deaf. Nina blushed with shame as if every person in line had heard the running monologue in Nina's head. What kind of monster was she? Thinking ungenerous thoughts about a deaf woman and her sweet little girl.

Michael had nursed his hangover, listened to public radio, and made a desultory attempt at the *Times* Sunday crossword puzzle, and still there was no sign of Nina. This was awfully long for her to be out without calling or leaving a note. Not that he was really worried. Although you did hear about things, sometimes. Missing people. You saw their pictures on the news, and then, weeks later, heard their bodies had been found in a park somewhere, or on the side of a highway, miles from home. He wondered about the parents and spouses of these missing people. When did they go from annoyance to concern to sheer dread? What would it take before Michael would actually consider picking up the phone and calling the police? How long was too long for someone to be out in the world on their own?

Preposterous. Nina was fine, wherever she was.

Adam had been upstairs an awful long time, too. And, like Nina, he was also fine. Michael suddenly remembered how long it had taken for Adam the baby to sleep through the night, how in the first few months of their newborn's life, night and day had become one big undifferentiated mush, and how he and Nina felt like the walking dead. They read Spock. They read Ferber. Called the pediatrician. Tried everything. Then one night, all on his own, Adam slept through. But when Nina woke up and realized her breasts were leaking and she hadn't been awakened all night long, she was convinced the baby was dead. She'd jumped out of bed and run to the nursery, where of course he had been sleeping, just fine, right the way they'd put him the night before, head turned to the side, pudgy cheeks, his little chest rising and falling ever so slightly, breaths as delicate as the whispers of grasshoppers. Michael had tiptoed in after Nina and stood at the door, watching as she leaned down into the crib, touching that soft face with the pad of her right index finger.

The phone jolted Michael out of his reverie.

It was Nina, not dead at all, but full of instructions. She wanted him to start the bread machine. She was going to make pizza. And make sure that Adam started his homework.

And tell Adam not to make any evening plans with his friends. They were going to have a family dinner. And by the way, could he pick up some of those moth traps they sell at the hardware store?

Michael might have gone straight from worry to annoyance, but for the fact that Nina was providing the very structure he'd been missing all morning. He started on his wife's to-do list, whistling.

They sat down to eat in the kitchen. Somehow the dining room seemed too formal, just for pizza, even homemade pizza, although Michael had set the table with real dishes, not paper. Nina realized that this hastily pulled-together family dinner was carrying the weight of her disappointment over last night's wretched potluck at the Unitarian Church; it symbolized some barely acknowledged yearning for them to act like a family again. When had they turned from a tight little constellation into three separate satellites, each marking a separate trajectory through the chilly black universe? And why had she spent the whole day escaping into the bubble of capitalism that was the Mall at Short Hills? Was it to punish Michael for drinking and playing poker the night before, or had she finally succumbed to her Long Island childhood and turned into her mother?

Nina noticed that both her men were fidgeting with their napkins and studying her, as if trying to read her mood or keep her on an even keel. Or maybe they were just waiting for her to become a warm and loving maternal presence, like Ma in the *Little House on the Prairie* books.

"Should we say grace?" Michael ventured.

"Grace?" Did he mean a prayer? They never said a prayer before eating.

Adam chimed in helpfully. "*Baruch Atah Adonai, Elohaynu Melech Ha Olam* . . . How does the rest go?"

"I don't remember."

"*Asher Kidashanu Bar Mitvah Tov?*"

What next, Nina thought, were they going to dance a hora, or break into a tune from *Fiddler on the Roof*?

"I don't think that's it," she said. "Why don't we just eat? Like we always do."

Michael persisted. "Why don't we join hands?"

Nina squinted at Michael. Something funny was going on in that head of his, but she couldn't think of any decent reason to object either. Very slowly, Nina reached her right hand over and put it on Michael's; then she took her left hand and found Adam's.

Michael bowed his head. "Thank you, Father, for the bounty we are about to eat—"

"Why is it always Father?" Nina snapped. "Why not Mother?"

Michael reached out and took Nina's hand again. "Thank you, *Mother,* for the bounty we are about to eat, for our health, for the beautiful weather, and for being together as a family."

"Amen," Adam said.

Nina looked at them both suspiciously. She felt a conspiracy afoot, as if Michael were hiding something from her, and Adam was in on it, too, but she was damned if she could figure out what it was or come up with one rational reason why the whole grace episode had made her so uncomfortable.

Monday

Adam had never been one to divide the world into Jews and non-Jews, but after Lisa Epstein's bat mitzvah, he couldn't help himself. Philip: Jew. Lisa Epstein: Jew. Joshua Gates: Jew. Aidan O'Toole: Gentile.

But what about Adam? What was he? His mother was a Jew, sort of. That is, she'd been born one. But it was very clear that she hated everything about being Jewish, hated synagogues, Jewish noses, Jewish hair, and especially Jewish American Princesses. On the other hand, Jewishness was supposed to pass through the mother, so technically speaking, didn't that make him a Jew?

Then there was his father, who'd really been raised nothing—but was some sort of Protestant, of course. And there was the Universal Unitarian Church, where Adam's family worshipped, although *worshipped* was really the wrong word, because you were allowed to believe in anything you wanted, and there was no God with a capital *G*, no big man with a white beard. No bar mitzvahs and no Jesus, certainly. Just the same kind of tree-hugging, love-your-neighbor stuff you got on *Sesame Street*.

So what did that make him, in the end? One of those mixed-religion kids, a mongrel, a mutt.

And his family didn't even do that right. Other kids— Delphi Lewes, Chris Schwartz, Sean Goldsticker—all celebrated Christmas and Chanukah, a present every night, effectively doubling their December haul. Adam just got Christmas. Yeah, he got Chanukah presents from his grandparents and his aunts and uncles, but he would have gotten presents from them anyway, no matter what religion they were, whether they called it Christmas or Chanukah or Kwanzaa. It was the kids who celebrated Chanukah and Christmas at home that really racked up. The Summer family, of course, didn't celebrate Chanukah. His mom had always wanted to celebrate Christmas growing up, and now she got to, although she called it Winter Solstice if Adam's grandmother was around.

Adam liked Christmas, so he'd never questioned any of his family's arrangements when it came to religion. And he'd never envied Jewish kids who had to go to Hebrew school twice a week. It was such a drag, they said, always having to go every Monday and Wednesday. But now, he was getting invited to bar mitzvahs and bat mitzvahs, well, yowza! Talk about your promised land! Lisa Epstein's bat mitzvah, of course, was going to be the best in show. Adam couldn't stop thinking about it. The games, the DJ, the stilt-walkers, all the cool stuff they handed out. Every time he thought about the butterflies, of course—and kids were reminding him of this all day long on Monday—he started to get an erection, requiring him to keep a book or notebook always at the ready for instant camouflage.

Mostly, though, it was the dough.

Think what a kid could get with that kind of dough. An iPod Nano, a laptop, front-row tickets to the Nets . . . Shit, a kid could even get his own Segway scooter if he wanted.

That Monday, walking around school, without knowing it, Adam continued a time-honored tradition of assimilated American Jews, a tradition that his grandparents had all enjoyed but that had somehow, in the case of his own parents, skipped a generation. He began playing a simple game, portable enough for car trips, flexible enough to be played alone or with others: Jew or Not Jew? In the shower room in gym, Adam discovered he'd developed a sudden curiosity about circumcision, and sitting behind girls in class, he found himself rating hair thickness on a scale of one to five. Adam played the game in his own head, and he played it with Philip, who provided fascinating clues and inside information, until he had classified every single kid in the eighth grade. When he ran out of classmates, Adam went onto sports and entertainment figures.

Coriander walked in, again without stopping to knock, but this time Nina realized she'd been hoping for Coriander's visit all morning. It was like when you had a crush and the object of your affections suddenly walked in; Nina felt happy, excited, and a little scared. It wasn't exactly a crush, more like if the Magician card in Nina's tarot deck suddenly jumped out and started waving around a wand. The air seemed to crackle when Coriander was near, as if she could tune into deeper, more exciting frequencies than everyone else and therefore brought secrets from another world.

"This is a good time, right?" Coriander asked.

Of course it was a good time—in fact, a perfect time, right between classes. Nina, who was midbite in a peanut butter–and–alfalfa sprout sandwich, nodded vigorously and tried to voice her enthusiasm. "Mmmm, mmmm," she mumbled. "Mmmm yes."

"Good," Coriander said. She reached in her bag and pulled out a red string fitted with several old coins and dropped it in Nina's free hand. "Housewarming present. Brings good luck." Then Coriander pulled out a compass and walked around the room, holding up the compass and squinting hard.

"Of course I know what direction your studio faces," Coriander explained, "having the space directly underneath. But I have to see first if your room energies are out of balance. Mirrors create confusion. Can disturb the mind. Deflect good chi."

Nina jingled the coins on the string Coriander had handed her, enjoying the pleasant clink. "Is it okay to put on music?" she asked.

"Something yang," Coriander said.

Something yang? Nina looked at her collection of CDs: Mozart, New Age, Joni Mitchell, and pulled on a collection called *Tubular Bells,* one of her favorites. It was yang, she supposed, all those tinkling bells. But was it yang enough? Maybe the Beach Boys, with their songs of sun and summer, were the kind of yang Coriander was thinking of. But then, of course, Nina didn't have any Beach Boys. She put *Tubular Bells* in her boom box.

Coriander stopped looking at her compass momentarily and smiled. "I like that."

Nina felt like a dog that had just been petted.

"Energies not drastically out of alignment. Now," Coriander said. "Let's go see what went wrong with your fountain." She strode into the waiting room that had been the site of Nina's flood. "Water features are very tricky," she explained, sounding very much like a tour guide. "Like mirrors. Much risk of misfortune."

"Misfortune?"

"A misplaced water feature can make your man leave you,"

Coriander said. "And you know how dangerous toilets are, right?"

Nina felt a flutter of anxiety. It was disconcerting to think that a common everyday object like a toilet could be dangerous.

"In the northwest corner, a toilet flushes all your wealth down the drain. A well-known fact." Coriander bent down and looked at the blister of linoleum that had formed from Friday's flood. She traced her finger on the floor, like a cop dusting for fingerprints. "So here." She pointed to the exact spot where Nina's meditation fountain had been. "The fountain was here."

"Yes?" Nina squeaked.

"Doubly inauspicious. Northwest corner, wealth corner, and draining water feature. Also, against the flying star formula."

Doubly inauspicious, Nina thought. Just terrific.

"Actually," Coriander said. "If you want a water feature, you'd be better off with a single goldfish in a bowl."

Nina nodded.

"But first things first. We have to get rid of the energy of the bad ballet teacher."

Michael's job for the day, for that day and the next day and as long as it took, was to get a job. To that end, he planned to register on Monster and type up a new résumé and call some of his meteorology friends in Princeton and New York. There were a couple of guys in private practice around, guys who made a living advising insurance companies on the probabilities of catastrophic storms and serving as expert witnesses in lawsuits over "acts of God." It was possible, he supposed, that one of these firms might have an opening. But New Jersey wasn't a big market for meteorologists. In New York, of course, there were a few jobs for bozos who wanted to stand in front of a TV camera and make jokes about the weather, but Michael suspected that, even if he wanted such a job, which he didn't, his growing bald spot might preclude consideration. Boulder was the place to be a real atmospheric scientist—he knew lots of friends from college who wound up there—or Washington, D.C., but asking the family to relocate seemed out of the question, especially with Nina's new studio. Besides, why move to a pricey place like Boulder when the job of predicting the weather, obviously, could be done anywhere? Why not move to the Philippines, or Timbuktu?

By eleven-thirty, he'd registered on Monster, typed his new résumé, and left three phone messages, which left the day wide open.

He felt bitter, bitter and a little scared, thinking about the mortgage and all the other bills that would continue to make their inexorable way to his mailbox, whether there was money to pay them or not. He'd never seen their life as particularly precarious, though of course, as a meteorologist, he should have known that the world was in constant flux, that everything changed, that no pattern could sustain itself forever, that mudslides could bury whole villages, tsunamis turn a coastal paradise into a graveyard. He should have foreseen that jobs could move, too, just like fronts and pressure systems. Why, he wondered, were humans so inextricably tied to a single place? Native Americans hadn't been. They'd been flexible, moving from place to place in the great big wilderness of North America, like dandelion seeds floating in the wind. That was how to be. Except, of course, it hadn't turned out so well for the Indians, who were now tethered, too, to their reservations, blackjack tables, and a way of life as divorced from nature as any white man's.

Naturally, Nina had given him a list of things to do: groceries, laundry, putting away the backyard furniture for the winter, taking in the hoses, shutting off the outdoor water, and calling the plumber about a leak in the third-floor bathroom. Just looking at Nina's itinerary exhausted him.

What would he be doing now, he thought, if he were at

work? He'd be tracking Tropical Storm Ida, now sweeping through the Caribbean, on the cusp of being upgraded to a hurricane. And of course, seeing what tropical depressions were coming up the pike. He'd be running models, checking out the effects on all Aeronautica's routes, advising dispatchers. Lives could be at stake. Captains, crews, businessmen, lovers, families. Taking the gas grill down to the basement for the winter was such a pathetic substitute. It was chore for a Saturday, when real men did chores. Even though he knew, better than most, that the weather was turning and that it was time to prepare the yard for a new season.

Michael found himself gravitating to the NOAA Web site. Ida, he saw, was getting to be a big girl. The probability that she would become a hurricane was now 80 percent. The numbers predicted her to come in as a category 1 or 2, but there was still a chance that she'd gather to 3 strength, and a slight chance she'd become a really big storm, a category 4 or 5.

Michael clicked through the various images of the storm: infrared, shortwave, water vapor, Dvorak. He was frustrated at how slowly they loaded on the sunroom computer, even with broadband. Yet liberated from the responsibility of interpretation and prediction, he noticed how intricate, how beautiful the pictures were. He wondered if he liked paisley ties because of hurricanes. That's what Ida looked like now: a paisley. A paisley? Was *paisley* even a noun?

When the phone rang, Michael reacted as if someone had set off a firecracker. He jumped, literally, and his heart sped up. Fight-or-flight, he recognized immediately. But why?

"Hello?"

"Oh, Michael," came the voice, his mother-in-law. "I was expecting Nina."

There was a little edge to her voice, Michael thought, suddenly remembering that he wasn't supposed to be home on a Monday, not if Nina was keeping his unemployment a secret. "She's at the studio," Michael said.

"Right, I keep forgetting. The studio. And you? How come you're not at work?"

Yes, caught out, all right. *Not at work.* She'd put her finger on it, hadn't she? He was home on a Monday: a slouch, a slacker, a loser, a bum, a man who couldn't support his family. It was hard to get anything by Belle Gettleman. It had taken one day for her to discover the truth. Well, she didn't know the truth exactly. She'd just sort of stumbled on some evidence. How could he throw her off track? Like most scientists, he was a lousy liar.

"Oh." Michael manufactured a little cough. "A cold. I have a cold."

"Vitamin C," Belle said. "Max and I always take vitamin C when we start to get a cold. Take as much as you can. It can't hurt you. You know what Linus Pauling said. We like the chewable. You do have it, don't you? Nina does buy it?"

What a freaking busybody. "I think so," Michael lied.

"And tea, of course, with honey. But I'm glad I got you anyway. So tell me, Mr. Weatherman, what do you think about Ida?"

Michael was relieved to be back on solid ground. Ida, the tropical storm. "I was just online at the National Hurricane Center. It's on track to become a hurricane by early Wednesday. Most likely a 1 or 2."

"Yes, smarty-pants, I know all that," Belle said. "I watch the weather, too."

"Well, what do you think I know that the weathermen down there don't? We all use the same maps." Was it possible to please this woman? No wonder Nina didn't want her to know he'd lost his job.

"I don't want the probabilities. I want the bottom line. Not is it likely to be a two or three, but is it safe to stay in Florida? Or should we come up to you?"

Oh, Michael thought, now there was a loaded question.

Having her parents visit was the last thing Nina would want, Michael knew. And Ida, even if it became a hurricane, was still looking like a 1 or 2. Still, he'd never hear the end of it if his in-laws got stuck in some high school gym or armory, sleeping on cots, or if, God forbid, something worse happened.

"I think you're safe," he said honestly. "But I'll let you know if anything changes."

After a few more admonitions to take vitamin C, Belle finally let Michael off the phone. Yes, he thought, he'd go out and get some, the chewable kind. Why not? But the cars in the Gettleman-Summer household apparently had their own minds this week, or at least were following the unconscious desires of their drivers. Michael got in his car and found that it retraced the old familiar roads, the Parkway headed south, Lyons Ave. in Irvington, Route 78 east, the little curlicues of service roads that looped around Newark Airport. The car wanted to make its familiar trip, to the employee lot, but Michael remembered suddenly that he didn't have a space there now. He went, instead, to a corner in the daily parking lot near Terminal A with a decent view of a runway, where he watched, with the wide-eyed wonder of a little boy, as plane after a plane roared into the lower cloud stratum, defying gravity and physics.

Adam walked briskly through Risdale Park, his head down and his forehead furrowed in concentration. *Temple Mchachacha,* he was thinking. *Temple Shrimp Is Okay but Ham Isn't. Temple Macher, Macher, Macher, and Macher.* These were just a few of Philip's nicknames for Temple Beth Shalom, the suburban bar mitzvah factory that had turned out Lisa Epstein, Asa Samuelson, and all the rest, and which Adam hoped would be the ticket to his own salvation. Or at least popularity and riches. Why not be a Jewish kid? Wasn't that his birthright? But when he actually pushed the buttons for 411, Adam felt a small stab of panic. Could he really pull this off? He walked even faster, rehearsing what he would say if he got the rabbi, if he got the secretary, if he had to leave a message. At the same time, like someone reaching for the cookie jar, he kept looking right and left to make sure no one was watching.

"Your listing?"

Synagogue nicknames continued to dance through Adam's brain: *B'nai Liebowitz and Epstein. The Synagogue at Christopher Court Pointe.* Adam stopped, suddenly, aware that he couldn't talk and think at the same time.

"Temple Beth Shalom," he said finally.

"Please hold while I put you through."

Adam had bolted as soon as last period was over in order to make this call. He didn't want to run into Philip, who might slow him down or somehow ferret out his plan. Philip was the last person Adam wanted to know he was thinking about a bar mitzvah—well, the last person besides Adam's mom. The whole thing was too fresh, too tender, too virginal, too untested—too open to ridicule. And there was his own ambivalence. Was there a single crumb of sincerity in this whole idea?

"Temple Beth Shalom. May I help you?"

Adam suddenly felt like the Cowardly Lion. *I do believe in spooks. I do believe in spooks. I do I do I do I do I do.* He sucked in a breath and scrunched his eyes, trying hard to summon his nerve. *I do believe in God,* he said to himself. *I do I do I do.*

"Hello?"

If he didn't say something, the woman in the temple was going to hang up. Then he'd either have to start all over, or give up entirely. If he was afraid to call a synagogue, how in hell would he tell his mom? How would he tell Philip? Dare to send out invitations? Adam gummed up his courage. It was no harder, he told himself, than stepping up to the plate in a late inning when your team was behind. His mouth was amazingly dry, but he swallowed hard, producing some saliva, and finally blurted it out.

"May I speak with the rabbi?"

"The rabbi's busy. But I can take a message. Can I say who's calling?"

Adam looked at the phone as if it were a live grenade, and stabbed the END button. Then he noticed the display. Seventeen seconds. Seventeen friggin' excruciating seconds. How in the world was he going to ask for a bar mitzvah?

Tuesday

Off the west coast of Florida, the atmospheric disturbance formerly known as Tropical Storm Ida was now Hurricane Ida, and was in the process of becoming a rather imposing whirlwind. By the middle of the night, the howling gusts she produced had reached eighty miles an hour. Ida was big and growing, three hundred miles across and fifty thousand feet from the Atlantic's now unpacific surface up to the tip-top of her funnel. She was expected to make landfall Wednesday morning, and to pound Florida's west coast with a foot or so of unremitting rain.

A respectable hurricane, Michael thought, but no record-breaker. There was still just a 15 percent chance Ida would crank all the way up to a category 4 or 5 storm. Yes, Ida looked a lot angrier today than she had yesterday, but she still wasn't in the league of a Katrina or a Camille. Not even close.

Michael wondered how the meteorologists in the Philippines, the ones replacing him, would do with Ida. Sure, they had access to all the data Michael had, but they were used to Pacific typhoons, not Atlantic hurricanes. Would they have a feel for the way hurricanes moved? For the geography of the East Coast? Would they even know, for God's sake, that Georgia was north of Florida?

He wondered how long it would be before his mother-in-law called.

Coriander had left Nina a photocopied sheet with instructions about how to purify her studio to rid it of the bad "mankind luck" energies left by the ballet teacher. Nina kept rereading it as if it contained greater truths—the secret to life, perhaps—folding and refolding it, putting it in her purse, taking it out of her purse, fingering it like a talisman.

1. Take white cloth. Soak in water, leave outside in the sun.
2. Wipe down all surfaces, including floor.
3. Open all windows to allow for exchange of air.
4. Start at front door. Light scented incense and move around entire doorframe.
5. Repeat for all doors/windows in the studio.

Five instructions, as simple as a basic recipe. Yet unfortunately, some of the steps were open to different interpretations. This is why Nina had always hated multiple-choice quizzes in school. There were always multiple interpretations. Some of the instructions were quite specific: *Take white cloth,* not pink, not yellow, not beige. But what kind of cloth? Should it be cotton? And just about every other instruction suggested as many questions as it did answers: *Soak in water.* What kind of water? Hot water, cold water, room-temperature water? Should the water have soap in it? She supposed not, or it would have said. *Leave outside in the sun.* For how long? And where outside, exactly? Would her own yard do? The studio didn't come with any land, unless you counted the municipal parking lot, or the roof deck.

Nina obsessed about the various interpretations through both her intermediate and beginner classes, parsing Coriander's instructions while sitting in half-lotus and reminding her students to empty their minds. The weather had turned overcast, so could she leave the soaked white cloth outside today? Would that be considered sun? What if it rained? What if it rained all week? She made a mental note to ask Michael whether it was supposed to rain. All the while, she was telling her students, *Take a deep breath; hold it, hold it, hold it; let it out with a deep sigh. Let your face soften. The only thing you need to concentrate on is your breath.*

Nina wondered: Should she knock on Coriander's door and ask for some clarifications? You never knew. It was true that Coriander just seemed to waltz into Nina's studio whenever she pleased—although, with her aura-reading skills, she probably had a sixth sense about the best time to come. But did Nina dare interrupt Coriander the same way? You couldn't knock on a therapist's door, and a feng shui expert was kind of like a therapist, wasn't she? A therapist for luck? What if Coriander was seeing a client? She might be angry. Nina didn't want to take a chance at making Coriander angry. It seemed, to use Coriander's word, inauspicious. Even if there wasn't a client, Nina didn't want Coriander to see her as overly neurotic or needy.

Nina finally decided, after much consideration, that the best kind of cloth to use for her purification ritual would be a cotton diaper. Organic cotton, preferably. After all, what could be more delicate—more symbolic of the purity that Nina aimed to achieve through this exercise—than a baby's tender skin? But where to get a cloth diaper? It had been more than a dozen years since Adam had been a baby. Of course, she'd used a cloth diaper service then. It was more time consuming, sure, but how could she have contributed to the ecological catastrophe of disposable diapers: putting human excrement in landfills, polluting underground water supplies, not to mention the profligate waste of paper and plastic? But even if she could remember the name of the service—Soft Cheeks?—they would never deliver just a single diaper. She remembered, vaguely, the deliveries for Adam. You got *bushels* of the things.

Nina looked around the room at all her students resting, considering who might still actually have a child in diapers. There was April Shandone—Nina seemed to remember that April had a toddler—but with her shellacked fingernails and Louis Vuitton bag, April didn't seem like a cloth diaper kind of gal. Amy Friedman was young enough, and a little more likely. Well, after class was over, she'd ask. Explaining, of course, that she needed it for feng shui.

The answer, it turned out, was simple: They sold cloth diapers at Toys "R" Us. Amy Friedman was quite sure. People used them as spit rags. Nina looked at her watch. It was eleven forty-five. She had a break before her next class, at one-fifteen, a break she'd scheduled around the local ladies' lunch hour. If she hustled, she was pretty sure she could make it out to Route 46, pick up diapers, and be back in time for class.

She was most of the way down Valley Road before a disturbing thought occurred to her: What if the diapers were a cotton-polyester blend?

Michael had drifted from Hurricane Ida to the virtual reality of *The Sims*. It wasn't such a stretch, when you thought about it. Meteorological models were based on probability and projection, and used bright graphical interfaces. It was all simulation, pixels on a screen, right? *The Sims* was just a little more playful. Michael was amused at the messages that flashed across the monitor while the game was loading: INVERTING CAREER LADDER . . . ADJUSTING EMOTIONAL WEIGHTS . . . CALCULATING MONEY SUPPLY . . . LOADING CHAOS GENERATOR. Clever, very clever. Of course, in the meteorological version, you didn't need to load a chaos generator. It was there automatically. In science, they called it the butterfly effect.

Michael had also heard of a game called *SimCity*, where instead of creating families and building bathrooms, you constructed an entire urban infrastructure and decided the cyberfate of whole communities. Maybe he'd use his time off to develop his own *Sim* game—*SimWeather? SimAtmosphere?*—where people could play God and move around the heavens and earth. Cause an earthquake? Why not? Stop a tsunami? It couldn't be easier. Be careful or you'll melt the polar ice caps! Given the interest in climate change, it just might be a hit. Educational, too. Maybe they'd get rich. Or so he was thinking when the phone rang and his mother-in-law interrupted his entrepreneurial fantasies.

"You're still sick?" she asked. "Did you take the vitamin C like I said?"

Michael detected a little wedge of suspicion in Belle's voice, which reminded him to cough. How long was he going to have to keep up this little charade?

"Yes. I found some in the kitchen cabinet."

"Make sure it's not too old. Check the expiration date."

"I will," he promised.

"So, what do you think of Ida?" Finally, Belle was getting to the meat of the matter. And here, Michael noticed, the tenor of her voice changed. She sounded a little vulnerable—not the dragon lady inspecting his medicine cabinets from a thousand miles away. Belle wasn't just passing time; it wasn't idle speculation about the weather. He could tell his mother-in-law was worried. He recognized the same tightness in her voice that he heard in Nina's when the wind picked up and she started worrying about the oak trees in the backyard falling on Adam's bedroom. Belle Gettleman was a force of nature, but even she knew there were forces bigger than herself.

"Well, I won't lie to you," he said. "She's getting worse."

"Max!" Michael could hear Belle turning away from the phone to spread the news through Delray Beach. "He says it's getting worse."

He heard Max shout back, "How much worse?"

"It's still just a category one. But there's a good chance it could turn into a three. And a very, very small chance it could get up to a four or a five."

"He says it's going to be a four!" she shouted to Max.

"No," Michael said, annoyed. "I said there was a good chance it could turn into a three, a *small* chance it could be a four or a five."

"But there is a chance?" she said.

"A chance, yes."

"Do you think we should fly up?"

"It could be bad," he said. "But I doubt there's time. It's supposed to make landfall by tomorrow morning." That was the honest truth. It probably was too late to get a flight out. He felt a little guilty, because even a category 3 storm, which was now likely, could be a hell of a thing for his in-laws to endure, depending on what path it took. Yet deep inside, in a place he could barely admit to himself, let alone anyone else, he really didn't want to be sheltering his mother-in-law from anything less than a category 5. He'd seen the two storms collide before—Hurricane Belle and Hurricane Nina—and there wasn't a category on the Saffir-Simpson Hurricane Scale to describe it.

"Make sure you have batteries and flashlights and candles," he said helpfully. "And water. And make sure your cell phones are charged."

Nina had hated Route 46 from the very first week she'd moved to New Jersey. The traffic was demonic, the signing and the ramps idiotic. You had to come to a complete stop to merge, and then once you lurched into the flow of traffic, you had to look out for all the cars creeping into the right-hand lane from the endless succession of chain stores. America in all its glory. The intersection of Routes 46, 80, and 23 had been described once, in something Nina had read, as "the scariest intersection in America," and she believed it. But the closest Toys "R" Us was on Route 46, and she had just a little over an hour to buy the diapers and get back in time for her one-fifteen. She grasped the wheel tightly. She didn't want to sail right by the store and have to go north on Route 23 to turn around. And where was the Toys "R" Us on Route 46? Was it before the Motor Vehicles office, or after it?

But there it was, suddenly, and though she had to slam on her brakes to let a semi go by in the right lane, she somehow made it safely into the parking lot—though her nervous system had taken quite a beating in the process. What irony, she thought, if she'd been killed on an errand to rid her studio of bad karma.

She pulled into a spot and allowed herself a deep breath before getting out. It was amazing, she thought. The whole world could change. Babies could turn into teenagers. Dictators could fall and democracies spring up in their place. But the one thing that would never, ever change was a Toys "R" Us parking lot. Through all eternity, every Toys "R" Us parking lot would always be an indistinguishable rectangle of sad-looking asphalt, filled with sad-looking minivans and SUVs, edged on one side by a four-lane highway and on the other by a bravely cheerful storefront and oversize shopping carts. Or maybe it was just that being at a Toys "R" Us unleashed long-forgotten memories of rummaging through racks of powder-blue baby clothes with football appliqués or waiting in long lines with a toddler bawling full-throttle over her principled refusal to buy a toy gun.

Well, this time would be different. She didn't have a toddler in tow, and she was shopping for just one simple commodity.

But how cavernous it all was, Nina thought as she passed into the main part of the store. How cavernous and mazelike, with the prospect of an endless march down countless aisles in search of a single package of cloth diapers! The baby aisle, she vaguely remembered, was in the front half of the store, partway down near the cash registers. Though maybe it was a different Toys "R" Us that she was remembering. One in Brooklyn, where they'd lived until Adam was six months old, or one down in Florida that she went to while visiting her parents. She looked for a clerk—but what was more elusive in American retail these days than a clerk?—and not seeing one, finally discovered a young mother, cradling a small child against her hip and pushing a baby in a stroller. "The baby aisle?" she asked. "Could you tell me where it is?"

The woman, it seemed, looked at Nina skeptically, as if she were the last person one might expect to need the baby aisle. Sure, Nina had been in perimenopause for a year or two, but she still had the equipment to produce babies if she wanted! Did the woman think she was a grandmother? Or was Nina just being paranoid, reading something into the woman's look that wasn't there?

"Niños?" the woman said. *"Está alli."* She shrugged toward the back of the store, where Nina remembered the books and computer games being.

Nina had to pass down the truck and car aisle, and she noted with indignance that there were plenty of Hummers, but not a single Prius on the shelves. Even more exasperating were the endless aisles of pink plastic—Barbie dolls and tea sets and ballerina costumes and magic wands. Sugar and spice and positively antediluvian. No wonder women all had such body issues! It started when they were four, playing with the male fantasy of what a woman should look like. And the tea sets! As if girls still ought to be trained in pouring tea and setting out cookies. What about girl astronauts? Girl reporters? By the time Nina found the baby aisle and a package of cloth diapers (cotton after all, she was relieved to discover), she was a teapot herself, clattering at a raging boil. She bought the diapers, noting with irritation all the candy by the cash registers, set out to give kids something to scream for while their poor mothers fished in pocketbooks for credit cards. She could hardly wait to flee the store and get back.

In her hurry, Nina put the Prius into drive rather than reverse, heaving into the blue car in front of her with a hideous crunch, the telltale sound of metal scraping metal. *Oh fuck fuck fuck fuck fuck,* she thought. Just what she needed. Insurance companies, police reports, being late for class! Nina quickly peered into the car she'd hit. No one was in it. She checked her rearview mirror—no one walking by—and the sideview, too. There was only a black Lab, panting in the front seat of a Chevy Suburban in the row behind her. Nina surveyed the damage, from safely inside her car, inspecting what she could through the windshield. Why get out and draw attention? *Breathe,* she ordered herself. *Just breathe.* It was nothing really, just a little nick on the bumper. The blue car was just some old shitty American model anyway, a poor person's car, like the one her cleaning ladies drove. Probably some immigrant, who wouldn't want to get the police and insurance involved. Besides, the back left taillight was already smashed, and not (she was pretty sure) by her. Actually, Nina decided, it would be the charitable thing to just drive away. What immigrant would want to get involved with police reports or insurance companies?

Nina put her car in reverse, checking multiple times to make sure she had it in reverse and not drive, and backed up slowly. And though the black Lab started howling as she pulled out of her space, Nina managed to get to the exit before any cars or pedestrians appeared. She merged onto Route

46, a little more aggressively than usual, and realized that, for the first time in her life, she was happy to be there.

Belle hung up and walked around the kitchen counter to face Max, who was leaning forward on the plaid sofa and flipping channels for news on the storm.

"I don't like it," she announced.

"None of us do," Max said. "But it's part of living in Florida."

"Not the hurricane. *Michael.*"

Belle had pronounced Michael's name with such vehemence that Max looked away from the TV and waited. Belle always had a theory, and 90 percent of the time it was negative. She saw the worst in people, imagined conspiracies, perceived slights, picked fights. What was wrong with Michael, Max wondered.

"Why is he home two days in a row?" Belle sputtered. "And during a hurricane?"

"He said he had a cold, right?" Max felt it was his job to disarm the conspiracy theories. And in the interest of solidarity toward the male sex, and in having his oldest daughter remain married, to defend his son-in-law.

"A cold," Belle said. "A *cold.*" She spit the word out like it was a stray piece of hair that had gotten tangled in her pasta. "Who stays home for a cold?"

Max picked up the flipper and started changing channels again.

"He didn't say he had a fever," she said. "Or bronchitis. Or pneumonia, God forbid."

"So why is he home?" Sometimes it was better just to indulge her. "What's your theory, Sherlock Holmes?"

"I don't know." She lowered her voice to a whisper. "An affair?"

"Yes, he stays home *shtupping* some, some—" Max couldn't

think who Michael might be shtupping. "—and taking phone calls from his mother-in-law."

"He could. To deflect suspicion."

"Belle! Leave it."

"I'm calling the airlines. We're going to New Jersey."

Max pushed the clicker, returning to the Weather Channel. "Listen," he said, appealing to Belle's preoccupation with the coming storm. "They're discussing Ida."

But Belle wasn't nearly so distractable. She walked over to the sofa, snatched the remote, and turned off the TV. "You close the hurricane shutters," she commanded. "I'll pack."

The drive to Newark Airport seemed even more natural than it had on Monday. The Parkway, Irvington, I-78. This time Michael remembered not to head for his old space in the employee lot, and instead pulled neatly into daily parking.

Michael rolled down his window, relaxed, and again looked out at the sky, wondering how in all these years as a weatherman he'd forgotten that the forces of nature actually played out in colors and shapes and textures, not just charts and readings and measurements. It was beautiful, all of it, even the thin layer of stratocumulus undulatus that grayed up the sky today. And mesmerizing, watching the planes take off and land, over and over, as if their landings and takeoffs were an elaborately choreographed ballet, arranged for his personal pleasure.

Tomorrow, maybe, he'd bring a camera. There might be some cumulus clouds. . . .

Adam raced out of ninth period gym, ran to his locker, and quickly grabbed the books he needed for homework that night and deposited those he didn't need. He wanted to keep his backpack light, because the synagogue was several miles away. He moved efficiently, not looking up, because he didn't want to make eye contact or start a conversation with anyone—least of all Philip. He just wanted to get on his bike and get it over with.

It being Tuesday, he wouldn't run into any of the kids he knew, because Hebrew school was on Mondays and Wednesdays. Tuesdays were safe. And the rabbi at Lisa Epstein's bat mitzvah had seemed like a pretty nice guy, at least as far as you could tell. He'd made some jokes, mentioned some movies. Maybe it would all work out, Adam thought, giving himself a little pep talk as he unlocked his bike. Maybe he'd get to the synagogue, tell the rabbi that he wanted to return to his faith and study for a bar mitzvah, and the rabbi would embrace him as a long-lost son of Judaism. Riding down Bancroft Avenue, Adam began to fantasize about standing on the bima, the rabbi resting a fatherly arm over his shoulder and telling the congregants how special it was, in this cynical day and age, to have a young man come to him with the desire to renew his bond with his forefathers. He imagined chanting Hebrew flawlessly, his grandfather beaming, and afterwards, relatives pressing envelopes on him. And the chair! His friends and his uncles lifting him up, with music, and below, a roomful of people clapping, doing the hora. . . .

But when Adam got to the synagogue and saw the rather plain-looking brick building and the nearly empty parking lot—no bands, no DJs, no beaming grandparents—his fantasies slipped away and his mouth went dry.

He locked his bike and walked warily toward the synagogue's main door, but when he pulled the handle, it didn't budge. Then he noticed a small card, taped to the window, instructing weekday visitors to press the buzzer, and the office staff would let them in.

It was just a minor inconvenience, but it made him nervous and reminded him of the audacity of his mission. He'd counted on just walking in, not having to state his purpose into an intercom. Adam wanted to turn around, hop on his bike, race home. But he'd done the equivalent of that yesterday, hadn't he, on the cell phone? And where had that gotten him? Nothing ventured, nothing gained, right? The butterflies at Lisa Epstein's bat mitzvah, weren't they a sign that he was supposed to be doing this?

Adam held down the buzzer and was greeted by a muffled voice.

"May I help you?"

"I want," Adam said, and then he stopped. He wanted a bar mitzvah, that's what he wanted. He wanted a big party, with a DJ, dancers, everything. He wanted the chair, the ten thousand dollars. But of course he couldn't say anything of that. "I want," he finally said, "to talk to the rabbi."

"The rabbi isn't in, but maybe I can help you? Can I ask who this is?"

Adam felt his whole being deflate.

What should he say? Adam Summer, a name the voice would never recognize? He could say Philip Tanner; they'd know that name and let him in. But they'd see immediately that he was a fraud.

"I'm just . . . a kid."

The buzzer sounded, and Adam was able to pull the door open. He walked into the lobby he'd seen several times, always on a Saturday, usually crowded with people in suits and fancy dresses, kissing and hugging each other. Now it was empty. He noticed a display case filled with Judaica—he didn't even know how he knew that word, but he did—Stars of David, Passover plates. All the stuff his mom hated.

He spotted a little sign that said TEMPLE OFFICE and walked in. There was a giant photocopying machine, mailboxes, desks, computers. It had never occurred to Adam that a synagogue was, well, like a business. He'd never been in a synagogue, or even the Unitarian Church, for that matter, during business hours, and he found it strange. There was only one person in the office, a temple secretary, and she was talking on the phone and writing an e-mail at the same time. Adam stood politely and waited, watching as the minute hand lurched from 3:22 to 3:23.

Finally, the temple secretary hung up and waited for Adam to state his business.

"I'm interested." He gulped. "In having a bar mitzvah."

The secretary raised her eyebrows and looked at him as if this were the first time she'd ever heard the word *bar mitzvah*. Adam then became aware that he was being inspected, from baseball cap to ratty Converse sneakers, and wondered if synagogue secretaries had some kind of X-ray vision to check for circumcision, too. "You're not a member?" she said finally.

Adam shook his head.

"You have to be a member. If you're a member, you get a bar mitzvah date three years ahead."

"Oh," Adam said, blushing a deep crimson. He started to imagine himself as a sixteen-year-old, standing up their reciting Torah, and imagined Lisa Epstein in the back row snickering.

"Do you belong to another synagogue?"

He shook his head.

"Well." The woman walked over to a file cabinet and opened a drawer. "Here's a booklet explaining all about Beth Shalom. Membership, dues, High Holidays, application form." She thumbed through the gray booklet, licking her finger every time she turned a page, until she finally found what she was looking for. When she'd found it, she flattened the booklet on the desk and pointed to the page. "Here's everything about *b'nai mitzvah*. Hebrew school requirements, mitzvah projects, and stuff for your mom—the *oneg* and all that." She dog-eared the page, closed it, and handed it to him.

Adam took the booklet. "Thank you," he whispered, then turned around and rushed out.

Adam slipped the synagogue brochure into his backpack, unlocked his bike, and tore off. What a fool he'd been! How naïve! His heart was beating so hard, he didn't even notice his best friend, Philip, who'd just been dropped off in the parking lot for a bar mitzvah lesson with the cantor.

A man in a navy blue Windbreaker sat in a little booth for collecting parking fees, only the little *X* on the lane leading to the booth indicated it was closed. Actually, it was always closed. Patrick McCarthy, the man with the Windbreaker, sat in a dark corner, out of sight of drivers, looking at a small array of computer screens and peering out the tiny back window.

McCarthy now spoke into a headset hooked around his ear. "Jack," he said. "Parking lot A, section one, fourteenth row. Do you see the white Honda?"

"Copy on the white Honda," said the man named Jack.

"It looks like there's a guy in there, just sitting."

"Copy on the guy sitting."

"That's odd, don't you think?"

"Affirmative."

"Do me a favor and run the plates, okay?"

Nina made it back from Toys "R" Us with fifteen minutes to spare and, realizing she was famished, ran to the bagel store for a bite. She hated herself for giving in to carb cravings, but really there was nothing like a bagel to fill you up. Nothing so fast, or portable, or—she suddenly realized, as she ran into Coriander in the lobby of her building—quite so undignified as to be caught eating.

"Oh," Nina said, hastily wiping the vegetable cream cheese off her lips and gulping down a big lump of sesame bagel. "Thanks for those instructions for purifying my studio. I just ran out to get the white cloth."

Coriander closed her eyes in tight concentration, as if listening for a signal from some distant radio station.

"I figured a diaper would be good, a cloth diaper, I mean . . . of course, cotton. But of course if diapers aren't good, I could always get something else . . ." Nina was conscious of blathering, a nervous habit she sometimes suffered when confronted with her spiritual superiors. It happened when she went to yoga retreats. Nina actually had to bite down on her bottom lip to stop the meaningless babble. At the same time, she wondered if she had time for another mouthful of food, as long as Coriander's eyes were closed.

The bagel was halfway to her mouth when Coriander's eyes opened. "Oh, it doesn't matter," Coriander said. "About the cloth. As long as it's white."

Nina felt crestfallen, like a student who'd done extra-credit work only to find out it wouldn't bring up her grade after all.

"But I'm feeling a different vibration from you today."

Nina felt a sudden tightness in her chest. "Vibration?" She could barely get the word out.

"Your aura. I'm sensing something. . . ."

Nina felt alarm at having her soul examined. She flashed to the day in third grade, when her Sunday school teacher told the class that God closed the Book of Life on Yom Kippur, sealing in a year's worth of decisions about who would live and who would die. Nina felt sick thinking about every little bad thing she'd done that year, every cookie she'd sneaked without permission, every time she'd pinched her brother, and wondered if she would die, or perhaps one of her grandparents would be killed because of her indiscretions. Talk about tough love; Nina was glad she'd spared Adam that superstitious claptrap. But now, she felt the presence of a judgmental omniscience once again. She felt sure that Coriander had detected something about her little fender bender in the Toys "R" Us parking lot, and was judging her accordingly.

"Well, I wouldn't worry," Coriander finally said, forcing a little smile. She pushed open the door and walked out of the building, leaving Nina feeling more insecure than ever.

Adam was a little surprised to find his dad's car gone and the house empty when he got home. But it was convenient, too, since he felt like he was smuggling something illicit into the house. He went up to his room, unzipped the bag, and opened the booklet to the page the lady in the temple office had dog-eared.

1. To be eligible for b'nai mitzvah, a girl must be 12 years old and a boy 13 years old.
2. The family must be a member of the Temple Beth Shalom in good standing. All dues from the previous fiscal year must be *paid in full.*
3. The student must have attended religious school since the third grade. Religious education at synagogues other than Temple Beth Shalom will be considered on a case-by-case basis. Additional tutoring in Hebrew can be provided, for a charge, when necessary.
4. Temple Beth Shalom respects and welcomes interfaith families. However, the bar/bat mitzvah candidate cannot be attending the religious school of any non-Jewish place of worship during his/her education at Temple Beth Shalom.
5. Each bar/bat mitzvah student must complete a six-month mitzvah project, approved by the cantor. Examples include

Adam stopped reading.

It was hopeless. Stupid. Of course he couldn't have a bar mitzvah. What had he been thinking? They didn't give away prizes like that—big parties, huge checks—just to anyone who had a Jewish mother! You had to be a member of a synagogue. Duh! Philip been going to Hebrew school, every Monday and Wednesday, for as long as Adam could remember. Adam had always felt sorry for him, especially in good weather, being stuck inside, learning his Hebrew letters. And on Rosh Hashanah and Yom Kippur, when they had school days off, and Adam got to hang out on his bike or go to the movies, but Philip had to get dressed up in a suit and go to temple. Now he understood. Philip did it all for the payoff!

Adam looked down at the synagogue booklet—now useless to him—and wondered what to do with it. He did what was most expedient, stuffing it under his mattress.

Well, he'd tried, hadn't he? And there was still Christmas.

When Nina walked out into the hallway to lock up her studio for the night, she almost stumbled on a pile of books that had been left outside her door. A little gift from Coriander, of course. Nina smiled, bending to read the titles. *Total Feng Shui, Harmonizing Your Home, Home Energenics,* and—suddenly her smile withered—*Detoxifying Your Soul.*

Detoxifying your soul? Clearly, Coriander had read evidence of today's little parking-lot fender bender in Nina's aura when they bumped into each other at lunch. It was disturbing enough to think that her own guilt or remorse or whatever you wanted to call it was so easily detectable to the aura-minded, like psychic fingerprints or something. But what really alarmed Nina was the word *toxic.* Did she now have a blot on her soul? Were there karmic consequences?

Nina stopped by Kings on the way home to pick up a few things. They needed brown rice, coffee, broccoli. But when she got home, Michael, wearing her old Zabar's apron, was making dinner while Adam sat at the kitchen table, quietly doing homework. The perfect domestic tableau. Michael turned around from the sink, where he was peeling carrots, and bent to kiss her. Sure, he dripped a little water on Nina when he leaned in, but still, she was moved by the gesture.

As dinner was moving along without her, Nina opened the refrigerator and found half a bottle of chardonnay. She poured herself a glass, and was about to sit down, when it occurred to her to check the phone for messages. Sure enough, the telltale *beep-beep-beep* of answer call indicated that there was at least one message. Michael, naturally, hadn't even thought to check.

"Doesn't anybody check messages around here?" she snapped, tapping in her passcode.

"Sorry, I forgot."

Michael sounded wounded by the way she'd put the question, and it made Nina wonder if her soul did, perhaps, need some detoxification. But she didn't linger on the thought long, because the next thing she heard was the throaty growl of Belle Gettleman.

"Nina. It's Mom. Daddy and I are trying to fly up before the storm. We don't know for sure what flight we'll be on. We'll let you know."

Nina put down the phone and cracked her knuckles, something she always did when she was stressed. She sat down, threw back a glass of the chardonnay, then poured another one and waited for Michael to finish cooking. As Michael's concoction of eggplant, cauliflower, and peas simmered on the stove, Nina stewed at the thought of entertaining her parents during the course of Hurricane Ida.

"How bad is the hurricane?" she said. "I mean, is it really necessary for them to evacuate?"

"There's no formal evacuation order."

"Well, then, what did you say? You must have said something that made her feel like she had to come up."

"I didn't say anything. In fact, I said it was probably too late for her to get a flight out of Florida."

Nina snorted. "Oh! That's like waving a red flag in front of a bull. She had to get a flight—just to prove you were wrong."

This was the last thing she needed, her mother, here, now. With Michael out of work. She'd been so jittery ever since the flood, and now with Coriander reading her aura and finding it toxic . . .

"I don't get it," Adam said. "What's wrong with Grandma and Grandpop coming? I mean, aren't you glad they'll be safe from the storm?"

"Of course. Obviously. It's just . . ."

It's just . . . Well, what was she going to say? *It's just that I don't need my mother breathing down my neck and asking a million questions about Daddy getting a job? Whenever Grandma visits, she tortures me about housekeeping and the fact we're vegetarians?*

"Nothing, grown-up stuff. So, what happened in school today?"

The answer, predictably, was nothing, but at least it ended the discussion of Grandma and Grandpop's forthcoming visit. Nina made a mental note to be more discreet, in the future, talking about her mother in front of Adam. But it was infuriating the way Belle had just announced her visit, rather than *asking*, like a normal person would, if it was okay to stay. And the way her mother left it, they could arrive any time. In half an hour . . . the middle of the night . . . tomorrow morning. Which raised an immediate problem. What were they going to do about Michael being home? Nina really didn't think she could bear Belle's anxious suggestions about what to do with an unemployed son-in-law.

After putting dishes in the sink, they turned on the Weather Channel and watched the reports on Ida, which now had occasional gusts up to 120 miles per hour: a category 3. Evacuation centers were being set up in high schools and armories in south Florida, and at least a dozen people had died in Anguilla and Saint Maarten, which Ida had strafed during the day. "Well," Nina said, grudgingly. "At least they'll be safe here." She got out some fresh sheets and went upstairs to her yoga studio, where she'd have to put her parents, and anticipated the complaints about the stairs, and the fact that they'd have to sleep on a futon. The corners of the sheets kept popping off as Nina tried to make the bed, causing her to exhale in short bursts of annoyance.

She didn't like sharing her yoga and meditation room with guests. It felt like having people take up residence inside her, somehow, like parasites. This was her space, her god space, damn it, and it was being invaded. Finally, she wrestled all four corners of the sheet onto the futon and sat down to rest. She assumed, automatically, the full-lotus pose and closed her eyes, lengthened her breaths, softened her face. But that wasn't enough to release her from the stress she was under, so Nina got up, found her *Mystic Harp* CD, and returned to the mat, this time assuming the corpse pose. She felt her breath deepen and her stress release as her mind followed the harpist's chocolately progression up and down the strings.

Finally, feeling better, she went downstairs, changed into her pajamas, and got into bed with the feng shui compendium Coriander had lent her.

She began reading with a focused curiosity, eager to discover new secrets and unseen worlds, but she found the material way more complicated than she'd anticipated. It was filled with references to things auspicious and inauspicious— at first she couldn't remember which was which—and the bagua charts were incredibly complex. The directions always seemed to be changing, and which way were you supposed to hold the charts? It seemed at first that northwest was her most auspicious corner—she'd finally figured out that auspicious was the good one—but then there was the complicated Bagua Lo Shu formula, which started with a person's lunar birth year and proceeded like an equation out of advanced trigonometry. And the matriarch's corner was in the *south-west*.

But all that was just a bad day in math class compared with the thing she suddenly discovered, which stabbed her like an icicle through her heart. The Gettleman-Summer house had the most inauspicious sign of all—a cross street pointed straight at its front door, known in feng shui as a poison arrow.

Nina was sitting in bed in her blue pajamas, a pained expression on her face, when Michael came in. He knew she wasn't happy about Belle and Max coming up, and he expected Nina to be irritable, but she actually looked stricken, like someone who'd just awakened from a nightmare.

"Look," he said. "I know you have issues with your mom, but she's not the Wicked Witch of the West."

Nina didn't answer. Michael noticed that she had three books, one on her lap, one on either side, and that all of them were open.

She looked up, her face devoid of color, her eyes looking sunken, dark, hollow. Michael could see the skull that her face would one day become. He quickly shook his head, to banish the image.

Finally, Nina spoke. "Poison arrow."

Poison arrow? What was she talking about?

Michael was used to Nina's New Age pronouncements. He'd heard of chakras, mantras, auras, karma, Kabbalah. It was all silly, as far as he was concerned, though basically harmless. He dealt in the world of measurement, empirical evidence, statistical models—science, in other words. Nina's propensity to embrace every New Age concept that came along used to be one of her endearing qualities when she was in her twenties, a wearer of embroidered blouses and peasant skirts. He'd gone through something of his own hippie stage himself, years ago, when he'd met Nina behind the cheese counter of the neighborhood vegetarian co-op. But in a grown woman, one who shared his mortgage and his child, in someone whose hair was starting to gray, this New Age business had begun to seem less charming and more eccentric. A poison arrow? Had she added Native American lore to her retinue of odd beliefs?

Michael started to move toward the bathroom to brush his teeth. Nina grabbed his wrist.

"What?" he said.

"A poison arrow," she repeated, this time pointing to an illustration in one of her books. It showed a road, facing directly into a house—an exact diagram, almost, of the way Cedar Lane pointed directly at their house.

"So?"

She picked up a book and started to read: " 'The single most inauspicious sign in feng shui is the poison arrow, which can be caused by any straight line aimed directly at a front door. A poison arrow can be created by a tall tree, a telephone pole, the sharp edge of a building or a street or road pointed directly at the principal opening of an abode. Poison arrows produce bad luck: illness, financial disaster, even death.' " Nina shut the book emphatically. "Financial disaster. Michael, don't you see? Your job! The flood, my parents, everything!"

"Nina." Michael struggled to hide his exasperation, trying instead to convey patience, love, rationality, just as he would to a child who had come in after a bad dream. "Nina, we've lived in this house for twelve years."

"We've got to move."

"Right, Nina." He shook his head, smiling, and again started toward the bathroom.

She grabbed his wrist, harder. "I mean it," she said. "Unless Coriander can come up with some kind of cure. Something . . . And one more thing. I need you to be gone, during the day, while my parents are here. I can't have them driving me crazy about you being out of work."

"You want me to hide? To lie? To pretend I'm at work?"

"Not lie, exactly. Just, I don't know. Lay low. Go to the library. Maybe they won't even think about it."

"And Adam? What do we do when he brings it up? Because of course, he will."

Nina looked down at her lap, thinking of the conversation at dinner, of Adam wondering why she was unhappy about her parents coming. "I don't know," she said. "I'll figure it out."

Belle had wanted to ask Michael for his employee discount or at least use some of his pull to help get a flight. But then, since half the purpose of her visit was checking up on him, she felt it wouldn't be quite kosher to start asking him for favors. Besides, why would she think he'd lift a finger to help? Hadn't he as much as said that what she was trying to do was impossible? Well, he might know airlines and he might know weather, but he still had a thing or two to learn about Belle Gettleman. A hurricane was a hurricane; you couldn't fight with God. But airlines were run by human beings. And when it came to dealing with human beings, Belle didn't have any doubts.

They arrived at the airport at 7 P.M., and Belle ordered Max to sit in the waiting area with their one suitcase until she returned. Then she proceeded to the ticket counters.

She tried Aeronautica first and had to wait half an hour before she could even get to the window. There was one last flight out, at eleven o'clock, the stressed-out blonde behind the counter said, but it was already completely booked. She looked apologetic.

"But there's always a seat or two reserved, just in case?"

"No." The blonde's smile grew tauter. "Booked means booked."

"But what if a dignitary showed up, at the last minute, and

needed a flight to Newark Airport? What if, for example, the president showed up?"

"The president flies on Air Force One."

"But what if Air Force One was in the shop? What if—?"

The smile disappeared. "Ma'am," she said. "There's a lot we all have to do in preparation for the hurricane. I myself have two small children at home."

"I was just saying—"

"Do I have to call security?"

The conversation repeated itself, with slight variations, at three more airlines. Belle looked nervously at the departures board. Canceled, canceled, delayed, canceled. She was starting to have her doubts about getting to New Jersey, tonight at any rate. Maybe she could fly to LaGuardia?

Her cell phone rang, and she fished for it in her pocketbook. "Yes?" she said.

"Have you given up yet?" It was Max. Through the telephone, Belle heard the same airport loudspeaker calling flights that she could hear overhead. Only there was some split-second delay in the cell phone version that made it sound like an echo. "Passengers flying on Delta 386 should report to the gate immediately. Passengers—"

"No, I haven't given up yet."

"Because my knee is hurting me. And they're saying on the TV there are no more flights."

"Look at all the people around you!" But even as Belle said it, she realized that there were far fewer people in the airport than there'd been an hour earlier.

Max sighed.

"Just stay there. The last thing I need is to find a flight and then have to come looking for you."

She snapped the phone shut and strained to hear a muffled announcement coming over the loudspeaker. Something about boarding a plane headed to Chicago. Chicago? Why hadn't she thought of that before? They didn't have to fly straight to

New Jersey just to avoid Hurricane Ida. They could fly anywhere, and make a connection to Newark later.

Belle stepped back to get the longest possible view of all the
counters. She'd pick the one with the shortest line and fly
anywhere—anywhere in the continental United States—that
was her newest plan. The longest line was at Continental. It
snaked around, doubling back several times, full of people
with hot tempers and anxious faces. US Air was about half as
long. American the same. But the very last counter, Belle noticed, was empty. She looked at the big green sign above it.
Gator Airlines?

She ran to the waiting area where she'd left Max. He was
leaning back against the molded plastic seat, his head tilted
up at the TV, his eyes half-closed. She grabbed his arm.

"What? Huh?"

"Come with me," Belle said, grabbing the suitcase. "Now."
She pulled the wheel attachment out from the bottom of the
suitcase and started pushing the large bag with a grunt.

"You're supposed to pull it," Max said, hobbling to keep up.

"I am pulling."

"You're pushing."

"Shut up, or I'll push you."

They arrived at the Gator window breathless, their cheeks
flushed, their hair spread wildly about their faces.

The young man behind the counter sported spiky blond
hair and a nose ring. He looked like he belonged on a surf-
board, not behind a ticket counter. "Dude," he said. "Can I
help you?"

"Two tickets," Belle barked. She was panting.

"Where to?"

"Anywhere!"

"Although," Max piped up. "We would prefer Newark."

"But we'll go anywhere." An hour and a half of waiting in
lines had made her desperate.

The guy behind the counter looked at Belle again, staring

down his nose at her as though looking through bifocals, although there were no bifocals. She looked over the counter, expecting to see him enter their request into a computer, but there was no computer either. Instead, he looked up at a chalkboard, which had been heavily erased and which displayed a succession of tally marks.

"Well," he said, cracking his gum. "We do have two seats leaving Florida, but they're not together."

Belle and Max exchanged looks.

"We'll take them," Belle said.

"One is to Chicago at 10:05," the man said. "Five hundred dollars."

"One way?" Belle squeaked.

The man nodded. "And the other is to Boston at one A.M. Eight hundred."

Belle slapped a credit card on the counter window. "I'll take Chicago," she said. "He'll take Boston."

The man looked over the counter at the single suitcase. "And where should I check the baggage?"

Wednesday

Michael woke up to find Nina already out of bed, which was unusual, because waking up was one of his wife's least favorite activities. Adam had long been trained to set his own alarm, get dressed, and pour his own cereal, and it was usually a toss-up to see who would get to the kitchen first, father or son. But never Nina, who often fought the demons of insomnia until the middle of the night, and who—until now—had always scheduled her yoga classes to start safely in midmorning. Those days, however, were over. Having a studio, paying rent, required Nina to hold more classes—even early-morning classes—and forced her to set an alarm for the first time in years. Michael felt he could count on his fingers the number of times in their marriage that his wife had risen before him, yet this was the second time in the past couple of days.

He figured that she was probably up in her attic space, meditating, ahead of the category 5 storm that was Belle Gettleman.

But when he went downstairs to make some coffee, he was surprised to find Nina hunched over the kitchen table with a ruler and a legal pad, drawing something that looked like a stop sign, or the Pentagon, he couldn't tell which.

"Do we have a compass?" she said, not looking up.

"A compass? Well, I can tell you which way north is, if that helps." He pointed toward the pantry.

Nina put down her pencil and closed her eyes. She looked like a student who'd pulled an all-nighter, only to discover that she'd been studying for the wrong test. She rubbed her eyes and took a sip of coffee.

"Sorry," Michael said. "Adam gone already?"

"Yep. I guess little things like morning don't matter to you much anymore."

That was a cheap shot. How many years had Nina slept late, had Michael been the only one to see his son before he went off to school? He looked up at the clock. It was only eight-fifteen. It wasn't like he'd slept to noon. Michael studied his wife—her hair splayed Einstein-like in every direction, dark semicircles under her eyes, a look of avid concentration mingled with fear—and decided to let it go.

"So, what's with the stop sign? And the need for a compass?"

"I'm making a bagua."

"A bog-what?"

"A bagua. *Bog wah.* To see what else is wrong with this wreck of a house." From her accusing tone, you might have thought there was a huge hole in the roof and a foot of water on the floor.

"Oh, right. The poison dart."

"Arrow."

The phone rang. Nina leapt in front of Michael to answer it.

"Hello?" she said. "Yes. Hi, Mom. . . . Uh-huh . . . Uh-huh . . . What? . . . You can't be serious. . . . Chicago?"

Michael couldn't tell what his mother-in-law was saying, but he could hear her voice, fast and agitated, coming through the handset. It reminded him of those old Warner Brothers cartoons where a character would hold the phone a foot away from his head while a comically agitated voice bleated nonsensically through the handset.

"Gator Air?" Nina said. She was shaking her head and scribbling furiously on her paper. "God, Mom, could you make it any more complicated. . . . What? . . . *Boston?*"

Nina looked up at Michael and mouthed something, but he couldn't understand what she was saying. He never could read lips. Still Nina insisted, year after year, on transmitting silent messages. Finally, giving up, she shook her head. Michael waited.

"Look," she said. "Here's the plan. I'll give you Michael's cell number, and when you get in, you'll give him a call, okay?"

Nina continued drawing on her paper, retracing her original doodles with fierce dark strokes.

"Why not his work number? Because it's supposed to be for official business, Mom. Don't worry. He always has his cell. Okay? Good-bye." She walked back to the table where the phone usually sat, shaking her head as she replaced the handset.

"Of all the crazy things."

"What?"

"She's in Chicago."

"Chicago?"

"And Dad's in Boston. They couldn't get a flight to Newark."

Michael couldn't help it. He raised his hand as if to deliver a high five, but finding no hand to slap, lowered it. Too bad Adam wasn't there. Still, Michael allowed himself a tiny smile. "I knew it."

"Yes. But you didn't know my mother. Okay, here's the plan."

There was always a plan. Whether it was getting to a vacation house and deciding who would make the beds and who would go grocery shopping, or orchestrating Halloween, Nina planned any potentially complicated event as if she were staging a coup. And it wasn't just Nina. Once, down in Florida, when Michael, Nina, Adam, Belle, and Max were going to the Cheesecake Factory, a notoriously crowded restaurant that didn't take reservations, and where patrons were handed pagers when they gave their names to the hostess, Belle used the same expression, "Okay, here's the plan," plotting out who would drive, who would park, and whether, depending on the estimated length of the wait, they might go to a different restaurant. Michael had laughed when she said it—"Okay, here's the plan"—and Nina and Belle had both turned to him with identical scowls. "What's so funny?" Nina had said. "Nothing," he'd insisted. But they both kept scowling. It was funny how, despite her best efforts, despite an adulthood dedicated to New Age wholesomeness and the pursuit of progressive causes, Nina had really managed to turn into her mother anyway.

The plan, Nina explained, and Michael did his best not to smile, was for Michael to keep his cell phone on, and when Belle called, he'd pick her up at the airport. This way, Belle wouldn't discover Michael hanging out around the house, unemployed.

"And what about Max?"

"Call home for messages a couple of times an hour. Just stay away from the house, okay? I don't want you picking up the phone by mistake."

How long would Nina carry on this charade, Michael wondered, and what really was the reason for it? It was unsettling not to have a job, but it wasn't shameful. Not if you read all those *Newsweek* covers about outsourcing and white-collar unemployment.

The bagua chart, Nina could see, was hopeless. Everything was confusing. Why, in the book in front of her, was south at the top of the page and north at the bottom? What kind of *fershlugginer* system was that? You could apply the bagua chart to the whole house or to an individual room, but was the front door always supposed to be at the bottom?

Nina had been trying to draw the floor plan of her house, fitting it within the feng shui stop sign. The idea was to see whether the rooms and the furniture were arranged auspiciously (the bed positioned to encourage fidelity, for example) or inauspiciously (a bathroom in the wealth corner, literally draining the family's fortune away).

But her diagram was a complete mess. Surprise, surprise. She'd almost failed geometry in eighth grade, was terrible with angles, shapes, spatial relationships. What was a radius and what was a diameter and what was a circumference? She always got them confused. Trying to figure out puzzles like this made her brain hurt, and if her brain hurt too long, crazy things could happen, things she couldn't be responsible for. Like the time in Mrs. Wilcox's geometry class, when she'd been called to the blackboard to do a proof, despite not raising her hand, and got stuck halfway through. "Now, Nina. Remember your Pythagorean theorem." But that had only made it worse. She'd felt the heat build up in her cheeks as embarrassment flooded her like a sudden surge of hormones, and when her brain had been thoroughly doused with that adolescent mixture of humiliation and frustration, it went off like a bomb. To her classmates' astonishment, she'd yelled "Fuck you," flung a piece of chalk at Mrs. Wilcox, and ran out of the room. She fled out back with the kids who skipped class and smoked cigarettes underneath the bleachers. Her parents needed to get a lawyer to arrange for Nina to work in the library after school in lieu of getting suspended, and for good measure, Dr. Gettleman had helped sponsor the Math Team's spring trip to Orlando.

Oh, well. That was nothing compared to the kind of stuff that happened these days with kids going into schools with automatic weapons and shooting up their classmates. She looked at the diagram one more time, then tore the yellow sheet out of the legal pad and crumpled it into a ball. Why did it have to be so fucking complicated? But then she remembered that yoga seemed complicated to the uninitiated. First-time students were always complaining: Why did they have to *learn* to breathe? Wasn't it natural? Wasn't it something they'd been doing perfectly well since they were born? Spirited complaints about learning to breathe were, in fact, the hallmark of beginner classes, particularly those attended by the highly verbal: writers, lawyers, and professors.

Nina closed her eyes and took a deep professionally executed yogic breath.

Why did she feel such an urgency to master feng shui instantly, like it was a tea bag that you could just add water to? But it did seem urgent; everything seemed urgent. The flood in her waiting room on Friday, the near-fire in the kitchen Saturday—what were they but signs from the universe that the elements in her life were seriously out of whack? And Michael's sudden unemployment. Nina had barely had time to focus on that. Or maybe she'd just been repressing it. Michael had some severance pay, true, but after that ran out, they had savings to get them through a month, maybe two, without his salary. It was possible, she supposed, to renegotiate their home equity loan and take out some more money. But like just about everybody else in their cozy little suburb, with the big Victorian houses that guzzled desertfuls of heating oil each winter, they were house poor, oil poor, tax poor. They really couldn't afford their house even when Michael was working.

And the last thing Nina wanted to deal with when she was

undergoing a crisis—spiritual, metaphysical, or financial—was her mother.

She took another deep cleansing breath.

Her mother. Whose exact opposite—she suddenly realized—was Coriander. Nina smiled, as if she'd just solved a difficult mathematical proof. Think about it. Belle blustered into a room like a winter storm and commandeered it, exhorting on everything from salad dressing to golf. Coriander could slip in like a breeze. Belle, who was nothing if not fixated on the physical world: obsessed with the exact setting on the thermostat or whether a picture frame slanted a quarter of an inch to the left or the right. And Coriander, mistress of the intangible: auras, luck, shadows of the past.

Nina had studied with some real yogis years ago, in upstate New York, at the ashram where she'd first learned yoga. Real yogis radiated an undeniable grace. They operated outside the normal bounds of ego and stress. True, one of those yogis from the early '80s had been disgraced for improper sexual relations, but that kind of indiscretion happened to people in other professions, too. In Coriander, Nina thought she recognized something that she'd experienced so long ago in some of her teachers at the ashram: real transcendence, enlightenment, purity.

No wonder, then, that it seemed imperative to learn feng shui. It had started with the fountain. How naïve she'd been just to plug it in anywhere there was an outlet and not think about where it belonged! What foolishness that she hadn't done a thing to address the negative energy of the ballet teacher! But what *serendipity* that the water had overflowed into Coriander's office, immediately below. Who said there were no accidents? Freud, Tolstoy, Dr. Laura? No, the flood hadn't been an accident. It was the universe's sly way of introducing her to Coriander.

Nina walked over to the Mr. Coffee, took out the mug with stick figures doing yoga, which Adam had bought her for her birthday a few years back, and poured a cup. She really should be drinking more green tea. Unfortunately she hated how green tea tasted. This in itself sometimes made her feel like a fraud. The kind of person she wanted to be would not think green tea tasted like grass clippings. But as the caffeine began to percolate through Nina's bloodstream, recalibrating her brain's neurotransmitters to a more favorable balance, she felt a little better. She shouldn't have snapped at Michael, she suddenly realized. That wasn't nice.

Nina sat back down at the table again and started thumbing through the feng shui book in front of her. She'd skip the chart for now. She'd ask Coriander to draw one up; she'd pay for a full consultation. Still, Nina kept turning the pages, inspecting the diagrams, reading the Chinese words, feeling— despite the full-color illustrations—as if she'd found some mysterious dust-covered ancient text, and that if she only found the right page, the universe might split open and reveal its deepest secrets.

And then she came upon the paragraph she'd been seeking. *"The Yin Bagua, sometimes called the Bagua Mirror,"* she read, *"is one of the most powerful bad-luck cures in feng shui. It can even deflect poison arrow energy."* Nina stared at the illustration. The Yin Bagua was just an octagonal mirror with Chinese writing around the border. But the book said it was extremely powerful, even dangerous. Placed inside the house, it could harm—even kill—the people who lived there. Nina studied the illustration, her pulse quickening.

Maybe, just maybe . . .

Belle was sure that people had been watching her all night while she tried to sleep. She'd been huddled up in a chair at the gate, trying to find a comfortable position while remaining relatively ladylike and guarding her purse at the same time. Actually, various gates. At first she'd been relieved when they'd dimmed the lights where she was resting, but when she looked around and didn't see anyone else spending the night, she got spooked, so she moved to a gate that was closer to airport security, and seemed safer. It had crossed her mind to book a hotel for the night, but why spend $139 for five or six hours in an airport hotel room, where you'd hear all the flights taking off and landing anyway? Besides, it wasn't like she had a nightgown to change into. The suitcase had been checked onto Max's plane.

But in that half-awake, half-asleep state, in the dark corners of a strange airport in the middle of the night, Belle felt inordinately aware of the vulnerability of being a sixty-eight-year-old Jewish woman traveling alone. Maybe it was all the focus on airport security since 9/11—which should have, technically speaking, made her feel safer—but when she saw men walk by wearing mechanic's overalls and talking in a foreign language, she was certain that they were terrorists. When a young couple with spiky Technicolor hair and piercings from their eyebrows to their belly buttons took a seat a few rows behind her, the girl on the boy's lap, Belle became convinced they were on drugs and that, if she allowed herself to fall back asleep, they'd stick her with a dirty heroin needle and give her AIDS. Even an ordinary, well-dressed businessman filled her with fear. Why wasn't *he* staying at an airport hotel?

But in the morning she'd woken up quite alive, if cold, wrinkled, and ill-rested. She always had a hard time imagining the weather where she wasn't, and she usually underpacked for New Jersey, but she certainly hadn't anticipated a trip to Chicago or an overnight at O'Hare. When she woke up in her totally inadequate lime green linen-blend sweater, she was shivering. And then there was the problem of morning mouth. Belle's toothbrush was in the bag she'd sent with Max, and she'd gotten into O'Hare so late that she hadn't even been able to buy any mints.

Even though it was early, Belle found a little convenience store and spent $7.50 for a toothbrush and a tiny little travel tube of toothpaste. Talk about your highway robbery! Then she went into a ladies' room to brush her teeth. Just as she was spitting out, a little girl and her mother came out of a toilet stall, the girl looking at Belle and the sink with wide, disbelieving eyes—as if she'd just watched someone urinate on a public street. The girl's mother whisked her off to another set of sinks, making Belle feel dirty, like someone from a third-world country, a refugee. Of course, Belle *was* a refugee. A refugee from Hurricane Ida.

After brushing her teeth, Belle had called Nina, who seemed disgusted about the whole thing, about the fact that she and Max had left Florida at all, especially on two separate planes, as if it all had been arranged for Nina's own personal inconvenience. What was the saying? One mother can take care of ten children but ten children can't take care of one mother? Now Belle had to find a flight to Newark, which probably meant going back out past the security gates and standing in line at the ticket windows of the various airlines until she found something. She ought to call Max and see if he'd found something out of Boston. And call the neighbors at home to check on the house—although it was probably still early for the hurricane to have hit.

She called the neighbors first, the Rubells, and when she heard the fear in Esther Rubell's voice, Belle was glad to be up north, even in Chicago. It was still too early to tell how bad Ida would be. Rain was heavy and the wind was blustery, but that was all on Ida's periphery. The real storm hadn't hit. She tried calling Max next, but just as the number began to ring, there were three quick bleeps and her phone went dead. It wasn't something she'd thought of in the hurry to leave Florida—recharging her phone or bringing a charger with her.

Max Gettleman got off his Gator Air flight in Logan Airport, his eyes bleary and his knee aching from the tight position he'd been in all night. If he'd slept an hour the whole time, it was a miracle. When Belle had slapped her credit card on the counter, she hadn't bothered to ask anything about the flights. Whether they were, for example, nonstop. Max had gone to Boston via Houston and then, of all places, Chicago. Trudging through O'Hare at 5 A.M. to make his connection, he tried fruitlessly to spot Belle in the shadows. Maybe she'd gone to Chicago by way of Boston.

On the first leg of the trip, there'd been a baby three rows behind him, who was either teething or possessed by demons. On the middle leg, he was sitting next to a huge woman who had to lift the armrest to fit into her seat, and whose blubbery arms and midsection puddled against him. After the leviathan disembarked in Chicago there was a little more room, but midway through the flight someone tried to smoke in the bathrooms and set off such a loud and insistent alarm that Max and all the other passengers awoke with a start, wondering whether there were hijackers or the plane was crashing.

He had to wonder if it was worth it, just to get out of the way of Hurricane Ida. He'd been planning to wait out the storm in the small walk-in closet in their bedroom. He'd bought new flashlights and batteries for his little portable TV. They could have brought pillows into the closet, too. There wasn't much room to stretch out, but there was more than there'd been next to the woman in 11B between Houston and Chicago.

And now, here he was finally in Logan, unsure what plane he'd take next. He followed all the other passengers, who walked like zombies to luggage, and seeing that their bags hadn't come out yet, sat down on the edge of the empty luggage rack behind him while he waited for his American Tourister to emerge. He thought about Belle, wondered what indignities she might have suffered and where she might be this very moment. Then he considered her suspicions about

Michael. What did she think? That he had some kind of floozy on the side? No, it wasn't in his son-in-law's character. Belle was always so suspicious, seeing scams everywhere, sure she was being cheated. And anybody who didn't share her view of the world was, in her opinion, hopelessly naïve. It was a terrible worldview to have, Max thought.

When the conveyer belt he was leaning against started moving, unexpectedly, Max lost his balance and lurched onto the floor. The next thing he knew, he was lying on his back, looking up at a circle of concerned faces, insisting that he was all right. But of course, he wasn't sure of that at all.

SEVEN

Everybody in school knew about Lisa Epstein's new 60-gigabyte video iPod. She'd had a Mini, which she'd already passed to her best friend, April Jacobson, like it was a half-eaten tuna sandwich. Lisa had taken some of her bat mitzvah money to the Mall at Short Hills on Sunday and, in addition to the iPod, she'd acquired a new Prada bag, Jimmy Choo shoes, and a poncho made by the same inmate who'd crocheted Martha Stewart's famous good-bye poncho. Adam recognized the iPod, but he couldn't have identified a Prada, Jimmy Choos, or a penitentiary poncho if they'd all been labeled and placed in a glass case. But it was impossible to miss with all the girls squealing in the hallway, and Lisa Epstein herself was in Adam's Spanish class, where the legendary iPod was confiscated by Señora Ramos after three increasingly annoyed *por favors*—leading to a rumor that Señora Ramos would be enrolling in the Witness Protection Program before the marking period was over.

By lunch, Lisa's malignant glare at Señora Ramos had become the newest nugget of school lore. It kept the subject of Lisa's bat mitzvah alive for another day, which led to a few more winks at Adam about the butterfly episode, and kept just about everybody in eighth grade in a good mood. But not Adam. He couldn't help thinking about what he'd buy if he had all that bar mitzvah money (Lisa's take was now rumored to be fifteen thousand dollars, and he was certain that if he had that kind of money, he'd spend it with a great deal more taste and flair than Lisa Epstein. Adam wanted one of those really small micromini digital video cameras and a MacBook— he'd heard you could make movies on them, real easy—but what he really fantasized about was a Segway scooter. He imagined zipping to school, zipping into town, a motorized boy—no, if he had a bar mitzvah, that would make him a motorized *man*—never having to ask his mom or dad for a ride anywhere, ever.

Only he wasn't going to have a bar mitzvah. That's what he'd learned yesterday, and it's what he should have known all along. This was what he got from having a mother who thought she knew more than generations of ancestors. What was he going to get with a mother like that, a walk through a churchyard labyrinth followed by a potluck supper?

It wasn't fair. Wasn't he also the grandson of Max and Belle Gettleman, just like his cousins Tyler and Madison and Hannah and Zach, who'd all had bar or bat mitzvahs of their own? Had *he* asked not to go to Hebrew school, not to belong to a synagogue? It was his mother who'd thrown away his birthright: a five-thousand-dollar self-balancing personal transportation device.

Philip plopped down into the cafeteria chair next to Adam and slid a tray with two brownies, french fries, and chocolate milk onto the table. "They say Señora Ramos is dead meat."

Adam shrugged. "Yeah, I was there."

"Oh, I forgot. You're in Señora's third-period class with Lisa. That must have been awesome. Was she really passing the iPod around in class?"

Adam tried to think of something titillating to add but couldn't even feign interest. "Can we talk about something besides Lisa Epstein?"

"We could," Philip said, "but then, why would we want to?"

"I'm just sick of it." He was sick of it, sick of the nonstop ego trip that was Lisa Epstein, sick even more of bat mitzvah talk, especially talk about what bat mitzvah money could buy—because he knew now that he was never going to get the pot of gold at the end of that particular rainbow.

"Okay, then. What were you doing yesterday at Temple Beth Shalom?"

The question—so sudden, so unexpected—landed like a slap. How the hell did Philip know? He'd picked a day when there was no Hebrew school, and he'd been there all of five minutes. Adam felt exposed, like someone had just barged in while he was in the crapper. Damn Philip. This was a secret wish, wanting to have a bar mitzvah. He wasn't ready to have it inspected.

Adam took his plastic fork and started making patterns in the leftover whole-wheat macaroni and cheese his dad had packed. It was cold, of course, and appealing as cardboard, but he'd gotten used to cold whole-wheat macaroni and cheese. It was just his lot in life.

"I know what you're up to," Philip persisted.

"Oh, I forgot. You're all-seeing, all-knowing, just like God."

"No. My mom had just dropped me off for bar mitzvah lessons. I saw you coming out."

"Okay, so you saw me at your synagogue. What was I doing there?"

"Trying to have a bar mitzvah, of course."

Adam put down his fork. Was it that obvious? Did Philip

know what he wanted to buy, too? Or the dream he'd had about Lisa Epstein and the butterflies?

"So if you knew why I was there, why did you ask?"

Philip ignored Adam's question. "So how did it go?"

"Can we talk about this later? After school or something?" It was bad enough that Philip knew, but he didn't want everyone in junior high school in on his little fantasy.

"Sure, pal," Philip said, his smile somehow both smug and conspiratorial. They decided to meet at Risdale Park after school. For just a few minutes. Philip had Hebrew school.

On her way into yoga class, Nina dropped by Coriander's studio, but the door was closed, and no light showed in the crack underneath. After her first class, she went downstairs to check again, but the only change was the appearance of a big bundle of mail. Nina felt a growing panic as she imagined catalogs, magazines, and bills piling higher and higher, while Coriander lingered on some Mediterranean island and the inauspiciously arranged forces of water, wind, wood, and fire all wreaked havoc with Nina's life. *Perfect, just perfect,* she thought. *I've got a poison arrow pointed right at my house, my husband's unemployed, my mother is coming, and Coriander is nowhere to be found.*

She went back upstairs and taught her ten-thirty, but she was just going through the poses mechanically; there was no grace, no transformation. Even the yoga nidra at the end of class seemed somehow lacking. After the last student had rolled up her yoga mat and stacked it in the corner, Nina ran downstairs to check again. Still the closed door, the untouched stack of mail.

Nina would have to wait. As Michael had pointed out, they'd been living in the same house with the same poison arrow for twelve years.

But she couldn't wait. It was one thing to have an unknown

hazard in your life, another to see the danger and do nothing. Desperate times called for desperate measures. Floods, fires, pink slips, hurricanes—what was Nina waiting for? She had to get a bagua mirror, and she had to get it *now*—even if Coriander wasn't around to supervise.

Nina's first thought was the Internet. You could find anything on the Internet. But even if she ordered one immediately, it could take a week or longer to arrive. No, she couldn't wait. She needed one *now*. But this wouldn't be as easy as just driving to Toys "R" Us. They wouldn't sell them at Target or Kmart either.

And then Nina was struck with an extraordinary inspiration. She knew a place—a veritable Hong Kong, where fish glistened on tables and shops were stocked with teas, amulets, luck charms—where she could buy a bagua mirror. Chinatown. She could get there, by train, inside of an hour.

Energized by her plan, Nina bounded back to her studio, found a piece of paper, and made a sign: *Today's PM Yoga Classes Canceled.* Taping it to the door, she chewed her bottom lip, wondering if she should go through with it. Was it really wise, canceling a yoga class? There were so many yoga instructors in town. It was a buyer's market. And yet, since she'd seen the poison arrow, she hadn't been able to get it out of her mind. She picked up her pen and added four more words: *Due to Family Emergency.*

It seemed absurd to Michael that he had to leave the house. Couldn't he just not answer the phone? On the other hand, what was so terrible about getting out of the house? It was better than moping around in a bathrobe. He could go to the batting cages; he hadn't done that in a while. He could spend some time at Starbucks. Or maybe he could call one of the guys from the poker game. Find out what they did all day, unemployed in the suburbs. Then he remembered, yes, the airport.

He'd been planning to go again, as he had the last two days, and this time he'd bring the digital camera to take pictures of takeoff, the moment when man's creation pulled free of the force of gravity and soared, the junction of metal and clouds.

First, though, he'd take a quick look at Ida. He opened the National Hurricane Center's page and was astonished at how the storm had behaved overnight. Ida was turning into an interesting piece of weather. She'd blown offshore and gathered strength—briefly blustering into a category 5 storm—and then stalled in the western Caribbean. The various models were all over the place in terms of predictions. One model expected Ida to stay a 5 and not hit Florida at all, possibly taking a straight path north for a direct strike at Halifax later in the week. Another model had the storm weakening to a 3 and going inland around Miami. Still another model saw Ida hovering offshore for several days, soaking the mainland with a foot or so of rain, but not producing much in the way of wind damage.

Michael turned off the computer. Well, maybe his crazy mother-in-law wasn't so crazy after all—at least to have gotten on a plane to escape the hurricane. He went upstairs to get his camera, then left for the airport. It surprised him to discover that this simple mission, going to his former workplace to take photographs of clouds and airplanes, seemed to make him happy.

Nina looked out the train window and watched town recede; then she opened her feng shui book, *The Art of Channeling Wind and Water,* a different one than she'd studied at home. Yin Bagua, bagua mirror. The phrases buzzed in her head like a secret password or prayer. She found a photograph of the object on page 119, stop sign–shaped, reflective, red, with strange Chinese characters. *"The most powerful cure for bad luck,"* the book said. *"Excellent for deflecting poison arrow, sharp edges, negative energies. But"*—and here Nina felt her heart tighten—*"be very careful in its use. Do not use inside the home, or allow the mirror to reflect energies back to a neighbor. It is irresponsible to unleash the mirror's potent powers on someone else."*

Nina closed the book and thought for a moment what exactly she would do with the mirror once she procured it. Just how powerful was it? Would it be dangerous to carry it in her handbag? Could it cause a transit accident? Maybe the shopkeeper would wrap it in some heavy velvet, something to neutralize its powers until she was ready to give it a permanent home. Certainly she couldn't risk bringing it inside the house. But if she left it on the front porch, carelessly, it could point at the Grimeldes or the Baskins. Mr. and Mrs. Grimelde were old, and their children had grown up and gone to live in other parts of the country, coming back only rarely, but with increasing broods of little Grimelde grandchildren. Mr. Grimelde still took care of his own lawn and had a passion for sealing his driveway with cans of black tar. Every time Nina saw him pushing the lawn mower or shoveling his own snow, she expected him to keel over on the spot. The Baskins, Nina had heard, had been trying unsuccessfully to become pregnant for several years. Not that Anita Baskin, who sold real estate and drove a silver Jaguar, looked like someone who wanted to be weighed down with a child.

Still, Nina thought, neither the Baskins nor the Grimeldes needed bad luck any more than she did. She'd have to be very careful, just as the books said. She certainly didn't want to add bad karma to her list of woes.

Risdale Park was right behind the middle school and in addition to a basketball court and two baseball diamonds, it featured a small playground, a graffiti-covered public bathroom, and a small retinue of drug dealers, who plied their trade despite the sign forbidding their business within five hundred feet of a public school. Two young mothers—one black, one white, as if supplied by Politically Correct Central Casting—were holding their toddlers on a teeter-totter, allowing them to go up and down, but carefully preventing any unexpected bumps. Adam was half-surprised the children weren't equipped with helmets. Adam's mom didn't like him hanging out in Risdale Park, even though the county had been fixing it up lately, adding some benches and fancy signs teaching joggers how to stretch. You heard stories every couple of years about the police finding bodies there in the middle of the night. But kids cut through Risdale on their way home from school all the time. If you were seen there at three-fifteen, nobody would think a thing of it.

Philip was already there when Adam arrived, occupying one of those swings that curves up around your butt. He was idly kicking up the little brown rubber fake mulch pellets with his feet, but as soon as he saw Adam he stopped.

"Come on," he said impatiently. "I have Hebrew school."

Adam plopped into the swing next to Philip's, feeling defeated already. Hebrew school: just an inconvenience for Philip, but for Adam a symbol of everything he'd never have. "So." Adam dug his feet into the pellets. "You saw me?"

"Yeah, I saw you."

"You think I'm an idiot."

"Why would I think you're an idiot?"

"Because they wouldn't touch me with a ten-foot pole. I haven't been taking Hebrew since third grade. My parents don't belong to a synagogue. We belong to the Unitarian Church, for Christ's sake."

"So they wouldn't take you?"

Adam shook his head.

"But you want a bar mitzvah?"

Adam jumped off the swing. "Yeah, I want to have a bar mitzvah! I want a DJ and a huge party and people to hold me up in a chair. I want my ten thousand dollars. Is Lisa Epstein more deserving than me? Are you more deserving than me?"

"Okay," Philip said. "I get it."

The mothers with the toddlers turned and squinted in Adam's direction, as if evaluating for possible threats. Adam felt his cheeks start to burn. He'd made a scene. Like it wasn't embarrassing enough just to want what he wanted, and to be caught by his best friend, now the local Mom Squad was looking at him as if he were a drug dealer.

"Hey, pal. Chill," Philip said. "I've got an idea."

Adam sighed. Philip always had ideas. He was always pulling miniature tuxedos out of bags in the backs of limousines. But what kind of trick did he think he had to turn Adam into a Jew? "What?" Adam said.

"Have you heard of the Chabad?"

"Huh?"

"Chabad. The guys with the long black coats, the black hats, the beards, the sideburns? Who go around every year in December in a van with a menorah on top of it?"

Adam thought. He guessed he'd seen guys like that in New York City, the really weird, Amish-looking guys who worked in electronics stores selling computers and digital cameras. Sort of creeped him out.

"I think so," he said cautiously. "In New York City."

"Well, they're out here, too," Philip said. "In New Jersey."

"So? What does that have to do with me?"

"It has plenty to do with you, my friend," Philip said. "Your mom is Jewish, right?"

"Yeah."

"So you're a Jew!"

"Well, sort of."

"No," said Philip. "Automatically. Your mother's a Jew; you're a Jew."

"Okay. What's your point?"

"The Chabad guys will take anybody. They're like missionaries for nonobservant Jews. They don't care if your mom is a yoga teacher or thinks she's a Unitarian. They don't care if your dad is Episcopalian or Lutheran or a Moonie. Your mom was born a Jew, so you're a Jew, no questions asked."

"What's the point?" Adam said. "I'm going to become an Orthodox Jew?"

"No. That's the beauty part. They do outreach. Their whole mission is to take Jews like you—lost Jews, Jews who never set foot in a synagogue—and make them more Jewish. So, if you want a bar mitzvah, they'll give you a bar mitzvah."

"They'll give me a bar mitzvah."

"Yes," Philip said. "But I've got to go. Hebrew school." He backed all the way up on the swing, so that he was standing. Then he kicked his feet up and let the swing lift him forward, dismounting with a neat little jump.

Philip picked up his backpack and started walking away. He stopped about ten feet away from the swing set and turned around. "Google it," Philip added. "Chabad. *C-h-a-b-a-d*."

I'm a Jew, Adam thought, watching his friend walk slowly across the park toward Hebrew school and Judaism and his own inevitable champagne-fluted bar mitzvah. *I'm a Jew. Automatically.*

He reached into his backpack and pulled out his planner and a pen, writing down the word *Chabad* before he forgot it.

Once Nina arrived in Penn Station and walked outside, the optimism with which she'd started her mission began to fade. The canyons formed by Manhattan's office buildings immediately cut what light there was in half, and the sense that the sun was more than midway through its daytime trajectory, that time was running out, made her panicky. What was she doing in town anyway? What was she thinking leaving a sign up and abandoning her afternoon classes? Adam would be coming home from school, her mother could show up at any moment, yet here she was in New York City on this insane wild-goose chase. She stood there for a moment on Seventh Avenue and thought about turning around, taking the train right back. The nonstop motion of bodies going around her in every direction reminded her of a filmstrip she'd seen in school as a kid, with ants all speeded up and moving in a hundred different directions, digging tunnels, dragging back food, communicating without any kind of spoken language, all in service of the queen.

No. She was here. She might as well do it.

Nina followed the signs to the subway, trying to remember which ones went to Canal Street and then, looking at a map, saw that they all did. As she walked down the stairs to the platform, her sense of being an ant, or surrounded by ants, only increased. There were more people, moving in all directions, and of course, no natural light at all. And she was in an underground tunnel, just like an ant. It was hard to feel solid in such a place. Or, to use the language of yoga, to feel rooted. And it was this thought—this not feeling rooted—that made her realize, in a crushing instant of self-recognition, that she'd become a suburbanite. All of this—this subterranean grittiness, with its hipsters and its homeless and its incessant motion and the screech of brakes and the omnipresent stench of urine—was dirty and unpleasant. *She was becoming her mother.* But then, at the far end of the platform, she heard someone playing something classical on a violin, and briefly she was cheered.

At Canal Street, Nina climbed back up the stairs toward the light, but there was no relief from the moving swirl of humanity. If she stopped for a moment on the sidewalk, to orient herself, to figure out which way was east, the people behind her would smack right into her and they'd all topple like dominoes. She had to keep moving, despite the fact there was no longer a compass, no World Trade Center marking due south. She moved with the crowd, either propelled toward Chinatown or away from it; she had no choice. Then suddenly her nose sucked in the strong sewerlike odor of the Chinatown streets—raw fish—and there they were, dead-eyed, openmouthed, and glistening with water sprayed on them to keep flies off, like something from another century or another continent. She looked up, and there were all the booths with the hats, scarves, gloves, purses, backpacks. The newest fashion: long scarves made of fluffy balls that looked like rabbit's feet, strung together like a chain of sausages.

Nina suddenly became aware of someone talking to her. "Gucci? Prada?" She pulled her attention back to eye level and there was a woman, inches away, beckoning her toward an alley. Nina shook her head, but every few feet there was a new woman—five foot two or shorter, black short hair, middle-aged—saying the same words, asking the same questions—"Gucci? Prada? Watch? Rolex?"—a question, an offer, a temptation. She didn't remember such insistence before, didn't remember people in Chinatown coming on like drug dealers. "Gucci? Prada?" Had Chinatown changed, or had she? Did she now look like a kind of suburban matron, an easy mark for cheap designer knockoffs?

Still, she wasn't seeing what she wanted. Why didn't they whisper "Yin Bagua"? There was something worthy of whispers and dark alleys, a thing so powerful, it could repel bad luck. Or cause it.

Nina kept walking. What she was looking for was farther down. Pell, Mott, and that crooked little one, whose name she could never remember, bent like the inside of an elbow toward the Bowery. She remembered dozens of stores with chopsticks and jade Buddhas and ginseng tea, and, she was sure, some secret and powerful feng shui cures, things she'd always, in her ignorance, overlooked.

And yet, when she got to Mott, when she got to Pell, when she started going into stores whose wares she thought she remembered, she found no bagua mirrors, no three-legged toads to bring prosperity—none of the feng shui cures or luck charms she'd read about in the books. There were plastic windup toys, miniature Statues of Liberty, cell phone covers, bootlegged CDs, and cheap snow globes that froze the Twin Towers in an eternity of glittery ash. And still, people asking, "Gucci? Prada? Rolex?"

Yes, a wild-goose chase.

Nina picked up a pincushion in hot pink and stared at it idly when the proprietor of the store, a sprite woman with twinkling eyes, suddenly grabbed her forearm. "Back of store?" The woman's lips stretched into a winking leer. "Many special things."

Many special things? Secret sex toys? Heroin, cocaine, crack? Nina looked at the back of the store, and all she saw was more of the same. Chinese pajamas hanging on cheap wood paneling. But then the woman pressed against the wall and there was a door, a secret passage, like in a Nancy Drew book. The woman put her finger to her lips—"They find this, they shut us down"—and led Nina into a secret back room.

There, in a tiny room the size of a walk-in closet, were a thousand secret handbags, most still wrapped in plastic. Not sex toys but, Nina had to acknowledge, an almost orgasmic profusion of leather, suede, chains, buckles, designer labels. At first, Nina felt a wave of disappointment—not the feng shui warehouse she'd hoped to find—and then, almost against her will, a thrill. "Gucci, Prada," the woman said, pointing to various corners. "Coach, Fendi." Deep down, under everything, at her core, Nina was still a Long Island girl. She found herself gravitating toward a chocolate-colored bag with a Prada label. She reached under the plastic wrapping to caress the bag's soft skin. Suede was the chink in her vegetarian armor. She wouldn't eat meat, but suede was soft, like a memory of childhood. She couldn't stop herself from wearing it.

"Sixty dollars," the proprietor said.

Nina took her hand away, as if she'd touched a hot stove. This wasn't what she'd come to Chinatown for.

"Fifty dollars."

She hated herself for wanting it, for allowing herself to be distracted. But it was cunning, this suede bag. Reluctantly, Nina turned around, back toward the front of the store.

"Thirty-five dollars, my final offer," the woman said, resolute, her arms folded, as she blocked Nina's exit from the store.

"Okay," Nina said weakly. She knew she shouldn't, with Michael out of work, and everything up in the air. But the hunter hunts. The shopper shops. The spider sees a fly and it pounces.

"You not disappointed," the woman promised. And she wrapped the bag in a bigger plastic bag as Nina reached into her own purse and found money.

But she was disappointed. Not with the bag, or the price she got it for, though she knew of course that it was a knock-off. But with herself, for succumbing to her own Princess tendencies, always under the surface, even after years of political enlightenment and feminism and practicing yoga. She hated the way her heart raced when presented with a bargain, the way she could be distracted from her mission. And she was disappointed with Chinatown. Where was the mystery, the wizened herbalists cooking up bitter broths of chi-enhancing tea? China, the world's oldest living civilization, the bosom of Buddhism, of Tao, of acupuncture . . . and the best Chinatown had to offer was Prada knockoffs?

Well, if she wanted to go home with what she'd come for, she was going to have to ask. But she felt shy, suddenly, asking about a bagua mirror. Maybe she'd mispronounce it; after all, she'd only read about it in books. Nina had been to restaurants in Chinatown where she'd asked for certain dishes that the natives were eating, and they'd steered her instead to blander ones they thought a Westerner would like. So what would happen if she asked for something a whole lot more exotic than Eight Treasure Sea Cucumber? What if they knew what the bagua mirror was and looked at her like she was a criminal? What if they didn't know what she was talking about? She smiled, thinking of how men could never stop and ask for directions. She felt that way now. Like her mouth wouldn't open, like she'd rather walk for hours than ask a question that seemed, oddly, embarrassing.

The woman in the store handed Nina the purse inside the plastic bag, and her change, and smiled broadly. "Tell your friends," she said, though she was already starting to scan the street for fresh customers.

"Wait," Nina said. "I was looking for something else."

"Watch? I have Rolex."

"No," Nina said, struggling to release the words. "Yin Bagua?"

The proprietor looked confused.

Nina tried again. "Bagua mirror?" Nothing, no glimmer of understanding. "Good-luck toad? Feng shui?"

"Ah," the woman said, smiling. "Feng shui. Lucky toads. Yes, yes. I know where you go. Manhattan Luck Company. They have everything. Everything lucky. Bamboo . . . Chinese coins . . ."

"Where?" Nina asked. Nothing could be too far in China-town, but the sun was getting lower all the time, and any minute her mother could be landing. She hoped it was on a street that she'd heard of, or at least somewhere close.

"SoHo."

The sky was so blue, it looked like it had been painted with a children's art set, and it was filled with startlingly white cu-mulonimbus clouds, so billowy that Michael wanted to sink into them and fall sleep—even though he knew that they were actually nothing more than water vapor. It was strange, see-ing clouds this way—as forms to be appreciated. Strange, ac-tually, really *seeing* any part of the weather. He was used to observing weather on computer screens—an abstraction, a series of measurements, graphs, probabilities—and always as a potential liability. Weather as a threat, a hindrance, an encumbrance, a danger. Never a thing of simple beauty.

The clouds suddenly brought to mind his summers visiting cousins on the Michigan peninsula, lying in a hammock and staring skyward for hours at a time. He hadn't thought about that for years, Aunt Florence and Uncle Joe, those lazy Augusts in the house by the lake, before he was old enough to be expected to work as a waiter or a lifeguard. He could practically feel the hammock, the way it hugged his body, the gentle almost imperceptible undulations, time so open and spacious, you could afford to waste it. And the pleasure of watching the clouds float away like dreams, and sinking into dreams himself. Until, of course, one or both of his cousins came and jumped on the hammock, laughing and tickling him, demanding that he come with them and hunt for frogs or go skateboarding or, as he got older, go out waterskiing. All the harmless summertime pursuits of Sault Sainte Marie in the 1960s and early 1970s.

Was this where his interest for weather began, in those summers, in that hammock? Surprisingly, he'd never thought of it. Or maybe it was just that he hadn't thought about it in years. He'd always imagined it was Hurricane Agnes, that big bully of a storm that bypassed the usual stop in south Florida to hit hard in Pennsylvania just as his family was driving home one summer from Michigan. They'd listened nonstop to news about Agnes on that drive, all leaning toward the little radio in the family station wagon, while the rain beat down so hard, it was impossible for his father to see two feet ahead. His mom's job was to tune the radio, and she turned the knob frantically, whenever the static carried a news station away, as she tried to convince Michael's dad to pull over to the side of the road and wait. His father, meanwhile, gripping the steering wheel and looking as pallid as a ghost, argued that it was safer to keep going. He was afraid that if he pulled over, and other people were doing the same thing, somebody would rear-end them, maybe even a huge rig, and that would be the end.

They'd wound up stopping in a town—he didn't remember the name and he doubted his parents would either, although it would be interesting to look on a map and try to figure it out—and staying at an old hotel with a saloon in its lobby, a place that he and Nina today would probably find quite charming, but which his mother, preferring a Holiday Inn or any chain that provided sanitary strips across the toilet seats, was sure would give them bedbugs or lead to their deaths in some awful and violent way. The lights had gone out hours before they got there, and Michael's family was given a few candles, and then huddled in the room, listening to the rain that sounded like it would never end, until finally, his dad talked his mom into letting them go down to the saloon, which had a gigantic polished wooden bar and a million bottles of whiskey behind it, and an old mirror the same length as the bar, lit by candles, making the whole thing look like something out of the Wild West. His mom drank Tab, his dad drank scotch, and Michael and his sister, Jean, were allowed to drink White Russians.

Hurricane Agnes became part of the family's canon of awful vacation stories, but Michael and Jean remembered it fondly as one of the few real adventures of their youth, and it had inspired Jean, during her twenties, to work as a bartender herself. Michael had always assumed it had something to do with his developing interest in weather—although now, remembering the hammock, he realized his vocation might have even earlier roots, those lazy afternoons in Michigan watching the atmosphere gather and reform.

He pulled into the daily lot and found a space off by itself, where his view wouldn't be obstructed by a minivan on one side and an SUV on the other. Of course, people were so predictable. You could do a probability chart on what parking spaces people would choose and in what order. People parked closest to the terminals, and liked to park at the end of a row, but instead of following the pattern, Michael parked all the way in the back, by himself.

He turned off the engine, but then turned the key halfway so he could hear the radio, because he was listening to Lenny Lopate interview some new indie film director and wanted to hear the end of the conversation. Then he spread out, taking his time, pulling his camera bag from the back and spreading his lenses and his filters out on the passenger seat. It was an old camera, ancient, a Nikon from college, and it shot film.

Michael was looking through his lens filters, trying to remember the best one for shooting a bright daytime sky, when there was a knock on the window. He jumped, literally, and when he looked out the window the first thing he saw was a gun, tucked into a waistband. Michael's heart began to pound. Was he being carjacked? The man at the window had red hair, buzz cut, and was wearing a dark blue Windbreaker and khaki pants. He wasn't any carjacker, Michael could tell instantly. He was way too clean cut. Some kind of cop, or security guard. The kind of guy Michael had seen around the airport a thousand times, but never paid any attention to. But here was a piece of cold metal, just inches away from his face.

Michael very slowly and deliberately rolled down his window and made his face as neutral as he could. "Hello?"

The man leaned in, inspecting Michael's hands first, and then squinted disapprovingly at the camera equipment in the front seat. He thrust his chin forward, like a pit bull straining to get past a tall chain-link fence. He was chewing Juicy Fruit, and Michael found himself wondering if that might be the last thing on earth he might ever smell.

"What's that?" the man barked, indicating the camera on the front seat.

Duh, Michael wanted to say. But he'd stopped trying to act clever around cops years ago, the summer between his sophomore and junior years in college, when he'd driven across country and learned, the hard way, that in a showdown with a guy in a uniform, the uniform always wins. He was determined to be polite, obsequiously so. "A camera," Michael said.

"What the fuck are you doing with a camera?"

"I was planning to take pictures of—" He was going to say "the sky" but then he realized how lame it sounded. He started again. "I'm a meteorologist," he said. "And these are some of the best examples of cumulonimbus clouds I've ever seen."

"And they don't have these same clouds in Jersey City?"

"Well," Michael admitted, "I wanted to take pictures of the airplanes, too."

The man reached into his pocket, nearly causing Michael to have a heart attack, but luckily all he pulled out was a laminated piece of identification and a metal badge. "Homeland Security. Get out of the car. And keep your hands away from your jacket."

Michael stepped out, putting his hands up, the way he saw in movies. "What's wrong?"

The man flipped him up against the car in half a second, patting him down to check for guns. "Don't you know it's against the law to take pictures at secure facilities? Airports, naval bases. Shit, haven't you noticed the signs on the Lincoln Tunnel?"

"Look," Michael said, twisting his head around to look at his captor. "This has to be a mistake. I'm the last person you have to be worried about. I don't even cheat on my taxes."

"Shut up and turn around," the man ordered. "Keep your hands on the car." Out of the corner of his eye, Michael saw the man keep his left hand on his gun and use his right to pull out a walkie-talkie. Shit. What kind of nightmare was this? Less than a week ago, Michael could go anywhere he wanted in Newark Airport. He had a laminated ID and a nodding relationship with half the security guys in the airport. Now he was being treated like a terrorist.

"Jack," he said. "This is McCarthy. I'm with this bozo way out in Lot A. Here are the plates. New Jersey. JZ BH68. See if this is the same clown who was here yesterday. Uh-huh. Uh-huh. What? Okay. Thanks. Over."

The man named McCarthy pulled Michael away from the car.

"Pop the trunk," he said.

"What?"

"Pop the trunk."

Michael reached inside the car window and popped the trunk, and McCarthy inspected, finding just two bags of Nina's clothing discards intended for a donation box. McCarthy peered into the backseat and then, making Michael wince, dumped the rest of the contents of Michael's camera bag. When no contraband appeared, no weapons, he pointed to the Nikon and said, "Take a picture."

Michael picked up the camera, looked through the viewfinder, and aimed it at McCarthy. He started to spin the lens into focus, when McCarthy said, "Not at me, fuck face. And just shoot the damn thing." Michael turned toward a distant spot in the parking lot and clicked.

"Okay," McCarthy said, apparently satisfied that the camera wasn't a bomb. "Now scram. We ran your plates. We know you worked here. And as far as I'm concerned, any ex-employee showing up a high-security facility the week after he's been fired is bad news. But there's no weapon and no priors, so today's your lucky day. I'm letting you go. But I don't want to see this crappy little piece of Japanese engineering here again. Do you hear me? And no cameras at airports, tunnels, subways, or even the Empire fucking State Building. You got plenty of clouds in your own backyard."

Michael backed into the car, put both hands on the steering wheel, and turned on his ignition while McCarthy glared. His heart was thumping like a bad transmission. He wanted to feel outrage. He could imagine how Nina would react if this happened to her, how she'd be on the phone within an hour to the ACLU, calling well-placed friends, writing letters to editors. But he just felt like he had in third grade when Miss Kuretsky had made him stand in the corner, punishment for having smuggled a comic book into class inside his spelling book. He hadn't told his parents about the comic book incident and, he decided, turning the radio back on, he wouldn't tell Nina either.

Adam didn't notice any cars when he got home, but after he unlocked the front door, he stood for a moment in the foyer, listening, just to make sure. "Mom? Dad? Grandma?" Good. The coast was clear. He put down his backpack, got a yogurt out of the fridge, and sat down at the computer in the sunroom. As he booted it up, he felt vaguely guilty, as if he were preparing to look for porn. Well, given his mother's feelings about Judaism, he might as well be searching for naked breasts. He pulled out his planner, looked up the word that Philip had spelled for him at Risdale Park, then typed it into Google. Chabad . . . *C-h-a-b-a-d*.

Chabad came up—1,630,000 results—and Adam narrowed the search by typing in *New Jersey,* and then his ZIP code. And there they were, just like Philip said. Men in black hats, beards, coats, looking just like the dancing Jews in some old-fashioned painting his grandmother had in her living room in Florida. But these guys in the long coats and the black hats weren't in some stupid old painting; they were right here, in real life, in New Jersey, now, in the twenty-first century. Just one town away, practically in his backyard. He even recognized some of the scenery in the background.

Jesus! What a freak show! This wasn't anything like Lisa Epstein's bat mitzvah. Where were the limousines, the girls in spaghetti-strap dresses, the ice sculptures, the shrimp? This had nothing to do with his fantasy, of a party in his honor,

125

people handing him envelopes with money, his friends hoisting him aloft in a chair. This was weird shit, the kind of stuff his mom hated, and for once in his life he could see why. It was weird-looking Jews like this who gave normal Jews a bad name.

Still, he kept clicking. It was almost irresistible, like looking in some old issue of *National Geographic* at African tribesmen who lengthened their necks and turned themselves into human giraffes. Freak shows were interesting. That's why people paid to see bearded ladies at the carnival.

Adam clicked on a tab that said SOFTBALL. Amazing. They actually had a slow-pitch softball team that had come in first place in its division. Strange-looking dudes: these guys in beards and baseball caps with weird fringes hanging out of their uniforms. It was impossible to imagine any of them sliding into second. And yet they'd won their division. The record stood for itself.

Adam started randomly clicking on buttons, pulling up pictures. One tab said PURIM, and Adam saw little kids dressed up as if for Halloween, only there was snow in the background, and the little Bat Men and Supermen wore yarmulkes. He pressed on CAMP. He pressed on CELEBRATIONS, and there it was, just like at Lisa's bat mitzvah, a kid being held aloft in a chair with a crowd below, clapping and dancing. There was even a picture of guys doing Russian dancing, their arms crossed, their butts almost on the ground, their legs straight in front of them. How did they keep from falling?

Adam clicked on the FREQUENTLY ASKED QUESTIONS:

Do you have to pay dues to study or pray at the Chabad?
No. Contributions are welcome but not required.

Do we welcome Jews from Reform or unaffiliated backgrounds?
We believe that labels like Reform, Conservative, and Orthodox

divide rather than unite. We invite Jews of all backgrounds to study with us, and to extend their Jewish educations, no matter what level of practice they are at currently.

What about bar and bat mitzvahs?
We are honored to prepare Jewish children of bar/bat mitzvah age, no matter their affiliation or experience, to learn Hebrew and engage in a ceremony of commitment to Judaism.

Adam read that sentence again. "We are honored to prepare Jewish children of bar/bat mitzvah age, no matter their affiliation or experience, to learn Hebrew and engage in a ceremony of commitment to Judaism."

So Philip was right. But then, maddeningly, Philip was always right.

Adam found the address of the Chabad center, entered it in MapQuest, and saw that it was less than five miles from his house. Straight uphill, from what he could remember about that road, but still biking distance. He printed out the FAQ.

Adam wondered whether he had the stomach for going to visit Rabbi Mendel Abraham. For one thing, he'd have to pretend that returning to his religious heritage was coming from a genuine place in his heart, and not an empty place in his wallet. And for another, well, he'd have to hide it from his mom. At least initially, until he was ready to spring the bar mitzvah on her. It was like a double life, like something in a spy movie, and he didn't know if he could pull it off, or if he even wanted to. Maybe having a bar mitzvah was a dumb idea.

Nina left Manhattan Luck Company with her coveted bagua mirror tucked into the new purse she'd picked up at Chinatown. Mission accomplished. It had been slightly awkward, asking for the funny little mirror by name, and it had seemed to her that the salesclerk had eyed her suspiciously, as if she'd been buying a gun or something. Or did everybody who had anything to do with feng shui have the power to read auras? The store was a little weird—sterile as an operating room, minimalistic as an art gallery—and the woman had insisted that Nina place her credit card in a red envelope before handing it over to be scanned. Some kind of Chinese custom. Oh, well. She had it—her secret weapon—that was the important thing. She bounded up Broadway, headed to the subway, on her way to Penn Station, suddenly at one with the city. Why had she found it so threatening before? Why had she felt overwhelmed by all the people moving in different directions, by the ant-farm aspect of it? New York was exciting, vital, brimming with chi—the life force. Nina patted the plastic bag she'd gotten in Chinatown, which contained her new brown suede Prada knockoff, inside of which she'd tucked a weapon powerful enough to repel a poison arrow. Nina felt triumphant and suddenly equal to whatever her mother had in store.

Belle had planned to take a taxi to Nina and Michael's house. The element of surprise was always helpful when you were checking up on someone. But by the time she landed in Newark, she was exhausted, and didn't feel like waiting in a taxi line or enduring the smell of secondhand smoke. All New York City cabs, and New Jersey cabs, too, smelled like smoke as far as she was concerned, and she didn't care what she might have read or heard about various smoking bans. Taxicabs would always smell like cigarettes. Even if they didn't smoke in front of you, cabdrivers all smoked while they were driving around looking for fares, stinking up their whole cars. And if their cabs didn't smell like smoke, they smelled like incense, or like those awful car deodorants, shaped like pine trees, that hung from rearview mirrors. Besides, she held the opinion that most cabdrivers were dishonest. They'd take you to New Jersey by way of Queens, and charge you three times what they were entitled to. And a lot of them were Muslim. That bothered her. So even though she was suspicious of Michael, wondering why he'd been home two days in a row, and even if his car was never particularly neat, a ride from him was still preferable to one from some guy named Muhammad.

Since her cell had run out of charge in Chicago, Belle looked around for a pay phone to call her son-in-law. Pay phones, she quickly discovered, were not in such great supply in airports these days. There were plenty of Starbucks and kiosks where they sold cell phones and cell phone accessories, but there wasn't a single phone booth in sight. Where, she wondered, would Superman change if he was fighting crime in the metropolis of Gotham these days? She sighed heavily and asked the airline lady, checking in passengers for the next flight, where she might find a pay phone. "Down there," the woman said. "Past the security gate." It figured. Phone booths would be considered a security risk at an airport these days. Someone could plant a bomb in one and rig it to go off when the phone rang.

Belle finally got to the bank of phones and pulled out the number Nina had given her. She put in thirty-five cents and pushed the buttons, but soon got a recording asking for her to deposit another dollar. That wasn't easy. She was afraid to show her wallet in public—there were pickpockets everywhere—so she blindly rummaged at the bottom of her purse for coins. Finally, cleared by the mechanical voice for three minutes of talk time, Belle heard the phone ring. And ring. And ring. Then Michael's voice. "This is Michael Summer, please leave a message at the tone." She slammed down the receiver. Good-for-nothing son-in-law, not even picking up the phone when he was supposed to. And she didn't have enough change to try again. She waited by the pay phone for five minutes, in case Michael saw the booth's phone number on his caller ID and called her back. Then, dispirited, she walked out to the cab line.

Michael wasn't even a hundred feet away from McCarthy when his cell phone rang. He pulled it out of his pocket and glanced at it, keeping it down below the level of the dashboard. PAY PHONE, the display read. Fuck. It was Belle. It had to be. Either Belle or Max. He didn't want to pick it up. Couldn't. After what he'd just been through, he didn't want to break any laws, not even the laws against driving and talking on a cell phone at the same time. He didn't want to give McCarthy any excuse to throw him up against the car. And he sure as hell wasn't going to circle back and pick Belle up. He pressed the IGNORE button. What choice did he have? He'd make up some excuse later.

Adam tucked the computer printouts about Chabad into the brochure he'd gotten from Philip's synagogue and smuggled the whole thing back under his mattress. What he was saving them for, he didn't know. Could he actually go through with this? Bike up the big hill to talk to some guy with a beard? His mother was contemptuous enough about dropping him off at the temple where Lisa's bat mitzvah had been. He couldn't even imagine what she'd think if she could see him talking to guys who looked like they'd stepped out of *Fiddler on the Roof.*

As he tucked the printout under the mattress, he noticed an old copy of *Playboy* from 1978. He'd forgotten that it was there, but suddenly remembered how it had come into his possession. Philip, of course, worldly Philip. He'd plucked it from his father's collection, hidden in an antique chest in the attic, and given it to Adam for his twelfth birthday. Adam had studied it at the time, the centerfold, of course, the cartoons that showed orgies, even some of the stories. And then, his mother had knocked on the door to give him a good night birthday kiss, and he'd hurriedly shoved it under the mattress. He'd consulted it regularly for a few months, then forgotten about it.

Adam felt his heart and his breath speed up. His boner was so strong that he felt his jeans couldn't contain it. And then he remembered: he was all alone in the house. His mother was out at the studio, teaching. His dad was . . . Well, he didn't know where his dad was. But who cared? Adam opened up the magazine to the centerfold. The bunny had blond hair flipped up in an old-fashioned hairdo and looked like a cross between a high school cheerleader in an old movie and that foxy house-wife in the old *Bewitched* TV show, all innocent but for the fact that her legs were spread open to show the slit that was her vagina. Adam imagined sticking his finger in that slit, imag-ined what would happen to the girl if he could do that. Would her back arch in pleasure? Would she wrap her legs around him?

Adam walked over to his bedroom door, and despite the fact that the house was empty, locked it anyway. He returned to the bed and the magazine and pulled down his pants. In the thirty seconds it took to do the deed, the blond cheerleader from the 1970s had morphed into Lisa Epstein. When the milky stuff squirted out, Adam quickly wiped it off with the printout from the computer and stuck the whole mess back under the mattress.

Nina's triumphant mood began to evaporate as soon as she got to the New Jersey Transit terminal in Penn Station. It was late afternoon, and the waiting room was already thick with commuters, their eyes riveted to the departure board as if expecting to see a miracle, when the only miracle they could possibly see was the appearance of a gate number next to their train. For some reason, that made Nina think about the Rapture, that crazy fundamentalist idea that the Messiah would come and all the good Christians would instantly vanish, transported up to heaven, leaving only the damned (people like her, in other words) to walk the earth. She wondered what it would be like if the Rapture arrived, like a gigantic express train at rush hour, emptying out Penn Station in an instant. The idea depressed her. Not the empty train station—that would be great—or the version of the story that had Jews and other infidels writhing in agony afterwards, but the fact that there were people who actually believed such crap. Transported, like something out of *Star Trek,* straight up to heaven? Yeah, right. And yet millions of people believed it.

The commuters all around her did look damned, like the living dead, and Penn Station was a kind of purgatory. The people seemed gray—their clothes, their expressions, their skin—as if all their life force had been slowly drained over months and years of traveling between the suburbs and boring desk jobs. Some of them seemed so bled of life, they were in danger of becoming living fossils, like the women who still wore running shoes with skirts and carried their high heels in plastic bags, a fashion relic left over from the transit strike of 1980. Why did women still feel the need to wear grotesque foot-maiming pumps anyway? It was a modern version of Chinese foot binding. What was the purpose of shoes you couldn't walk in? One pair of comfortable shoes—some decent flats, some cute boots, or, in the summer, sandals—was all a woman should have to wear to work. And how about the fact that these sneakers were always worn over socks over pantyhose? She shuddered at the thought of a life that would require pantyhose five days a week, of legs encased like sausages and the creepy feeling of nylon rubbing up against the ends of her toenails.

Nina scanned the room, hoping not to see anyone she knew. She didn't want to share a seat, to have to carry on a conversation on the way back home, to explain her sudden impetuous errand in New York City. She shifted her weight and rearranged her bags, and suddenly thought about which way the bagua mirror was facing. She wouldn't want to acquire any bad karma by unintentionally shining some bad luck in the direction of a hapless commuter. But the fact that it was wrapped and hidden inside her new purse, that would neutralize any hazard, wouldn't it? The mirror had to actually reflect something bad to be dangerous, didn't it?

And then she remembered her mother, who could be waiting at their house right now, for all Nina knew. The great and terrible Belle Gettleman. Nina dreaded the next few days, her parents as houseguests, everybody pestering Michael for updates on the hurricane, waiting for it all to be over so they could all get back to their lives. Why it seemed so unendurable, she couldn't say. Her mother was difficult, but so were a lot of mothers, and not just Jewish mothers; she'd heard stories about Greek and Italian mothers that almost made Belle look like a piker. Sure, her mother was loud and opinionated and wore bright fuchsia running suits, but why did that grate on Nina's nerves so much? Nina thought back to the psychotherapy she'd had in her twenties, and for the first time felt disappointed she hadn't stuck with it longer. She'd preferred a holistic approach to mental health, preferred to integrate body/mind/spirit through yoga, being a vegetarian, eating organic food. But now, waiting for the train back home, she felt as if she were walking toward a gallows. Belle Gettleman was like Nina's own private prosecutor; spending time with her was like being on the witness stand. Nina wished she understood her mother better. It might help disarm her.

There was no action, present or past, that got past Belle's critical eye. Why they'd picked their house, why they were vegetarians, why they weren't raising Adam Jewish. Lots of her friends' children had married non-Jews, Belle said, but they were still all raising their children Jewish. Studies showed—Belle Gettleman was always quoting studies, the kind you found in magazines—that kids did much better in life if they were raised something. And what was this Unitarian business? Anything that Belle was skeptical about she referred to as "this business": this yoga business, this vegetarian business, this New Jersey business. What an affront it had been to her mother that they'd chosen to live in New Jersey, of all places, rather than Long Island—as if Nina had selected the Garden State as a personal rebuke of her upbringing.

The board suddenly flickered—departures were moving up, track numbers were appearing—and the room of half-dead commuters suddenly thrummed to life. It was like a signal from the queen, sending armies of ants scurrying toward different underground tunnels. Gate 4. That's where Nina was going. She negotiated her way through the crowds, which crisscrossed in a free-for-all toward three separate gates, and then found herself at a dead halt at the escalator. What was this all about? Nina took two steps to the left, peering around the dozen or so people in front of her, and finally noticed a woman with a cane trying to get her footing on the moving stairs. Why hadn't she just taken the elevator, Nina wondered, irritated.

Finally, with the help of a young man behind her, the woman managed to climb onto the top step of the moving stairs, then tuck her cane under her arm so that she could hold on to the railing. Nina stared, riveted, as the woman hobbled awkwardly off at the end, the people behind her frantically clamoring backwards onto the stairs behind them to keep from smashing into her—a mad race between the cripple and the escalator. Ridiculous, Nina thought, how this stupid woman had put her fellow passengers in danger instead of just finding an elevator. And in that instant, Nina caught sight of the woman's face: Charlotte Hendricks, the slip-and-fall from Friday's fountain accident.

Nina did her best to hide behind the man in front of her, but still peeked out to see which car Charlotte was boarding—and then walked to the end of the platform to find a car at the opposite end of the train. Seated, she pulled sunglasses from her purse as an extra precaution against being seen by Charlotte Hendricks.

In front of her, a drab overweight mother, dressed shabbily in a sweatshirt and jeans, was trying to calm a yowling baby. The infant faced backwards, its mouth throttled to the fully open position, its eyes riveted on Nina with such an accusatory expression that it made her flinch. When the train lurched forward, the baby, amazingly, managed to clamor even louder. Nina thought about moving, but even knowing that Charlotte Hendricks had boarded seven cars back, she didn't dare take a chance of getting up. Besides, the motion of the train, once it started gliding through the Meadowlands, was sure to lull the baby into submission. Motion always did.

It was a few minutes later, when the baby mercifully turned its head on its side, its tearstained face making a dark wet blotch on its mother's shoulder, that Nina suddenly remembered the cloth diapers she'd bought at Toys "R" Us. In her rush to Chinatown, she'd forgotten about soaking the diapers in water. That was the feng shui cure she was supposed to be working on today, ridding her studio of the toxic energy left by the ballet teacher. Nina felt irresponsible and exposed, like an electrician who'd left out a live wire while running to a different part of the house to change a lightbulb. Until she scoured her studio clean, there could be more Charlotte Hendrickses. Nina sucked in a tense breath, thinking about more accidents: slipping yoga mats, faulty headstands, and the myriad dangers of Downward Dog.

The taxi was yellow on the outside, just like all the rest, but inside it looked weird, and smelled weird, too. Instead of glass, there were wooden brown beads hanging down between the driver's seat and the passenger seat. The man behind the wheel was black and had long black braids that looked like they hadn't been washed in months, if ever, and which stuck out from an ugly cap knitted in red, yellow, and green. The dashboard was cluttered with tchotchkes, things made out of bamboo and plastic, incense and ashtrays, statuettes of lions and flags in the same red, yellow, and green as the driver's hat.

"Yes, mon," he said to Belle, his eyes practically closed, his head turning only a millimeter in Belle's direction. "Where you going?"

Mon? What did that mean?

Belle froze. What was Nina's address? If she were back home, in her kitchen, she could scribble it on the front of an envelope without a second's thought. But suddenly her mind was blank. She knew the town, of course, and how to get there; driving her own car, she'd get there on autopilot—even if she had spent most of her adult years in Long Island, rather than this landlocked hellhole of a state where her daughter had chosen to live. But now, embarrassingly, she drew a complete blank; she was starting to feel fury, too, fury at Michael. It started with the fact that he was supposed to have picked her up, but it grew and blossomed into other resentments, new and old. Why, for example, hadn't he given her better warning about this hurricane—or Hurricane Ivan, for that matter? How come he'd never converted to Judaism? Why hadn't he picked up the phone when she called, and why had he been home two workdays in a row when he should have been at work?

Belle, usually so sure in the world, particularly in her relationships with hired help, suddenly felt insecure being separated from Max, God only knew where he was or if he was okay. It had been years since she'd taken a cab by herself. She never took them unless she and Max were on vacation. And Max was always the one who told the cabdriver where they were going, who paid and tipped the driver at the end. Now here she was in New Jersey, which she really didn't know, alone in a car with a strange man, and if he didn't rape and kill her, which was altogether possible, then certainly he was in the perfect position to rip her off. For all the force of her personality, Belle realized that she must look old and feeble, particularly after spending the night at O'Hare. And now—because of Michael!—this madman with the braids was going to take advantage of her. He'd take dangerous shortcuts through Newark, or long detours in areas she didn't even know, and the bill at the end would be hundreds of dollars.

And that, it seemed at the moment, was the good scenario, the one that didn't involved death and dismemberment.

Instinctively, Belle put her hand in her purse, fishing for her cell phone. But even as she wrapped her hand around the cool and reassuringly compact hunk of metal, she remembered that it was dead. So she couldn't even call 911 if the driver took her off on some deserted road.

"Mon?" the man repeated. He'd not pulled out of the taxi line yet, and the cabs behind him were starting to honk, but his voice was still placid. "Where to?"

"I don't know, okay?" Belle said. Her voice was both pleading and belligerent. "I mean I do know—it's my daughter's house—but I can't remember the address." The driver's eyes fluttered briefly, his only perceivable reaction. "I can get there, though," she said, not wanting to sound like a total flake. She named the town Nina lived in. "Once you get to the main street, I can find it easily."

The driver's jaw glided forward slightly in an almost imperceptible motion. He didn't seem angry or even annoyed. He snapped on the radio with an easy gesture and seemed relaxed almost to the point of being rubbery. With the most casual glance in his side mirror, he pulled out of the taxi line into traffic, and when a car already in motion honked and slammed on its brakes, he didn't flinch. He could have been sitting on a bus, or on a beach, holding a can of beer. His eyes, Belle saw through the rearview mirror, were at half-mast. Or lower.

His state of utter relaxation was beginning to make her nervous.

The music on the radio sounded familiar, but Belle couldn't exactly place it. She didn't know much about music, except for singers like Bette Midler and Barbra Streisand, but it reminded her of that little band that played outside Grand Cayman airport when you got off the plane—drums, bongo drums or congo drums, whatever you called them, and maracas or

139

caracas. Lively, tropical. It wasn't exactly her style, but not terrible either. Not like that horrible racket they called rap. But when she noticed the words the man in the song was singing, she detected a frightening undercurrent of politics, anger. "Get up, stand up. Stand up for your rights." Whose rights? The rights of cabdrivers in New Jersey? Or black men with long braids down their backs?

The cab merged onto Route 78, which the sign said would take them to the Garden State Parkway, but as usual the driver seemed oblivious to the threat of other automobiles. Their hurtling mass, speeding behind them and to their left, hardly seemed to register in his glazed eyes. Not only was this the last man on earth who would stand up for his rights, Belle thought, but it looked like he might fall asleep. At any moment. She glanced over her left shoulder at a tractor trailer rapidly advancing in the next lane.

"Hey!" she shouted.

He met her eyes in the rearview mirror.

"Yes, mon."

"Are you awake?"

"I'm talking to you."

Well, this was true. Undeniably, he was talking to her. Which meant he was conscious. To some degree, anyway.

"It's just . . . ," she said. "You just seem so blasé. Hardly paying attention to the other cars."

He listened without saying anything. She had to up the ante.

"I'm scared, damn it," she shouted, pounding her fist on her seat. "Don't you get it?"

"No need to be scared, mon," he said. "I never had an accident."

Belle squeezed her cell phone, even though she knew it was dead. Too bad it wasn't a gun, she thought, shocked that the idea had even occurred to her. Of course, even if she had a gun, it would be out of bullets, wouldn't it? Just like her stupid useless cell phone. Although she could pretend it was loaded, put the cold metal to his neck. She'd seen it in movies.

"Not good for your health, mon," the cabdriver added, "being so anxious."

For a split second, she saw it from his vantage point. An old Jewish lady, like Shelley Winters in some comic movie, too much makeup, overweight, overbearing. She shuddered. There was nothing so devastating as recognizing the cliché you'd turned into.

Belle closed her eyes, feeling that her life really was out of her hands. She couldn't even bear to look out the window anymore. All she could do was hope for the best. Deep breath, deep breath—isn't that what Nina would suggest? Belle inhaled sharply, but when she did, her nostrils twitched, detecting a new smell, something musky, almost sweet. Her eyes popped open. The driver was holding a fat hand-rolled cigarette and sucking it deeply. Bluish smoke curled back toward her seat.

Secondhand smoke, she thought angrily. Thoughtless. Illegal.

Belle coughed. "Do you mind?" she said, waving her hand in front of her.

"Certainly," the driver said, and passed the cigarette back to her.

She dropped it immediately, then stomped her feet on the floor to make sure it was out. That would be something, right, the car going up in flames right in the middle of the highway? She ground the butt into the floor of the van, and for the first time the driver seemed perturbed.

"You didn't have to do that," he said. He sounded sad, as if she'd just dropped a family heirloom.

Belle suddenly felt strange, as if her brain had atomized into a million little droplets, not unlike the feeling she sometimes got when she took allergy medicine. She noticed the cars on the highway speeding by her, but it felt, oddly, like a scene in a movie.

When Max took his topple at the luggage carousel, his fellow passengers were quick to respond, instantly surrounding him, the way crowds do when they perceive a minor emergency. Quick to respond, yes, but there being no apparent expert in the field of first aid among them, unsure of how to help. They called out warnings and instructions—"Elevate his head!"—"Don't move his head!"—"Get ice!"—drawing on wives' tales, TV hospital shows, and memories of first aid classes from fifth grade. Finally, out of the hubbub, a man of indeterminable age stepped forward, put up his hand, and yelled, "Stop."

The take-charge gentleman sported a gray ponytail, blue jeans, and work boots, and could have been an aging hippie, the owner of an antiquarian bookstore, or some dot-com multimillionaire. Probably the latter, because something in his manner commanded respect, and the crowd instantly parted, allowing him to kneel down next to Max and bend down toward his face. "Sir," he said. "Can you tell us your name?"

"Max," said Max. "Max Gettleman."

"Good. And do you know the date?"

Did Max know the date? A picture of a calendar formed in his brain, but he couldn't quite find the square on the calendar that corresponded to the date or see any number in it. They'd left in such a hurry, and he'd been traveling . . .

"I . . ."

"Who's the president of the United States?"

"George W. Bush," Max said, his lip curled in disgust. "Damn butterfly ballot."

There was laughter.

"And can you tell us what city we're in?"

What city, what city? West Palm . . . Chicago . . . Boston . . . Newark . . . Then suddenly he remembered the ticket window in Florida, and Belle's decisive order to the attendant with the earring. *I'll take Chicago. He'll take Boston.*

"Boston!" Max said triumphantly, as if answering a question on a quiz show. Then he lifted his own head, demonstrating that he wasn't paralyzed.

"He's fine," the ponytailed man pronounced. And so one by one the onlookers began to disperse, each responding to the gravitational pull of their own arriving suitcases, reassured that someone else in the crowd would help the old man in the rumpled Hawaiian shirt if he took some kind of turn for the worse. After all, it had been a red-eye for all of them. People wanted to get home, clean up, and go to work—or take off their clothes and slip into bed. It had been a long night. Max was just an old man—not a lost child or a woman in childbirth. There was no blood. He was conscious, talking. He'd even made a joke!

The last person to abandon Max, a statuesque blonde wearing a scarf in the manner of Marilyn Monroe, gave him one last chance. Was he sure he didn't want her to find a flight attendant? Or some other person who worked for the airport?

"I'm fine," Max insisted.

In the end, one lone suitcase circled round and round the luggage rack at Logan—Max and Belle's—while Max perched on the edge of the rack and caught his bearings. He closed his eyes, silently cursing Belle. Hurricane Ida, back home, couldn't possibly be as bad as this meshuggah trip. They'd been living in Florida all these years, and never been done in by a hurricane. Hurricanes were just a fact of life. But now . . . all this travel already, a whole night of sleeplessness and torture, and still he was only halfway done. He still had to book a ticket down to Newark.

Max tried to think of a rational way to find a flight. Go to Continental and just book the first one he could get? Or Aeronautica? Or should he try, somehow, to comparison-shop? He wished he'd been paying more attention last night, to see how Belle had managed things. But then, she hadn't managed things so well, had she?

Max lost track of the time. Without a flight to connect to, or a taxi to catch, he was that rare traveler who was not in a hurry. Suddenly, though, he noticed a worker in a hunter green jumpsuit that bore the logo of a maniacal alligator on the back, taking the last suitcase off the carousel and tossing it onto a wheeled cart. Slowly, it dawned on Max. That was his suitcase.

Max lifted an arm, waving to catch the man's attention, but it was no use—the worker was hooked into an iPod, not paying attention, and just kept pushing the cart toward some nondescript doors and parts of the airport that only people with special uniforms and ID necklaces could enter. Max thought about leaping up and sprinting after the man, but leaping and sprinting were a young man's game. It took everything out of him just to lift his frame up to a standing position, and by the time he'd accomplished this, the man was gone, the cart was gone, and his suitcase gone, too.

Suddenly, Max had a terrible thought. What if the protocol for unpicked-up suitcases these days was to bring in explosive-sniffing dogs or to prophylactically explode the suitcase on the tarmac. Unattended baggage, that's what they called it. Post 9/11, nothing was innocent anymore. Not even an old man's suitcase. And with his blood-pressure medication and clean underwear inside!

Max groaned imagining Belle's reaction to how he'd managed things. If she'd packed her makeup in the suitcase, he'd really be in trouble.

Michael wanted desperately to think, but his heart was pounding so hard, it felt like some kind of thrashing machine had accidentally gotten lodged inside his chest. It was all he could do to hold on to the steering wheel. He didn't know what upset him more: the security guard in the airport slamming him up against the car or the punishment he was going to suffer at the hands of his mother-in-law for failing to pick her up. And the worst part was that the one thing precluded the other. If he went back and tried to find Belle, he was risking . . . He didn't even want to think about it. Okay, he knew what he feared more. There was something about a gun—hard, cold, solid, lethal—that you couldn't quite forget, even if it was in the hands of a security guard rather than a thug. A bullet was a bullet, flesh was flesh, and cops shot innocent people all the time—look at Amadou Diallo.

The traffic on Interstate 78 flew by in a blur as Michael raced west. It was amazing how your instincts took over, how your car could retrace a familiar route all on its own, as if all there was to driving was resting your hands on a wheel. But after the Parkway, where was he going to go? He couldn't go home; he had strict instructions from Nina about that. Certainly there weren't going to be any more visits to Newark Airport. And the whole episode had soured his enthusiasm for amateur photography even if the clouds, as McCarthy had pointed out, were everywhere. You couldn't take a picture of the Statue of Liberty these days without being taken for a terrorist.

What had his world come to? His job had been handed over to a stranger in the Philippines; he'd had a gun pointed at him; he'd been banished from the airport and from his very own house. He was starting to feel like the hapless dad in the Sims, standing in his own kitchen and pissing on the floor. If he were a man of faith, maybe this wouldn't be so bad. Maybe he was being tested, like Job. But he wasn't a man of faith. He was a man of science, of math, probability, charts, weather maps, statistical models. Yet there was no science to guide him through the ache he felt, the sense of being displaced.

Thinking of Job reminded him of the visit from those church

ladies, the Jehovah's Witnesses, who'd come into his house and complimented him on his pancakes. A small piece of comfort it had been, but comfort nevertheless. They'd politely ignored the rubbery smell of the pan he'd burnt before Nina left for yoga class. They'd averted their eyes from all the dirty dishes in the sink. They'd acted as if a man making pancakes was the most remarkable thing they'd ever seen. Sure, their clothes were dowdy and their ideas outdated and quaint, but there was some essential kindness about them that seemed rare. He would have liked to share the experience with Nina, but he didn't dare. Hell hath no fury like a wife whose husband has given an inch to the Jehovah's Witnesses.

As Michael turned onto the Parkway, the bland interstate landscape gave way to familiar squalor—evocative little peeks into the backyards of people he'd never thought about. In his hyperalert state, the scenery seemed as exotic as some highway on the outskirts of Nairobi. There was the brick high-rise that had been modern in the middle of the last century, the overcrowded cemetery that hugged the highway on both sides, the factory where they made the silver packaging for Eskimo Pies, row houses with sagging porches, chain-link fences, and padlocked doors, and that were sided in odd colors like mint green. Did the Jehovah's Witnesses live in those sad little houses? Michael wondered. If you actually went inside, would you see kitchens with little flouncy curtains and crucifixes in every room? Or torn mattresses and discarded hypodermic needles?

Then suddenly, ending his speculation and signaling that he was now back in familiar territory, rose the towering orange sign announcing his local Home Depot.

Michael's right foot recognized the solution even before his brain did, as he mashed down on his brake and maneuvered into the right lane. Home Depot, a place he could actually go. Not the airport, not home. A safe refuge. No matter that he had no pressing home improvement projects. What did they need? Lightbulbs, cleaning supplies, faucets, gardening supplies? He had no idea, and it didn't matter. It was just a place where he could wander, in relative comfort and obscurity, until it was a respectable time for a suburban dad to arrive home.

But after he pulled into the Home Depot parking lot and turned off the car, Michael felt no hurry to go in. He turned the radio to WCBS, thinking he might catch something about the hurricane, and then absentmindedly watched the comings and goings of the parking lot. But twenty minutes rolled by and he realized he'd let the weather report go by twice, without hearing a single word. Add that to his list of losses: the ability to concentrate, even on the weather.

Michael turned the radio off and slumped back in his seat. That's when he noticed the seedy little side street on the far side of the lot, the back route home he occasionally took. In the middle of the block was a windowless building covered in pink stucco, with a sign out front that said THE VIXEN DEN. A gentleman's club.

Michael knew what that meant, and yet it seemed completely unreal. He'd been in a place like that only once, at his brother-in-law's bachelor party. That was long ago, and on Long Island, where all the Gettleman marriages took place. Michael felt himself harden at the memory of girls and pasties and poles. He'd driven past this Vixen Den dozens of times over the past few years, and never once had it ever caught his attention. Why was he thinking about it now?

Michael turned the key to the right, and started the car.

It was Nina's fault, he thought as he rolled away from the blandness of Home Depot to the forbidden pleasures promised right across the street. *She's the one who's banished me from my own home.*

Adam was lying on his back, staring at the ceiling, noticing a spiderweb up in the corner. He saw a spider dangle down, in a move that reminded him of Tom Cruise in the first *Mission: Impossible* movie. Watching the spider was mesmerizing. It climbed back up the tiny filament and disappeared, and then, after Adam had completely forgotten about it and his mind had drifted off to other things, plunged back down again. The thread the spider clung to resembled a tiny trail of saliva, and Adam wondered if that's what spiderwebs were made of, saliva. Or was it something more like semen? Perhaps the spider ejaculated his creation. Maybe a spiderweb was a monument to hundreds of hours of spider sex. Adam felt a slight throbbing between his legs as he considered this. He'd have to look it up on Wikipedia. But then he remembered: *Charlotte's Web*. It couldn't be true if girl spiders made webs, could it?

He glanced over at the clock. Four-thirty. And still no sign of his father, his mother, or either of his grandparents. Bliss, he thought, to have the house all to himself, no one nagging him to do homework or take out the garbage. His mom had acted all guilty when she first decided to rent a yoga studio, guilty that for the first time since he was born, she'd be working outside the house. Not that she was the kind of mom who put milk and cookies out after school. She'd always been busy and into her own thing, yoga clients upstairs on the third floor, or throwing clay in the basement when she was going through that phase, or growing organic alfalfa sprouts in their kitchen.

"It's okay, Mom," he'd assured her. "Really."

"But who's going to drive you places? Activities, clubs."

"I can bike, really," Adam had insisted. "Don't worry." The truth was he loved being a latchkey kid and having the house all to himself for a few hours each day. Just his luck that only a few weeks later, his father had to go get outsourced.

The spider bungeed down from the web once more, and Adam suddenly thought about what it would be like when Grandpa Max and Grandma Belle showed up at the house, all the tension there'd be. Whenever Grandma Belle showed up, Adam's mom worried about how the house looked, how she looked, how Adam looked. If they were going out for dinner, and Adam should happen to come downstairs with a hole in his jeans, his mom would stare knives at him. He had to unhook his Xbox from the TV in the den because it looked so "crappy" with all the wires all over the floor and besides it made it "impossible" for Grandpa to tune the television. At night, when everybody went to bed, Adam could hear harsh, angry whispers coming from under his parents' door.

But the worst was dinner, whether at a restaurant or at home, with Grandma Belle lecturing them about being vegetarians. Inevitably it would lead to a pointed discussion of Adam's height, and a cross-examination of his mother about proteins, vitamins, and doctor's appointments. Nina's voice would squeak higher and higher during these inquisitions, as she grew increasingly defensive and shrill, while Adam slouched ever lower, hoping to become not just short but invisible.

Adam glanced over at the clock again. Four-forty. Maybe he should take a ride up to the Lubavitch Center. As long as nobody was here demanding anything of him.

And then he heard what sounded like a small rock hitting his window.

He jumped out of bed, zipped his jeans, and walked over to the window just in time to see a stone smack against the glass. He noticed a little white spot on the window, a little nick on the glass. What the hell?

Then he noticed the unmistakable sound of girls giggling. He looked down to find Lisa Epstein and her entourage staring up at him. How did they even know where he lived? And wasn't Lisa supposed to be in Hebrew school, like Philip?

Adam felt his penis throb again, and decided to throw on a long shirt. Thank God his parents weren't home. It looked like his fortune had just begun to change.

Nina moved briskly once she got off the train, rushing toward her yoga studio. She was eager to soak the diapers in the water, per Coriander's instructions, in order to get the purification ritual under way. And she was anxious to get home, too. She was running out of time to give her house a once-over before the Inspector arrived. It was always distressing to see her home through Belle's hypercritical eyes, to anticipate the reproach, to figure out what she didn't have—or what she had too much of—that would result in one of her mother's exaggerated sighs. In fact, Nina realized, it was probably too late to tidy up. Belle was probably already there, giving the place the white-glove treatment.

Nina looked at her watch, saw that it was nearly five. Strange she hadn't heard anything yet from Michael. She'd made the plan foolproof, hadn't she? Michael would have his cell phone and pick Belle up at the airport when she called. Simple. What could possibly go wrong? Nina herself had made sure to check that Michael had put his cell in the charger the night before.

Nina was passing the overpriced florist and looked longingly at a bunch of sunflowers. It was always nice to have fresh flowers in the house, but ten dollars for four stems? She couldn't bring herself to pay $2.50 for a single flower. Besides, she realized with a shudder, there might be inauspicious feng shui implications about cut flowers. Who knew? She shook her head, fighting the impulse to spend money, and fished in her bag for her cell phone as she passed expensive delis and conservatively chic boutiques. When she finally unearthed the phone and called home, she waited the full four rings, only to get her own prerecorded message on the other end.

Strange. Someone should be home. If not Michael, at least Adam. Nina pressed END and punched in the number for Michael's cell. It sounded like she was going to get a message there, too.

"Hello?" Michael said, answering on the fourth ring. He sounded a little dazed. Or drunk? And there was loud music in the background. Loud music and the sound of men laughing.

"Michael?" Nina said. "Where are you?"

A pause. "Bowling."

"Bowling?"

"Well, you told me not to stay home. Right? What am I supposed to do all day, if I can't even hang out in my own house?"

Nina thought she heard a reprimand in Michael's voice, as if what she had asked of him was unjust. He understood, didn't he, how bad it would be, for all of them, if her mom got wind of the news that Michael was out of a job? He understood the cross-examination that would follow, didn't he? What were his job prospects? Why didn't he consider a job in television? What was his severance? What kind of savings had they put aside? What were their monthly mortgage payments? And on and on, until Michael had finally been browbeaten into applying for dental school and Nina had agreed that a nine-to-five job as a secretary would be much more practical than hanging up a shingle to teach yoga.

"Okaaaay," she said, returning to Michael. Though it wasn't okay. It wasn't remotely okay. She didn't quite know why, but she didn't like the idea of Michael hanging around, at close to five o'clock on a Wednesday afternoon, in some seedy bowling alley. And she didn't like his tone. But she decided, for the sake of expediency, to overlook it.

"Michael, have you heard from my mom?"

"No," he said.

"Hmmm, that's funny." Nina couldn't imagine that it would take her mom all day to get from Chicago to Newark. "Or Dad?"

"No. But then, my cell might not have had coverage for a little while."

"Not had coverage?"

"I don't know," he said. "There are some dead spots, you know, certain places. When you drive around."

"Did you check your missed calls? Your messages?"

"There were no messages."

Nina strained to listen to the background. Bowling alley? Something was strange. It didn't sound like a bowling alley, but Nina couldn't quite figure out why.

"Gotta go," Michael said suddenly, and Nina thought she heard the sound, now, of a woman laughing nearby. "My turn. Look, I'll call if I hear from Belle."

The phone went dead.

Nina checked to see if her mother's cell phone number was in her phone's contact list, but it wasn't.

She felt slightly deflated, like a balloon slowly losing air, and her stride slowed along with her sense of purpose. Nina liked to be in control—especially now, on the cusp of her parents' visit. But the triumph she'd felt on buying the Yin Bagua had faded after talking to Michael. Something felt wrong, but she wasn't sure what.

Suddenly, a woman stopped right in front of Nina, almost causing a full-body sidewalk collision. Nina dodged her at the last possible second. What the hell? What was wrong with people, almost slamming into you?

But the errant body had a face, and the face wore a warm expression. "Hello!" said a slight silver-haired woman carrying a large tote. "It's me. Bea Johnson? Beginners?"

"Oh." Nina struggled to place the face. "Right."

"Just worried about you," Bea said kindly. "Your family emergency. Is everything all right?"

Family emergency? Family emergency! Nina's sixth sense had been right after all. Michael, AWOL. Adam, missing. Her mother . . . the plane . . . But how did this woman know, when even Nina didn't?

"Family . . . emergency? . . ." she repeated.

"You know, the sign. On your door. About class being canceled."

"Oh, right," Nina said. "Right." That. She'd forgotten. Her excuse for not holding classes, when she'd decided to go into the city and buy the Yin Bagua. "Yes, fine. Just my son. You know how those school nurses are, calling for the least little thing. It was nothing. Ridiculous. But—"

"Well, I'm glad," said Bea, patting a rolled-up yoga mat in her tote. "I love your class. I'll try to catch it Friday."

"Yes." Nina smiled. "And thanks for your concern."

She nodded to end the conversation and continued walking toward the studio, but she still felt a residue of alarm at the words *family emergency*. It was like a distant rumble of thunder when you were at the pool, a sense of an impending threat. And then she remembered. Something her mother had always said. "Never lie about someone's illness to get out of something. It's tempting fate."

Yes, Nina admonished herself, she had tempted fate—and it appeared that fate had risen to the temptation. Because there *was* a family emergency going on, even if she didn't know what it was. She could feel it. Unconsciously, Nina traced the sign of the cross on her chest. Then, immediately, she wondered why. What was a nice Jewish girl—okay, maybe a nice Unitarian girl—doing making a sign of the cross? Must have been something she'd picked up from the movies . . .

As Nina pushed open the front door to her building, she wondered if she'd see Coriander and realized, with surprise, that she didn't really want to. Of course, she wouldn't mind some last-minute clarifications about soaking the white cloths, but she felt strangely vulnerable, and didn't want her soul exposed for Coriander to examine.

And then she had another realization, equally upsetting. Bowling pins crashing. That was what was missing from the background when she talked to Michael.

Adam hunched forward on one of the wicker chairs on his front porch while the girls—Lisa, Mara, and Jenna—crammed onto the porch swing across from him. It was Indian summer, warm enough that the girls were all wearing shorts, and their skinny suntanned legs were all over the place, rocking the swing chaotically. Lisa, of course, sat in the middle. Adam noticed that Mara's and Jenna's legs had Band-Aids and bug bites, like the appendages of normal mortals, but that Lisa's were as smooth and unblemished as wax fruit, and ended in spectacularly polished hot pink toenails. Apparently money and mob connections bought perfection, or at least a weekly wax and pedicure.

Lisa leaned back in the manner of a pasha, one used to giving orders and having grapes peeled and dropped into her mouth. Adam wished that Philip were there. Philip would be able to look her in the eye, match her attitude, and take any outrageous suggestion she made and top it. But Adam just felt like another groveler in the Lisa Epstein's posse, and he waited, with the others, to see what kind of boot-licking she desired. She had to want something. Girls like Lisa Epstein didn't hang out with the likes of Adam Summer just to pass the time.

"So you liked the bat mitzvah?" she said finally. "You had a good time?"

"Oh yeah, sure," Adam said. "It was great."

"And the butterflies?" She fluttered her eyelashes suggestively.

"Yeah, they were great, too." Adam found a little stress ball behind him on the corner of his wicker chair and started squeezing it. Great. He'd said *great* twice. The bat mitzvah was great. The butterflies were great. He felt like some kind of character in a Greek myth, struck dumb—or at least stupid—by the charms of a dangerous enchantress. If Philip were here, he'd no doubt have said something clever by this point, at least something cleverer than *great*.

The girls giggled, though, as if he'd been brilliant. "Well, they certainly did like you," Mara Peebles said.

Lisa ignored Mara and stretched out her long legs. She looked down at her toes as if inspecting them for a scratch or a drop of misapplied toenail polish. "So," she said. "You heard about Señora Ramos?"

Adam drew in a breath, waiting to see where she was going with this. Was she putting a contract out on Señora Ramos? Did she want Adam to be the hit man? He squeezed the stress ball harder, cutting its skin with his fingernail. Didn't Lisa have people for this kind of thing? Or at least Lisa's dad?

"Yeah," he said, trying to sound nonchalant. "Too bad. And a Nano video, I heard, too."

"How do you say *bitch* in *español*?" asked Jenna.

"*Cabrona*," Adam answered.

The girls hooted. "See," said Lisa, looking satisfied. "I told you he was our man." She turned back to Adam, her smile widening and growing more seductive. "How did you know that?"

"I'm a guy." Adam shrugged. "We pick up these kinds of things in the street."

"And cunt?"

"Excuse me?" He suddenly realized that she was looking for a translation. "That one, I'd have to look up."

Lisa purred, "And I bet you'd know right where to find it."

Yeah, Google, Adam thought. *But if she hasn't figured that out on her own, I'm not going to enlighten her.*

"Listen," she continued, and she now looked him in the eye as if he were the only person on earth. Adam could see that her irises were light brown, with little flecks of gold, and he felt, for a brief second, that he'd do anything, maybe even murder, just for the opportunity to stare into them, all by himself, from a few inches away. "I'm kind of looking for a favor."

Adam swallowed. He squeezed the stress ball again, trying to channel Philip.

"I want you to sneak into her classroom, during lunch or something, and cover her blackboard with *el shit-o.*"

Adam flicked the stress ball out of his hand and began to tap his fingers on the side of the chair. Well, now the agenda was finally on the table. He tried to picture it, looking up all the Spanish names for *cunt, whore, motherfucker,* and then sneaking into Señora Ramos's room, taking her chalk, and writing those words all over the blackboard. He liked Señora Ramos all right, had never had any trouble with her. Lisa probably deserved to have her iPod taken away. At least Lisa wasn't asking him to murder.

"Just think about it," she said. She stood up suddenly, indicating an end to the meeting.

Adam was thinking about it. He was thinking about how he could find out when Señora Ramos's breaks were, without drawing attention to himself. He was thinking about whether the chalk would squeak, what his mother would say if he got caught, whether he would be expelled or just suspended, whether disciplinary action in eighth grade went on your permanent record.

Mara and Jenna followed Lisa down the front steps. Lisa suddenly turned around, looked Adam in the eye, and winked. It was so perfectly executed—so fast—that Adam was momentarily unsure he'd even seen it. But as he watched her sashay down the sidewalk, her cute little butt wiggling ever so suggestively, Adam felt a growing recognition. Lisa Epstein already owned him.

The sight of his American Tourister vanishing through an un-
marked door finally snapped Max out of his reverie. In fact, it
produced a burst of adrenaline, the kind of thing they talked
about mothers having when their children were trapped under cars. He practically ran—okay, hobbled quickly—in the
direction of the disappearing suitcase.

But when he got to the wall that the man and his luggage
had disappeared through, Max noticed several nondescript
doors, not just one. All three were beige, the same color as the
wall itself, and without any signage or hint of what lay behind
them. It was like those modern corporate offices with their
endless cubicles, everything beige and identical. Max tried the
middle door, knocked lightly, and that bringing no results,
knocked louder. Then, speaking through a crack that he
hoped would carry sound, began a rather loud rant about his

wife, Belle, flying separately, a hurricane, going to see their daughter, falling down, and a missing suitcase.

The door still didn't open, but Max jumped when he felt a tap on his shoulder from behind. He turned to see a security guard with a nonplussed expression.

"Sir?" the guard said curtly. "May I see identification?"

"Boy, am I glad to see you!" said Max, eager to finally have the attention of someone in a position to help. "Somebody just took off with my suitcase. Just started rolling it and went through this door—"

"ID. I need to see ID."

Max reached into his back pocket, where he kept his wallet. But now, with great alarm, he discovered it empty. He patted every pocket he could find, but still no reassuring bulge.

"I can't find my wallet," he said.

"No wallet, no suitcase," the guard said, shaking his head. "And I suppose no plane ticket either?"

Max patted his pants again. "The one from last night must have been in my wallet. And I still hadn't figured what plane I was going to take to my daughter's . . ."

The man grabbed Max. "Come with me."

"I'm not a terrorist," Max protested. "I'm just an old Jewish man from Delray Beach. Plus, just a little while ago, I fell down." But he allowed the guard to push him through one of the beige doors into a labyrinth of behind-the-scenes airport bureaucracy, and then down corridor after corridor of ugly office furniture, boxes, luggage carts, and beat-up file cabinets. Finally, they came to a glassed-off room bearing a sign that said SECURITY.

"I fell," Max said. "Did you hear that? I could sue."

"Sit down," the guard said, opening the door and practically shoving Max down into a stained red steno chair. Then he spoke over Max's head to the man behind the desk, who brought out a ream of official forms. "No ID. No wallet. No ticket. No luggage."

"I'll call the docs at McLean," the man behind the desk said. Then he turned to Max with a fake smile that explained everything. Max was now, in the official view of Logan Airport, a crazy person.

It took Michael's eyes several minutes to adjust to the almost nonexistent light in the Vixen Den, and he felt like a nervous adolescent, unsure of the protocol and wary of getting caught. It was ridiculous, of course—a bordello, or some twenty-first-century version of one, smack in the middle of the suburbs, across the street from a Home Depot—and Michael didn't expect to do anything more than kill some time and drink a beer. He'd never expected to be sitting on a black leather couch with a voluptuous redhead astride him when Nina called.

But then nothing turned out as he'd expected. He'd ordered a gin and tonic instead of a beer, and then when the waitress brought him his drink, she'd mentioned her name and told him to let her know if there was anything she could do for him. *Anything* was the operative word, but Michael had latched on to the girl's unusual name. Xenon. Naturally, he recognized Xenon as an inert gas and a common component of scientific equipment, and nerd that he was, couldn't restrain himself.

"Xenon with an *X*?" Michael asked. "Like in the periodic table?"

"With an *X*. But I don't know about any damn table." Xenon nodded toward the back of the room. "We do have a couch."

Michael looked, his eyes opening wide. There was a couch, all right, where fully dressed men were receiving personalized up-close dances from barely dressed women, most young enough to be their daughters. He was shocked, shocked that this was all available, for sale, right here, across from the Home Depot.

"Want one?" Xenon said.

"What?"

"A couch."

"Couch? . . ."

"Couch *dance.*" She laughed. "Twenty bucks."

Michael calculated. The stirrings between his legs versus the tawdriness of the whole thing. Twenty bucks. It wouldn't break the bank, but he was out of work. Considering what he'd been through this week . . . considering what he'd been through just *today* . . .

Xenon cracked her gum and started to walk away. It was the sight of Xenon's satin hot pants, tight and high on her ass, that finally shook Michael into action.

"Wait!"

Xenon turned around and smiled.

Michael reached in his back pocket for his wallet, was embarrassed to discover he didn't have a twenty, and started counting out fives and singles.

Xenon waited patiently, then took the bills. "Wait there," she said, indicating the couch with a sweep of her bright red mane. "I have to get a beer for Mr. New Dad over there. Can you believe, last week, he shows me his kid's baby picture?"

Michael sat down, obediently, and waited. He watched Xenon and her hot pants tend to the new dad across the room, and he wondered if her pubic hair was red, too, and whether he would get the opportunity to see it. He listened to the gasps and grunts on either side of him, waiting impatiently for his turn, and Xenon came back, stripped down to a tiny G-string, removed her bra, and was rubbing her triple-Ds across his face when the cell phone rang.

Considering the timing of the call, Michael thought he'd handled it well. Especially (and Nina would be the first to appreciate this, though of course, he could never tell her) his breathing. But it had wasted half his allotted five minutes on the phone, and after he hung up, Xenon wearily informed him that he'd have to pony up another twenty to finish.

Well, Michael thought as he approached his bliss, what were credit cards for? Forty was steep for someone who'd just lost his job, but what was a guy supposed to do when his wife threw him out of the house?

Adam watched Lisa and her friends sashay down the sidewalk, giggling, always giggling, and it made him wonder whether he was the subject of their tittering, or if they were mocking Señora, or something else altogether. Even though he'd wished Philip had been there, he smiled at the fact that he'd faced the most popular girl in school on his own. She'd come to see him, after all—not Philip. She'd thrown rocks at his window, batted her mascara-caked eyelashes at him. It was a seduction, of course, though Adam didn't know if he was being suckered or getting the opportunity of eighth grade. He couldn't wait to tell Philip.

The girls weren't halfway down the block when a yellow taxi screeched to a stop in front of his house. The door opened, and there was his Grandma Belle, laughing so loudly that Lisa and her friends turned around and made little sour faces.

"Adam, *bubbeleh!*" Belle said. She reached for him with outstretched arms of shaking, jiggling chicken skin. "Come hug Grandma." After staring at Lisa Epstein's smooth brown limbs for half an hour, the fat dangling from his grandma's arms looked like a corruption of nature, like something that might make a Bible character turn into salt.

Adam gave his grandma a tentative hug, looking over her shoulder at Lisa Epstein, who appeared to be smirking from the other end of the block. He flushed, embarrassed, until he remembered that Lisa had a Jewish grandmother, too, the one who'd run shrieking from the ballroom when a butterfly had settled on her shellacked head. Then his nose twitched, picking up a smell on his grandma, a smell strangely musky and exotic.

Adam noticed a very tall black man with long dreadlocks, who got out of the cab slowly and gazed droopy-eyed at him and his grandmother.

"You know this lady?" he asked Adam.

"Yes."

"Thanks to God!"

Belle reached into her gigantic purse, rummaging for a wallet. She pulled out a glasses case, lipstick, a cell phone, handing each item to Adam as she excavated. The driver didn't wait. He walked back to his door, then looked at Adam over the taxi's yellow roof, shaking his head.

"Your grandmamma is crazy," he said before squealing off.

Belle looked perplexed, then dropped her wallet and the items Adam was holding back in her bag. "Meshuggah!" she declared. Then she turned to Adam, her face softening into a loopy grin, and fixed him with a big soggy kiss. "You're a good boy!" she blubbered. Adam was used to his grandmother appraising him with a shrewd eye, taking in his height, his grooming, and his attitude in a single disdainful glance. Wiping the saliva from his cheek, he kind of longed for the standard disapproval.

"Where's your suitcase?" he said, businesslike.

"Oh, Max has it."

"And where's Grandpa Max?"

Belle threw her arms around Adam again and began to sob. More wet grandma stuff smeared melted into his face. "Boston!" she cried. "But who knows? Our phones have run out of batteries!"

Pizza was the best that Nina could do under the circumstances, pizza and a salad. But even eking out a salad wasn't
easy. There was a bag of mesclun mix from Whole Foods that
had been sitting around for three days, and Nina had to carefully pick out the mushy black pieces that had started to rot,
and then try to rinse off the rest—although the muck of the
rotten vegetation couldn't really be removed from the delicate
leaves that remained. Aside from the mesclun mix, all she had
in the refrigerator in the way of vegetables were some carrots,
parsnips, and cabbage intended for soup, and her mother
shriveled her nose judgmentally as Nina chopped these into
small pieces and plunked them in the salad bowl.

"You don't peel them?" Belle asked.

"No, Mom," Nina sighed. "The skin contains all the nutri-
ents."

"And you don't have a little tomato or a cucumber anywhere?" Nina squeezed her eyes closed, preparing for the insult.

"For a vegetarian," Belle sniffed, "you certainly don't have many vegetables in the house."

The vegetable discussion paused when the front door opened, and both women waited for Michael to materialize. He walked in sheepishly, avoiding eye contact with Nina but apologizing profusely to his mother-in-law for missing her call. He mumbled something about Verizon phone drop-outs but didn't, Nina noticed, mention anything about a bowling alley. When he left the kitchen to check on the storm, Belle rolled her eyes significantly. Normally, it would have sent Nina through the roof, but Nina continued, stoically, chopping root vegetables. What she felt, but couldn't admit, was that her mother's skepticism might be warranted, that Michael was hiding something. Stiffly, she went into the pantry for napkins and paper plates.

There was a rumble of thunder outside.

"Max!" Belle cried. "My poor Max!"

It seemed absurd that Belle was taking the thunder personally, as if God were personally throwing thunderbolts at whatever plane Max was on, but at least it took the attention off Michael. Still, Nina had to wonder what was going on. Belle had been an emotional roller coaster since she'd arrived, careening from moments of elation to moments of despair, slobbering all over Adam one minute, sobbing like a war bride the next. Her icy critique of Nina's salad assembly skills, more typical of her repertoire, had almost been a relief.

"Why didn't he call?" Belle wailed. "It's not like him not to call!"

"Mom, we've been through this. His cell ran out of power, just like yours. And he was probably catching a plane."

"But it was hours ago that he landed!"

"We don't know that," Nina said reasonably. "Maybe there was a delay."

"Or maybe he never got to Boston. Maybe his plane went down in Florida. Oh my God. It would be my fault! He never wanted to leave. He was fine to stay."

Strike a postage stamp, Nina thought, *Belle Gettleman is admitting that something could be her own fault.* But given that her father would have to be dead for Nina to cash that chit, she let it drop, appealing to reason instead. "Mom," Nina said. "Don't you think we'd have heard if there'd been a plane crash in Florida?" Of course, she hadn't listened to NPR all day. Maybe, God forbid, there had been a plane crash. Suddenly, it occurred to Nina that Michael could make himself useful and try to track down his father-in-law. Certainly he knew how to pull up flight schedules on the Internet.

She walked into the sunroom to find Michael and Adam playing *The Sims.*

"So, how's the hurricane?" she said through clenched teeth.

"Moving north."

"And how was your bowling?" She put the word *bowling* in air quotes. Adam looked first at his mother, then at his father, quizzically.

"Fine," Michael said, staring at the screen.

"And what was your score?"

"I don't remember."

"Look," Nina said. "I don't really want to go into why you didn't pick my mother up at the airport today. I'll take you at your word about the cell phone. But why don't you make yourself useful and do something to track down my father."

"Your father's missing?"

"No one's heard anything from him since last night."

Adam cracked his knuckles, then cleared his throat. "Mom?"

"Yes?" Nina said.

"Grandma's high."

"What?"

"Marijuana. Don't you smell it? She got a ride from a Rastafarian cabdriver."

"Are you sure?"

"Mom, you used to smoke the stuff. Go smell her."

Nina ran back to the kitchen, pretending to need ice for a drink, and crossed close enough to her mother to draw a whiff. Holy shit! Adam was right. No wonder Belle had been acting so weird. Nina didn't know whether to burst into laughter or call Poison Control. She went back into the sunroom, where Adam waited for her confirmation, and sank into the futon. "Un-fucking-believable," she said. The thunder cracked again.

"What's the antidote for marijuana?" Adam asked.

"Sleep," Nina said.

"A stiff drink," Michael added.

"I think for Grandma," said Adam, "it might be television."

"Let's offer her all three," said Michael, standing up.

But Nina leapt up from the futon and pushed him back into the computer chair. "I'll take care of my high mother," she said firmly. "Make yourself useful and figure out how we can find Dad."

Belle had accepted a glass of white wine and eventually fell asleep in front of the television. She snored. It was a two-part snore—a long high-pitched windup followed by a short guttural blast. You couldn't call it a pleasant sound, under any circumstances, but it was a sure sign that Belle was sleeping, which made it safe for Nina and Michael to converse in a whisper.

"You weren't bowling," Nina said.

"I was."

"No, you weren't."

"How do you know?"

"No pins crashing. I would have heard pins."

"So I was in the snack bar."

"And it was your turn then? In the snack bar?"

"Listen, all you asked was that I stay out of the house," Michael said.

"Yeah, and that you pick up Mom."

"I told you, Verizon—"

The phone rang.

"Thank God," Nina said, reaching for the receiver. "It's got to be Dad."

Michael relaxed slightly. Saved by the bell. The current inquisition was over, or at least on hold. For now, he could stop defending his failure to pick up Belle and worry about the next puzzle: how to retrieve Max with that son-of-a-bitch McCarthy threatening an all-expense-paid vacation in Guantanamo if he got within a ten-mile radius of Newark Airport. And it wasn't like Nina was going to volunteer to pick up Max herself.

Michael suddenly realized, though, that Nina wasn't talking to her father at all. She was talking to someone else. She looked puzzled, and motioned furiously for Michael to pass her a pen and paper.

"Yes . . . this is . . . uh-huh . . . What?" she was saying. "And you have him where?"

Michael handed her the first piece of paper he could find: an envelope bearing an offer for a no-fee-ever credit card. A writing utensil was harder. The mug they used for pencils and pens was picked over, as usual, leaving the same dried-up ballpoints, broken pencils, and yellow crayons that were always there. Finally, Michael dug down and discovered a stubby pencil from a miniature golf outing.

"Can I talk to him?" Nina was saying.

Nina lowered the mouthpiece to below her chin and mouthed something to Michael while she waited. He couldn't make out her words, but he could tell she was puzzled and somewhat irked. She pointed to the phone, her index finger going in little circles, the universal gesture for "crazy." Yes. That was the word she'd been saying. Crazy.

"Dad, are you okay? Yes . . . yes . . . What happened to your wallet?"

Michael studied Nina's face, trying to guess what was going on.

"Yes, well, I doubt there are any more flights out tonight. But I'll send Michael up tomorrow . . . I know, I know . . . First thing, I promise . . . You'll be okay, right?"

Nina hung up, then closed her eyes and shook her head, looking deeply put upon.

"What?" said Michael.

"My father . . ."

"I gathered."

"Is still up in Boston. He fell down, got his wallet stolen, failed to pick up his suitcase, made a commotion when someone started to take it away, and was taken to airport security to be screened for, well, being a terrorist. Or crazy."

"Oh, Nina, I'm so sorry." Michael put his hand on hers in a gesture of solidarity. Then he remembered what she'd just promised her father—*"I'll send Michael up tomorrow"*—and he sputtered, "Wait. I'm going to go pick him up?"

Nina took a quick look to make sure that her mother was still asleep. "Well, I'm the only one in the family bringing in an income now, you know."

"But the storm—"

"What storm?"

"Hurricane Ida."

"What about it?"

"Well, if you want your mother to think I'm still working as a meteorologist, maybe you shouldn't take me away from my job during a major hurricane."

"Ssshhh!" said Nina. "Not in front of Mom." She checked again to make sure Belle was still asleep. "My mother will be beside herself about Dad. There's no way she's going to be thinking about your job and your hurricane."

Interesting, Michael thought. It was absolutely necessary to pretend he was still working—until it inconvenienced Nina. Suddenly, in the middle of the game, the rules changed. But he didn't argue. You couldn't argue with the weather, and you couldn't argue with Nina. Trying to fight when her mind was made up was like trying to reason with a low-pressure system.

On the other hand, Michael knew, he couldn't make that trip to Boston either.

The Weather Channel, on in the background all evening, was a mild diversion from Belle's histrionics. When she woke from her nap to discover that Max hadn't yet flown to Newark, that he'd fallen and been robbed, lost their suitcase and had been picked up by security, she was—just as Nina had predicted—beside herself. The hurricane quickly tumbled down Belle's list of concerns. Ida had finished her business in Florida anyway; by Wednesday night she was heading for the South Carolina coast.

Belle was furious that Nina hadn't woken her up when the call had come in from Boston. She was worried sick about Max, guilty that she'd put him on a plane alone, and, of course, still fuzzy from her contact high. One by one, she brought up new implications, increasingly dire. The credit cards! She'd have to cancel them. Which meant, of course, canceling her own credit cards, too, since they had all the same ones—and so what kind of money was she going to have to work with while she was visiting New Jersey? Max's medicines, her medicines. How could she possibly dredge up all their names and doses? Could she even get them up here? Would her doctor or her pharmacy even be in on Thursday to call the prescription in? What was the damage in Delray? Was power out? And what would happen to Max if he didn't take his blood pressure medicine for a few days? And with the stress of everything!

Nina played the part of the dutiful daughter. It wasn't a family role that she got much practice at, but it called on her training as a healer and nurturer, and made her feel grown-up and useful. She reassured her mother that her dad had sounded fine. He was alive and well. *Really.* She'd heard him with her very own ears. Nina helped Belle cancel the credit cards and assured her they could lend her all the cash she needed and purchase their airfare home. As for the medicines, she was sure that they'd be able to take care of it all the next day. She had a very good local pharmacist who would make the calls.

Secretly, Nina was glad that there was a crisis to take Belle's mind off the usual litany of complaints. Belle was too distracted to notice any pantry moths, worry about Adam's height, or raise suspicions about Michael. But like the little rubber ball returning to the paddle in that little toy she'd played with as a kid, Nina's mind kept going back to her cell phone conversation with Michael earlier in the day, the one from the "bowling alley." Each time, it disturbed her, though she dared not dwell on it, or bring it up, at least not with her mother around.

Even though Hurricane Ida was now past the point of hurting Belle, or her house, their heads would turn in the direction of the TV once in a while, to look at the pictures of the damage in Florida. "Oh, no!" Belle cried. "I should have had Max take the plants in. Oh, God. The back window is probably shattered!"

Nina smiled inwardly at the idea of her mother chastising herself, for a change. Whatever Nina had done wrong in her life, in her mother's opinion—deserting Judaism, becoming a vegetarian, moving to an old house that needed constant upkeep—there was no way she was responsible for the failure to bring the Gettleman plants inside before a hurricane.

Thursday

Michael had spent half the night reliving the moment when McCarthy slammed him up against the car to pat him down for weapons. He got palpitations thinking about McCarthy's gun. His heart hammered in his chest as he remembered driving away from the airport, his hands shaking. And mixed in with all that was the queasy, guilty feeling he'd had when Nina called him at the strip joint in the middle of his lap—um, make that couch—dance.

The alarm clock's orange digital display had mocked him throughout the night, reminding him of how long he'd gone without achieving asleep. 1:33, 2:46, 3:58. Now it was seven, and the radio had abruptly turned on, delivering the morning's dose of bad news. Trouble in the Middle East. Suicide bombers and failed diplomacy. And Hurricane Ida gathering strength as it went inland over the Carolinas. Michael stretched, opened his eyes, and looked over to Nina's side of the bed. Empty. There was water running in the bathroom. She was up, brisk and efficient. And he felt like crap.

She'd booked a flight for him to Logan at 9:55. He was supposed to be at the airport by eight at the latest. Which gave him just half an hour to splash water on his face, pull some clothes on, down some coffee.

Michael staggered into the bathroom, took up his position at the left sink, rubbed the steam off the mirror with a hand towel, and looked up at the pathetic face of a man who was afraid to drive to the airport and get on a flight to Boston.

Still, he knew, he had to get out of it.

The simplest thing, he supposed, would be just to tell Nina what had happened in the airport parking lot. If she knew, she'd understand. If she understood, she'd be willing to make other arrangements. To go to Boston herself, for example.

But he pictured Nina's face listening to his story. Her serious expression as she concentrated on his words, her raised eyebrows when he told her about bringing his camera to the airport, the sharp intake of breath when she heard about McCarthy and the gun, the glimmer of recognition when she suddenly realized why he hadn't picked Belle up.

And then (he imagined while shaving) the follow-up, and his frantic efforts to make up lies fast enough. So where did you go? Home Depot? So where was the bag? What? You were there for three hours and you didn't buy even a lightbulb? No, whatever story he made up, Nina would poke holes in it faster than he could patch them. He wasn't a good liar. He knew that.

No. He couldn't tell.

He could pick a fight instead.

A tiny spot of red bubbled up on his cheek. It was dangerous to shave when you were agitated. Michael went over to the toilet, wadded up a piece of toilet paper, and tried to staunch the blood. It blossomed into a little crimson flower, mocking him. Henry David Thoreau's brother had died from cutting himself shaving, Michael suddenly remembered from tenth-grade English. Lockjaw. *Most men lead lives of quiet desperation.* Thoreau had that right. And he hadn't even met Nina.

No. He couldn't stand up to Nina either.

Maybe—and the thought came to him like a gift, like manna to Moses wandering through the Sinai—what if he took Nina's car, the Prius, to the airport instead of the Honda? What were the chances that McCarthy had run plates on his whole household? It was the Honda that McCarthy had spotted two days in a row, the Honda whose plates McCarthy would recognize. The Prius would be safe to take to the airport. Who'd notice?

The immediate question was, how could he get Nina to switch cars?

Michael couldn't just suggest trading cars for no reason at all. Not just a lark. It would be strange—like asking to sleep on the right side of the bed. Or trading sinks. No, he had to have some logical reason. Something had to be wrong with the Honda. Something unsafe. Some reason to take it into the shop.

The brakes. Michael watched the corners of his mouth turn up into a little smile for the first time in days.

The brakes, of course. There was no way Nina would mess with that. No way she'd want him driving on the Parkway with bad brakes, especially not with her dad. But why was he just telling her now, this very morning, that the brakes were bad and that he needed to borrow the Prius?

Because the squeaking had just started yesterday! And he'd almost rear-ended a car on the Garden State! He would have told her last night, naturally, under normal circumstances. Only, her mom was here, and that was so distracting, and the crisis with Max up in Boston . . .

Yes, that would do. He was so sorry. Her friend Liza could drop her at the yoga studio, right? Unless she was ready to leave when he was. And surely he'd be back from Boston in time to pick her up at the end of the day.

Nina had slammed into consciousness by way of a terrible dream. There'd been a storm, in her dream, with blustering wind and relentless rain, and suddenly a huge oak tree in their front yard, which had been leaning dangerously for years but had been too expensive to remove, fell straight through the roof into their bedroom, smashing the house to smithereens.

Nina's heart was racing when she opened her eyes and saw Michael asleep next to her and the house still, quiet and intact. There weren't even raindrops on the windows. She willed herself to shake off the dream, to use what she knew of breathing and yoga to slow her heart down. Yet like a tongue poking relentlessly at a broken tooth, Nina's mind continued to probe the dream for associations even after she had mastered her breathing, turning it over and over until at last its meaning was perfectly clear.

Poison arrow.

Everything that had happened in the last week had been a warning. The flood in her waiting room, Michael's near-fire while making pancakes, everything she'd learned from Coriander and the feng shui books. And what a ditz she was, running into the city to find a bagua mirror when there was still bad karma collecting in her yoga studio! Still, it was the fact that Cedar Lane pointed straight at their front door—the classic feng shui poison arrow—that filled her with the most dread.

Suddenly Nina realized two more things about her dream. The first was that, in real life, there wasn't a giant leaning oak tree in their front yard. There was a weeping cherry, but it wasn't large enough to destroy their front porch, let alone the whole house. The second was a detail from the dream itself. It wasn't the windstorm that had toppled the tree, Nina realized. It was

175

Charlotte Hendricks, wearing a full-body cast, who had pushed the tree with a malicious little shove.

Adam's dreams weren't any better. He dreamed he was on his bike, riding up the hill to the Chabad center, when guys with automatic weapons started popping out of the nearby woods and firing at him. Being on a bike, he had no way to take cover, and if he slowed down (he felt in the dream) he would lose all his momentum and fall all the way down the hill. Another dream: he was being held high in a chair, smiling and waving to an adoring crowd, when someone came up behind him, slipped a wire around his neck, and strangled him. It was the last dream—finding Señora Ramos's head in his locker— that made him realize these were all cheesy Mafia nightmares, fed by *Godfather* movies and episodes of *The Sopranos*. Sure, in the movie, it was a horse's head in a bed, but the message his subconscious was trying to deliver was still pretty clear: Lisa Epstein's "request" to despoil Señora's blackboard was an offer he couldn't refuse. His world suddenly seemed overwhelming, fraught with dangers and impossible decisions.

Adam tasted something sour rise in the back of his throat, and realized he was starting to throw up. He refused. He clenched his mouth shut, tightened his hands into fists, made his mind go blank, and sat stiffly on his bed until the feeling passed.

"Listen," Michael said, suddenly appearing behind Nina, who was standing in front of the mirror on the landing and smearing some very expensive kohl under her eyes.

Kohl was one of Nina's compromises. She'd disdained cosmetics as a teenager, on principle, which of course had driven Belle crazy—makeup representing society's imposition of a tyrannical standard of beauty on women. And quite apart from politics, she'd found it "creepy," a mortician's tool. But it was one thing to take such an austere stance when you were sixteen and in the full blush of youth, and quite another when you were forty-six and age had begun to impose its own tyranny. Eyelashes were shorter, lips thinner, eyebrows paler, and—she hated to admit it, because it sounded so much like something her mother would say—she needed some perking up. Still, Nina refused to support the industrial-military-cosmetic complex, and insisted instead on finding natural beauty products, preferably from the third world, which of course had not been tested on animals and could be found only at Whole Foods. So Nina kohled her eyes and hennaed her hair and purchased Dead Sea bath salts and lipstick derived from mango butter.

"There's something I forgot to tell you about yesterday," Michael said. Nina lowered her kohl stick, even though one eye was underlined and the other wasn't, her heart pinched as she braced for news she certainly wasn't going to like.

"Oh, nothing bad," Michael said quickly. "Just the car. The Honda. Something with the brakes. They've been squeaking for a couple weeks. And then yesterday, on the Garden State, a car in front of me slammed on its brakes, and I almost rear-ended it. I mean, stepped on the brakes and *nothing*. Just on instinct, I went around it. Luckily the lane next to me was clear. I could have died."

Brakes, well, it could have been worse. Then it dawned on her: this was just another manifestation of the rapidly accumulating dangers of the physical world. The flood, the near-fire, now the brakes. It was almost as if the laws of physics had been rewritten over the last week with the explicit goal of bringing the Gettleman-Summer family to early graves.

"So I'd better take it in," Michael continued. "And take your car today to the airport."

She looked at her watch and quickly redid the calculus of her morning. "Fuck."

"I know. It's a big inconvenience for you." Michael touched her shoulder and pouted in a sympathetic manner. He laid out a plan that basically involved her driving him to the mechanic and then being carless all day.

"Fuck," Nina repeated. Then she remembered that Michael was doing her a favor by going up to Boston to rescue her father. It wasn't exactly fair to blame him for a problem with the brakes. If she were a good wife, she'd have been at least a little upset that he almost got into an accident on the Parkway. Still, it was just like a man—just like Michael, anyway—not to plan this a little bit better, to at least give her some warning the night before. Just like a man not to recognize the split-second timing her life required.

She couldn't help herself. "But why didn't you tell me this before?"

"I'm sorry," Michael said. "All that stuff with your mom, and the taxi, and your dad up in Boston. I completely forgot."

Nina wondered about that, how he could have forgotten, how he could have turned out the lights the night before without mentioning that there'd be a significant alteration in their morning plans. But then, as they said, men were from Mars. She had to keep reminding herself.

Michael was dressed and ready in five minutes, forsaking his shower, and also settling for the bitter dregs of yesterday's coffee, reheated in the microwave. A small price to pay if everything went as planned.

And why shouldn't it? He was a master at probabilities—if weather forecasting had taught him anything, it was how to read the odds—and the Prius ought to provide enough cover to get in and out of Newark Airport without attracting McCarthy's attention.

Nina was more than a little put off, acting as if the inconvenience of being without a car for one day was a major imposition, like being without electricity or water. Well, so what? His life had been nothing but inconvenience ever since Nina had demanded that he pretend he was still working. Having to fly up to Boston, that was an inconvenience, too. And a visit from Belle? The very definition of inconvenience.

Wisely, he kept his hostility well hidden, needing Nina to at least drive him to the garage and then hand over the keys to the Prius.

He'd dropped off the Honda keys quickly and asked Garvey, the only mechanic he'd ever known to wear a hairpiece, to change the oil and rotate the tires. No point in mentioning the brakes, which were fine. Michael rationalized: It was just a white lie, a sort of cosmic "get out of jail free" card, a way to keep Nina happy and avoid the overreaching hands of McCarthy and the Department of Homeland Security.

He dropped Nina off in front of her building, gave her a little peck on the cheek, and deliberately ignored her put-upon sigh.

Cruising toward the airport, Michael admired the smooth ride of the Prius and turned on the air conditioner just because he could. He coasted into daily parking and walked calmly toward the departures area. Without any luggage, it was quick work to get an electronic boarding pass and move straight to security. There, he felt a little spasm of nerves but luckily his profile had not been disseminated to the $11.35-an-hour airport screeners, and guilt-detection was not yet a standard part of their equipment.

And that was it. He was safely on the other side. Safe from McCarthy, with a minimum of fuss from Nina. There was even plenty of time to get a real coffee from Au Bon Pain. He sat down, waited for his flight to be called, and enjoyed the spike of fresh caffeine in his bloodstream. *Hold on, Max,* he thought, feeling suddenly magnanimous, even heroic. *I'm on my way.*

FOURTEEN

They'd had to dash off so quickly that it had been all Nina could do to jot a note for Belle and leave it on the kitchen table. She didn't have time to run upstairs and see if her mother was up, nor did she really want to. Not only was there the likelihood, no make that certainty, of complaint—Why a futon? Hadn't they offered to pay for a day bed?—but she really thought her mother needed the opportunity to sleep off the contact high from the cab ride, and the wine they'd given her to settle her nerves. Not to mention the fact that Belle had spent the night before that curled up in a tiny little seat at O'Hare. At least that's what Nina told herself. It was for Belle's own good that Nina ran out of the house without so much as a good-bye or the offer of a toasted bagel.

Reluctantly, Nina scribbled her cell phone number on the note, in case Belle needed something, or, God forbid, there was another disturbing call from Boston. Of course, if she left her cell number, she'd probably be forced to keep her phone on, violating her own rules about cell phones in the yoga studio. And writing her phone number down was almost like putting out a red carpet, an open invitation for Belle to interrupt.

On the plus side, getting into the studio early did give her the time—finally—to do the purification ritual that Coriander had prescribed. Nina stopped by the upscale hardware store on the corner to pick up a distressingly upscale and expensive bucket—wasn't there anything besides hammered copper to make a bucket out of?—then filled it with water and dumped in one of the cotton diapers from Toys "R" Us. As for where to put it to soak, she suddenly remembered the roof deck on top of the building. It would be safe from passersby. And at lunch, she'd retrieve the diaper and start cleaning. She'd scrub those bad vibes away until her knuckles were raw, scrub them clean out of her life.

Philip's locker was all the way down the science wing, about as far from Adam's locker as you could get, and even farther from Adam's next class. Still, the urgency of the situation required a quick consultation with his worldly friend. It was worth an after-school detention if he was a few minutes late for English. After-school detentions were just fifteen minutes—and that was a small price to pay compared with the punishment he could face if he did what Lisa Epstein had asked.

Even though the depravity of Lisa's request had wormed its way into his subconscious overnight and almost made him throw up that morning, Adam looked forward to surprising Philip with some big news. After all, it wasn't every day that a kid like Adam was summoned for a fatal mission by the most powerful girl in the eighth grade. But he wasn't altogether shocked to discover, when he reached Philip's locker, that his know-it-all amigo already knew.

"I've been expecting you." Philip continued to place texts and composition books in their rightful places. "And of course, you've got to do it."

"Do what?" Adam stammered.

"*Como se dice* 'cunt'?" Philip still faced forward and didn't even crack a smile. Adam looked around nervously to see if any teachers were around, but as usual Philip's timing was flawless. There was nobody within ten feet of them.

Adam put his backpack down on the floor next to Philip's locker.

"So you know?"

"Philip knows all."

"And you think I should do it?"

"Well, would you do it if Lindsay Lohan asked you?"

"Um."

"Jennifer Lopez? Paris Hilton? It's Lisa fucking Epstein, you moron."

"Okay, okay. I get your point."

"It's probably good for at least a hand job."

Adam tried to pretend he hadn't heard, and was grateful that Philip was still looking at his locker.

"The trick, my friend"—and here Philip finally turned around and not only faced Adam, but stabbed an index finger in Adam's chest—"is not getting caught."

"No duh," said Adam.

"I've got geometry." Philip snapped his locker closed and flicked the dial on his Master Lock. "But there are two critical elements, just as there are in any kind of sleight of hand—or a bank heist, for that matter. Speed, of course. You have to get in and out quickly. And creating a diversion."

"A diversion?"

"Yes. Attracting attention elsewhere. Having somebody else—your best friend, say, theoretically—create a disturbance that will make anyone who happens to be around look in the opposite direction."

He strode off without so much as a nod, like a corporate executive going to meet his board of directors, leaving Adam in dumb awe and, of course, late for English.

Belle blinked awake and saw an unfamiliar ceiling. She glanced to her left, where Max always slept, but he wasn't there, and before she could put the facts together and remember where she was, she experienced a shock of vertigo, as if being sucked upward by an out-of-control elevator. Then she remembered. Hurricane Ida. Evacuating. Gator Air. She was at Nina's house, on Nina's third floor, sleeping on the ridiculous futon that passed for guest accommodations. And Max, without a suitcase or an airline ticket, without so much as his blood-pressure medicine or a photo ID, was up in Boston.

She felt unmoored, completely adrift.

Where was everybody? Belle continued to lie still, but listened carefully, hoping to hear something—a voice, footsteps, water running, anything—to remind her that she wasn't as lost and alone as she felt. Nothing. At home, when Max got out of bed first, there'd at least be the comforting sound of morning television coming through the bedroom wall. But here, there wasn't even that. Not even the steady hum of a refrigerator.

Well, Nina must be down in the kitchen, two floors below. She'd probably have the radio on, even if Belle couldn't hear it all the way up here in Rapunzel's attic.

Getting out of the futon was no easy trick, not for a woman of her age and girth. She tried swinging her legs over the side as you would on a normal bed, but her feet remained, uselessly, at the same exact level as the rest of her body. She wished there were a safety bar around, like the kind she had in the shower at home, to pull herself up. But of course, there was nothing so helpful. Finally, she figured it out. Turned over so her stomach faced down, folded her knees underneath her chest, and put all her weight on her hands to push up. Gratefully, she realized that she'd managed to get through the whole night without having to pee. She must have really been zonked out. Thank God, she hadn't had to manage this trick in the dark. Or go down the narrow stairs in the middle of the night to the second-floor bathroom.

She got dressed—who wanted to have to climb these stairs again?—and went downstairs. But even on the second floor, the house was eerily quiet. "Nina?" Belle called. "Michael? Adam?"

She peed, washed up, brushed her teeth, but still no signs of life, and went down to the first floor to discover a deserted kitchen. The kitchen was a mess—how a person could go to sleep with dishes in the sink, Belle couldn't understand—and the table was covered with catalogs, newspapers, bills, and homework. Then Belle noticed a quickly dashed note from Nina. "Sorry, Mom. Car in shop. Had to leave early. Michael going to get Dad. If you need anything, here's my cell."

Belle had never thought of Nina as much of a hostess, but this took the cake. Not so much as a fresh pot of coffee or a shout up the stairs to say she was leaving.

There were several choices for the diversion, as Philip explained at lunch. "I can slip and fall," he said, stopping to savor the gruyère-on-croissant sandwich his father had packed. "That's the easiest. I slip, fall, make a big production out of it, make sure my glasses slide across the floor. And every teacher and janitor in sight bends down and makes sure there's no blood or head trauma."

"Ouch," Adam said.

"Right. The downside is that I actually could hurt myself,

ruin these nice corduroys or break my glasses. And in any event, doing a full frontal body slam isn't any fun."

"Option two?" Adam asked.

"I could get in trouble."

"How?"

"Slam a seventh-grader into a locker, for example. I've always wanted to do that."

"For the entire four weeks we've been in eighth grade?" Adam asked. He put down his plebian PB&J and gazed at the cornichons that accompanied Philip's croissant. "Look, I don't see the point of you getting in trouble just to keep me out of it."

"Well, then," Philip continued. "There's option three."

"Option three?"

"Dr. Pepper."

"Dr. Pepper?"

"Is there an echo?" Philip said. "Yes, Dr. Pepper, Cissy's hamster." Cissy was Philip's younger sister.

"The one that runs around on that stupid treadmill all day long? And occasionally squeaks?"

Philip patted his lips with the cloth handkerchief he always carried. "Never underestimate the power of a rodent to cause mass hysteria, especially in a place where ninety percent of the employees are female."

"So when are you going to bring in Squeaky? I mean, Dr. Pepper?"

"Oh, Dr. Pepper is here now," Philip said coolly. "Chilling in my locker. And don't worry"—he patted Adam's hand, as if to stave off the inevitable follow-up—"Dr. Pepper is just fine. What do you think the vents in the lockers are for?"

It had been a distraction, knowing that the cell phone was there, hidden under a yoga pillow but still on, during both her morning classes. And of course it made her feel like a hypocrite. Didn't she always tell her students to leave their concerns at the door, to turn off their cell phones, BlackBerries, and beepers, to devote the next ninety minutes to forging the connection between mind, body, and soul? She kept glancing over her shoulder at the pillow that was hiding her phone, anticipating the disruption, and she was sure that her distraction showed, that her backwards glances were like a "tell" in poker—signals to the observant that she was not centered and focused like a true teacher of yoga, a genuine maharishi, ought to be. To counteract her agitation, Nina tried adding velvet to her voice and called for more eye-closing and slow breathing. All to no avail. It was just like having Belle right there in the room.

Naturally the cell phone rang during yoga nidra, the time of deepest relaxation, when all the students were reposed in corpse position, listening to Celtic wind chime arpeggios and supported by under-neck and under-knee pillows and covered in blankets that Nina had so lovingly placed. Nina dived for the pillow, fumbled for the ringtone silencer, and fled outside the studio into her reception area, almost stepping on April Shandone's right hand in her rush.

"Mom," she whispered. "I'm in class. What's up?"

"Where do you hide your coffee filters?" Belle said.

To anyone else, Belle's voice would have sounded flat, matter-of-fact, almost toneless, but Nina could easily pick up the subtle undertones of reprobation. After all, with forty-six years of experience reading her mother's disapproval, it was one of Nina's most finely honed skills. On the surface, the question might have been neutral—the coffee filters? where were they?—but the word *hide* implied layers of judgment. First of all, the obvious: that Nina stored her coffee filters, and everything else in her kitchen, for that matter, in an illogical place. But right under the surface was a much more acid complaint. Why the hell hadn't she made coffee in the first place?

186

Or wait—forget that—why wasn't she there in her kitchen, to take care of her mother in her old age, her mother who had fled a hurricane and whose home was in God knew what condition, and whose life partner, Nina's *father*, for God's sake, apparently in early-stage Alzheimer's, was stranded up at Logan Airport without wallet or ticket or suitcase? What kind of house was she running? Was she totally lacking the milk of human kindness? How could Nina have run out of the house without so much as running upstairs and giving her mother a peck on the cheek—and maybe a hand getting out of that torture chamber of a futon? What kind of payback was that for ten years of piano lessons, for countless times waking up in the middle of the night to deliver cough medicine or comfort after a bad dream?

"In the cabinet over the spice rack," Nina said. "And you could lose the attitude."

"Attitude!"

And here is where the lid blew off. Criticism in the Gettleman household was supposed to go in only one direction: from Belle to everyone else.

"You have some nerve," Belle said. "I bet Ronnie Minkoff wouldn't talk to her mother that way."

Ronnie Minkoff! The bane of Nina's childhood. Nina couldn't believe her mother was still playing the Ronnie Minkoff card. Ronnie Minkoff of the perfect little gold tennis bracelet and the perfectly plucked eyebrows and her perfectly maintained teenage virginity. Ronnie Minkoff, who'd kept impressing all her mother's friends on into adulthood: a real *balabuste*, thrower of parties for hundreds, not just president of Hadassah but president of her whole *synagogue*. And whose home had been on the 2002 Rockville Centre house tour. The legend of Ronnie Minkoff grew larger every year, like Paul Bunyan's. She could feed a whole bar mitzvah with a single carrot and spin decorator showcases out of straw.

"Listen, Mom," Nina said, raising her voice more than she

187

intended, surely destroying the spirit of relaxation she'd so painstakingly created. "I've been listening to stories about Ronnie fucking Minkoff for forty-six years, and I'm sick and tired—"

"Oh, there you go with the F-word! You couldn't have made your mother a little pot of coffee before you left? That would have been so much trouble?"

"You know, Mom, it *would* have been too much trouble," she said. "Because Michael had to take a fucking day off of work to go up to Boston to get Dad. And it happens that the brakes in the car were shot, so I had to let him take my car."

The only problem with cell phones, it suddenly occurred to Nina, is that they couldn't be slammed, like real telephones, when the person on the other end was really pissing you off. You could press the END button—as she did now—but there was no physical pleasure to be derived by hanging up on someone that way. It didn't make any noise. Or allow you to let off steam. Even if you pressed the OFF button with the force of an elephant, it wouldn't make a bit of difference. The cell phone would turn off on its own schedule, playing its own silly little digital sign-off as cheerfully as ever. The only gesture that compared was to let a cell phone fly, to fling it across a room or against a wall, replacement policy be damned. So fling she did, and just as the cell phone left her hand, flying in the direction of the waiting room door, the same door opened.

The phone hit Charlotte Hendricks straight in the mouth with enough force to pop out several teeth. She stood there, leaning on her cane with an expression that slowly turned from surprise to confusion to anger.

"I wath coming to say let bygones be bygones," Charlotte said, struggling to maintain her dignity as she gathered up the bloody teeth that had dropped to the floor. "And twy your Thwursday relaxation class. I guess I was mithstaken!"

Charlotte stared at the teeth in her hand and looked vainly

in her yoga pants for pockets. Finally, like a fairy-tale witch invoking a curse, she stretched her hand out to display the teeth to Nina. "You'll hear fwum my lawyer!"

Nina, who'd been frozen in a state of disbelief, suddenly rushed to Charlotte's aid, blubbering apologies. But as she discovered a second later, doors—unlike cell phones—were excellent vehicles for demonstrating rage. Yet how Charlotte, burdened by her cane and a fistful of teeth, had managed to slam the door in Nina's face, she couldn't imagine.

When he saw the transformation that had taken place in his father-in-law, Michael suddenly understood how Logan Airport officialdom could take him as either a vagrant or a nut. It wasn't just his white hair flying in all directions, his shirt misbuttoned or the sour smell that clung to him; those things were all understandable, given the overnight flight, the long delay, the lack of a toiletry kit and access to a private bathroom. No, it was more profound than a temporary lapse in grooming or hygiene—though the idea of a dentist not having access to a toothbrush for two days was in itself heartbreaking—but more the *absence* of something. Sure, Max had always stood in Belle's shadow, but he'd always been an easygoing guy, with a shrug and a smile and usually a corny joke. It certainly must have been Max's good humor that had kept Nina and Belle from killing each other years ago. But the last forty-eight hours seemed to have sucked the juice right out of him.

"Pop!" Michael said, summoning a sort of back-slapping, middle-American, middle-twentieth-century bonhomie. Pop? Michael couldn't believe he'd actually said that. He'd never used it, not even with his own father. Was he channeling Jimmy Stewart?

Max looked up, but didn't seem to recognize him.

"Dad," Michael tried again. "It's me, Michael."

"I don't have a son named Michael." Max's voice was monotone, almost robotic.

Michael looked anxiously at the men in charge. The old man certainly wasn't making this easy.

"Look," he said to the bureaucrat behind the desk, who seemed burdened by a permanent scowl. "Can I have a moment alone with him?"

"Policy prevents me from leaving a detainee unattended. But I'll try to give you a little privacy." The guy stood up, walked to the door, and presented his back to them.

Detainee? Wow. That's what they called a feeble old man who'd fallen down, lost his wallet and his suitcase?

Michael slipped into the chair behind the desk, leaned forward, and looked straight into his father-in-law's eyes, which seemed to have acquired a dull, milky cast. "Max," he said. "I know you've had a tough couple of days. But this is Michael, Nina's husband, and I'm here to take you home." In a flash of inspiration, Michael took his wallet out. There must be a picture of Nina in there, he thought. But after fumbling through all the credit cards and plastic sleeves, he couldn't find a single one. Finally, hiding beneath his Costco membership card, he found a sixth-grade picture of Adam. He pulled it out and placed it the desk, facing Max. "See?" He waited a beat. "Adam. Your grandson."

Max touched the little photo, studying it, then rubbed his fingertip back and forth, as if trying to muss Adam's hair. "Nina's boy."

"Yes." Michael let out a long grateful sigh.

"Adam," Max said. "And you're . . ."

"Michael. Here to take you home." Michael gave his father-in-law a quick pat on the back. For all the resentment he'd felt about being Nina's errand boy, Michael now felt grateful to have been the one to rescue Max. Another day, and the old man might have been lost forever.

Processing the flight back took another two hours. A Boston police officer had to write up a report verifying that Max's wallet had been stolen and his ID lost. Michael had to sign a sworn affidavit as to his father-in-law's identity. They were screened with extra scrutiny—wanded, patted down, and subjected to a puffer machine to check for explosives—then escorted to the gate by two uniformed officers who stood with them until boarding.

Michael was, in a way, grateful for all the bureaucratic hurdles they had to jump, because it prevented any real conversation. Once they found their way to their seats and faced an hour and a half in the air, he worried that he might slip and tell his father-in-law about losing his job. He needn't have worried. As soon as the plane took off, Max's head rolled back against the window. Three minutes in, he was snoring. The woman on Michael's left looked over at Max with an exasperated expression, as if he were playing loud rap music through his nose. Michael shrugged and pulled out his *SkyMall* catalog.

Adam and Philip sat in Principal Drabyak's office, staring at their feet and avoiding eye contact as the principal finished taking a call from the central office. It was interesting how much the boys could communicate without talking, or even exchanging glances. Philip was saying, telepathically, "Let me do the talking." When Adam didn't respond, he added: "Keep your eye on the prize. Keep thinking about Lisa Epstein."

Mr. Drabyak was finishing a conversation about heating and air-conditioning, something involving valves, custodians, physical plant; who cared? The words—neutral, mechanical, boring—temporarily embraced Adam like one of those heavy aprons the dentist puts on you to take X-rays, leaden and comforting. As long as Mr. Drabyak talked about the physical plant, he was not talking about the hamster, or Mrs. Marzulli's heart seizure or arrhythmia or whatever it was that made her fall down unconscious when Dr. Pepper ran into her classroom between fifth and sixth periods, or about the awful words that had been written on Señora Ramos's blackboard and the telltale chalk dust all over Adam's pants.

Finally, Mr. Drabyak hung up the phone and picked up his pen, turning it over and over again, and clicking it on each rotation. He stared at the boys, clicking the pen, without saying a word, for at least thirty seconds—the full length of Final Jeopardy. It was Mr. Drabyak's trademark, that stare. Kids talked about it in the cafeteria. Bad kids, the kind of kids who got in trouble, kids like Lisa Epstein. But Adam had never heard the pen. It was like a metronome, or Edgar Allan Poe's "Tell-Tale Heart," meting out Principal Drabyak's disapproval with distressing regularity.

Adam's stomach suddenly lurched, and he tasted stomach acid rising to his throat just as he had in his bedroom that morning. He looked anxiously at the door to the left of the principal's desk. It looked like a private little bathroom. Yes, sure it was. But something about the protocol—prisoner facing his executioner—precluded a run for the john. Adam sat there, stoically, trying to will his fear and his bile down.

And then he heaved. Philip, acting quickly, grabbed a stack of papers off the principal's desk and held it up in front of Adam. Adam's half-digested lunch burst forth—brown, stinky, and studded with little chunks of carrot sticks.

Principal Drabyak finally put down his pen and sprang into action. He waved Adam into his private john, pressed an intercom summoning a secretary and a custodian, and looked down with disgust at the mess.

In Principal Drabyak's bathroom, Adam did his best to mitigate the damage. He wet a couple of brown paper towels and wiped around his lips, trying to remove the evidence of his cowardice and restore a shred of dignity. He blinked at his face in the mirror, wishing vainly for a toothbrush, or even a Lifesaver, and wondered how he'd managed to get into this state. It was hard to decide whom he hated more: Philip, his stupid know-it-all friend; or Lisa Epstein, that bitch, that cunt, that *conchuda*.

It turned out that Adam had vomited over the private personnel files of all the teachers in the school who were up for tenure. Mr. Drabyak's secretary would have the unpleasant task of cleaning them up, replacing the file folders that had been hit square on, and photocopying papers that had borne the full brunt of Adam's spectacular show of contrition. In fact, it was only the necessity of cleaning said files that delayed her call to Adam's house, to inform his parents of Adam's horrible misbehavior in Señora Ramos's room.

It had been hard to concentrate, between her blowup with Belle and Charlotte Hendricks's bizarre curse after the unfortunate accident with the cell phone, but Nina had no choice. She'd already missed a whole day of classes because of her trip to Chinatown on Tuesday, and she absolutely could not afford to miss any more. Michael was out of work and, God knew, it looked like she might be incurring some sudden legal bills. Nina concentrated for all she was worth, delivering the role of yoga teacher to the next two classes like she was Meryl Streep going for an Oscar. She positively radiated relaxation and centeredness, more attentive than ever to her students' various aches and pains, and delivered a yoga nidra session that could have put the Energizer Bunny into a coma.

But when it was time for a break, for the forty-five minutes of downtime she'd built into her Thursday schedule, Nina closed the door, lay down on a yoga mat, closed her eyes, and allowed tears to smudge her kohl and trickle down to her mat. Crying wasn't something that often overtook her, at least not since she'd started taking Prozac, and yet there was only so much a woman, even a seratonin-enhanced one, could handle. She was reminded of the previous Friday, the day the fountain flooded, when she almost electrocuted herself, and Charlotte Hendricks went skidding tragicomically across the floor. It felt just like that day, lying on her mat in the corpse pose, not knowing what to do, the day Coriander had come wandering in. . . .

The diapers! Nina suddenly remembered. In the bucket of water on the roof!

Reluctantly she forced herself to sit up, rubbing her eyes and redistributing the kohl, summoning the energy to stand up and mount the metal stairs to the fourth floor. Bad vibes, bad karma, and all because of that damn ballet teacher! Nina had to get rid of that bad energy, once and for all. She'd been paying for another woman's sins long enough. She started up the stairs sluggishly, but by the time she pushed open the door that led to the building's roof, there was a little spring in her step. She was ready, suddenly, for a transcendent cleaning experience.

She reached the rooftop just in time to see two smokers— nurses, it appeared from their white outfits and white shoes— deposit their cigarette butts in the designer bucket that Nina had left up there in the morning.

Nina's mouth dropped. Was there no insult the universe wasn't planning to deliver? Her 100 percent pure cotton white cloth, acquired at the expense of a trip on the dreaded Route 46 and a karmically compromising fender bender, now moldering in a makeshift ashtray! She would have screamed, strangled the nurses, but she didn't trust herself after the morning's cell phone–throwing incident.

Nina moved to the side to let the thoughtless smokers pass and go back down into the building. Then she went to inspect the bucket. It was filled with butts. Black, tarry, stinky butts, rendering the water suitable for absolutely nothing. Who knew there were so many smokers left to discard the filthy little souvenirs of their disgusting habit?

Nina would have emptied the whole sopping mess onto the sidewalk four stories down, but she was sure that if she did, Charlotte Hendricks would be crossing in front of the building at exactly that moment.

They arrived at Newark midafternoon. Max had slept the whole way, and Michael felt like one of those parents you occasionally see in airports at the end of a long trip from an orphanage in China or Korea or Vietnam, shepherding back a bundled-up baby. Even when Max's eyes did pop open, on landing, he had the confused wide-eyed blinking stare of a newborn. His father-in-law had definitely lost more on this trip than his wallet and a suitcase.

Max seemed frailer than his seventy-three years as he shuffled down the aisle of the plane, and the trip from the gate down to ground transportation was painfully slow. The old man had moved glacially for years because of his bum knee, but Michael was afraid that if he moved any slower, the earth, traveling the opposite direction on its axis, might catch up with them and it would be yesterday. The idea of escorting Max to the parking lot seemed excruciating.

Michael noticed a bench near the taxi line, maneuvered Max there, and sat him down. "Look," he said. "I'll go get the car. You wait here."

Max nodded.

"*Look* for me," Michael said, emphasizing key words and employing the firm tone he used when giving instructions to Adam. "I'm driving Nina's car. The *Prius.* It's light *green.*"

Max nodded again.

Michael glanced around, taking in the scene. Single mothers with toddlers on their hips, Wall Streeters back from morning meetings in Boston, supervising deals on ultrathin cell phones while they waited for limos—nobody that looked even vaguely threatening.

Michael put his hands on Max's shoulders and looked straight into his watery eyes. "Don't go anywhere," Michael said. "I'll be right back. *Five* minutes."

Then he bolted toward the parking lot with an ease of movement that felt exhilarating.

Adam couldn't remember exactly the last time he'd thrown up, but it had to have been so long ago that his mother must have wiped his face with a wet washcloth and tucked him into bed. Or maybe it was his dad who did the face-wiping in those days. He couldn't decide what was worse: the crappy taste that remained in your mouth *after* upchucking, or the shocking force with which the food defied gravity and rose up through your nose and throat. Actually they were both awful. The only redeeming thing that could be wrenched from the experience was pity. He knew that Principal Drabyak had let them off more lightly because he'd thrown up. They'd drawn a detention, not suspension.

He and Philip left the principal's office without glancing at each other, and Adam had no interest in hanging around Philip's locker after school and getting a lecture on how the plan had been brilliant, but its execution flawed. No. Philip had just been flat-out wrong, and the wild scrambling of the now dearly departed Dr. Pepper had served only to draw more attention to his nefarious deed, not less. Adam couldn't imagine what his mom would say, what kind of trouble he'd be in. He'd probably be forced to go to Unitarian potluck suppers for months to make up for it.

But now, more than anything, he wanted to be good.

How had he gotten off the track? Just a few days earlier, he'd had a plan to get a bar mitzvah, and then Lisa Epstein had come along, batted her eyelashes, and the next thing he knew, he was throwing up in the principal's office. Sure, maybe his motivation for the bar mitzvah had been less than pure. Maybe he had been thinking, at least a little bit, about the money. And the party. But now, he swore, he would get all those impure thoughts out of his head. He would go, today, right after school, ride up the hill and meet with the rabbi. He'd start studying. He'd commit himself to learning Torah or Talmud or whatever the hell it was, that thing that obsessed that boy in that book they had to read in seventh grade. Right, *The Chosen*. This whole thing—the temptation, the bad deed, throwing up—had been some kind of sign from God. It wouldn't kill him to learn a little bit about his religion. Maybe he could get back on God's good side.

His plan was simple. Go home, ditch his backpack, brush his teeth, and get his bike out of the shed. Then he'd start climbing the hill to the Chabad center. It was a big fucking hill. The only guys he'd ever seen climb it were those guys who wore those silly stretch suits and rode really expensive bikes. But it would be penance, or something, to climb that hill in the name of religion. He'd be like Moses climbing Mount fucking Sinai.

Of all the insults served up by old age, the inability to release a tiny trickle of water when you felt the urge was by far the worst. It was even worse, Max thought, than the waning quality of his erections. Urination was the most basic of human needs. Babies did it in their sleep, dogs did it in the street. And men, unfortunately, did it in front of each other. The sad state of Max's prostate made going to the bathroom hard enough under ideal circumstances—at home, in the condo—but doing it in a public bathroom, either at a urinal, or hiding girl-like in a stall, was pure humiliation. It was so bad that he'd worry about it the night *before* he had to spend a day away from home, and then he'd lash himself with pangs of self-loathing for hours *after* he'd stood at a public toilet, unsuccessfully bidding his bladder to release its burden.

The last twenty-four hours at Logan Airport had been pure torture. The man guarding him had insisted on accompanying him to the bathroom, and then stood over him the whole time, as if Max were storing liquid plutonium in his bladder and was just waiting for an unguarded moment to release it.

But now, son of a gun, he felt it coming. He felt for sure that he had to go to the bathroom.

Michael had gone to get the car, and told him very firmly to stay where he was. But Michael didn't have a clue what he'd been going through, and besides it would take just a few seconds, and he would be right back, waiting on the bench. Michael would never even know he'd left.

Belle had already wiped down Nina's kitchen counters and cleaned out Nina's silverware drawer. She'd thrown out years of menus from pizza places and Chinese restaurants. She'd attacked the stove, encrusted with the spills of hundreds of meals, and restored it to an almost pristine white. Not that Nina or her kitchen deserved these attentions, but it helped with the waiting. And it wasn't like there was a mah-jongg game down at the club.

But it was already early afternoon, and she still hadn't heard a thing. No call from Max or Michael. No car pulling in the driveway. Belle was on *spilkes,* but she was damned if she was going to call Nina again. Not after the way Nina had treated her when she asked a simple question about the coffee filters. What was wrong with that? Had she been such a terrible mother all these years, that Nina had all this pent-up rage? Was it such an imposition for Nina to have her parents visit for a few days, to give safe harbor to her own flesh and blood during a hurricane? Nina had a chip on her shoulder; she always had. What was the saying? *I love humanity; it's people I can't stand.* That was her daughter. No, Nina was going to have to call *her* back and ask for *her* forgiveness.

Belle had given up trying to figure out the four remotes, and was looking for a magazine that at least had a recipe or an interview with a celebrity, when the phone rang. She lunged for it, not knowing what she hoped for most: an apology from Nina or a call from Max saying that he was in Michael's car on the way home from Newark Airport.

"Mrs. Gettleman?" asked a woman whose voice Belle didn't recognize.

"Yes," Belle said nervously. *Mrs. Gettleman* was what strangers called her, people who were selling something, receptionists at doctor's offices. Her imagination lurched in the direction of plane crashes and car wrecks.

"Please hold for Principal Drabyak."

Oh, Belle realized. It was a call from school. Nina was the "Mrs. Gettleman" they wanted. Belle would never understand why women of her daughter's generation didn't just take their husband's names. Wasn't that the sensible thing? To have everybody in the same family use the same last name?

After a few minutes on hold, a man came on, and though Belle had planned on explaining the mix-up, that she wasn't the Mrs. Gettleman he was looking for, he launched so quickly into what he had to say that she didn't have a chance.

"Mrs. Gettleman," Principal Drabyak said. "I'm calling about Adam. I'm afraid I have to give him a detention on Saturday. He was caught in a serious infraction of school policy and, well, common decency as well. He was caught writing obscenities on his Spanish teacher's blackboard. They were in Spanish, but still . . ."

Belle felt like she'd lost the ability to speak. Adam? Was he really talking about Adam? Adam had never been a bad kid, at least not as far as she knew.

"Mrs. Gettleman?"

"Yes," she croaked.

"I'm quite surprised by this. I've never had Adam in my office before. In fact, he was so nervous that he threw up."

"Threw up," Belle repeated in a monotone.

"Mrs. Gettleman? Are you all right? I know the last thing a parent wants in the middle of the day is a call from their child's principal. Of course, we have to treat incidents like this seriously, but he is just in eighth grade. It doesn't go on his permanent record. . . ."

Belle had heard enough. It was bad enough that her grandson had done something like this, but the idea that the principal was now practically apologizing for having to punish him? That was too much.

"Look Mr. . . . Mr. . . ." She searched for the name.

"Drabyak."

"Mr. Drabyak. First of all, this isn't Adam's mother. I'm Adam's grandmother."

"This isn't Mrs. Gettleman?"

"This *is* Mrs. Gettleman," Belle said firmly. "I believe you're looking for my daughter, *Mrs. Summer.*" Belle felt a malicious little thrill, throwing the principal off track and invoking

Nina's proper married name, which she knew her daughter disdained.

"You're not Adam's mother?"

"No." She waited for the principal to get his bearings. She could almost see the mechanism in his bureaucratic little pea brain grinding away as he registered the fact that it was possible to call a student's house during the day and get his grandmother instead of his mother.

"I'm very sorry to have disturbed you, Mrs. Gettleman." Principal Drabyak now seemed doubly apologetic. "My secretary should have . . . I actually shouldn't have . . . Sorry, this is just . . . Well, we screwed up. Could you ask your daughter to call me back?"

The line went dead.

Belle shook her head. She was disappointed that Principal Drabyak had hung up, because now she had plenty to say. Plenty to say about kids these days, and parents and, well, *principals*. In her day, they wouldn't have been talking about a detention. It would have been a suspension. At the least. No wonder the world was going to hell in a handbasket.

Apparently it was a good thing that she and Max had come for this visit. It looked like the state of her daughter's household was even worse than she'd imagined. It would take Belle Gettleman to straighten things out.

Adam was panting hard before he was halfway up the hill, and by the time he reached the top, his lungs felt seared. The road through the reservation had switchbacks to minimize the grade, but there was no diminishing the elevation. Adam had never attempted it before, and he was amazed at his accomplishment. His first thought was to call Philip, but then he remembered he wasn't talking to Philip. Adam drained his water bottle in three long slugs, even though it didn't even begin to slake his massive thirst, then bent over, hands on his knees, to catch his breath.

The Chabad center was just a storefront, wedged between a children's consignment shop and an Italian deli. Adam slowly walked his bike down the sidewalk, trying to muster his courage. He didn't see a bike rack, or even a chain-link fence or a parking meter to lock his bike to, and for half a second that seemed like an excuse to turn around and ride straight back down the hill. But that would be like Moses climbing Mount Sinai and forgetting to pick up the Ten Commandments. No, Adam had committed to this plan. He'd practically incinerated his lungs with the effort. He wasn't going to go home without at least walking into the place.

He leaned his bike up against the side of the building and nudged open the door. A little bell chimed. "Hello?" Adam called tentatively. "Anyone there?"

The store—was it a store? a synagogue?—was filled with menorahs (some with eight candles, he noticed, and some with seven), books, calendars, and little paintings of dancing rabbis. There were also framed pictures everywhere of a bearded man, some of which said THE REBBE or THE GREAT REBBE underneath. Adam imagined his mother cringing. It was so very, very Jewish and old-fashioned. "The religion of my 'forefathers' "— she sometimes said, putting air quotes around the word *forefathers*—"is all superstition, fear, and sexism. A religion that hasn't changed since the time of camels in the desert."

But, Adam always thought when his mother raised this point, there were still camels in the desert, weren't there? It wasn't like a religion created in the days of unicorns.

"Hello?" he called again. If nobody answered this time, he was going home. After all, his bike was outside, unchained. Anyone could steal it.

A door opened in the back of the store and a man rushed out. Adam knew at once that this was the rabbi. He had a full beard the texture of a Brillo pad and wore the uniform of his sect: a black hat and a long black coat. This was what Adam had come for, yet he wasn't quite prepared. You might see a guy like this in New York City—that wouldn't be quite so weird—but you wouldn't be face-to-face with him and, if you were with Philip or with Adam's mom, you'd probably make fun of him from a safe distance. But this wasn't a safe distance, and despite the strange outfit and the beard, the rabbi was real. He looked at Adam, tilted his head, and smiled, as if trying to figure out a puzzle.

"You're not my typical customer."

"No," Adam admitted. "I guess not."

"Sorry, I was just in the storeroom, doing an inventory of my sukkahs. I'm Rabbi Mendel Abraham. What can I do for you?"

Should he just blurt it out? *I want a bar mitzvah.* Adam was afraid it would sound stupid, shallow, and that the rabbi would be able to see right through him. He might as well say what he really wanted: *I want ten thousand dollars. I want a hand job from Lisa Epstein. I really want to stick it to my mom.*

"Um," he said instead. "Is it okay to bring my bike in here?"

"Sure. Then meet me in the back."

Adam retrieved his bike, then found the rabbi sitting at a desk in the corner of the room. The floor all around him was covered with sections of PVC pipe. When Adam walked in, the rabbi looked up from his papers and leaned back in his chair. "So tell me why you're here."

Okay, Adam decided, gumming up his courage. *Just say it. Tell the guy why you're here and stop wasting everyone's time.* "I want . . ." He stopped, looked down at his hands.

"You want—?" the rabbi said encouragingly.

"A bar mitzvah." There, he'd said it. "I want a bar mitzvah! But I'm only half Jewish and we don't belong to a synagogue, and I've never been to Hebrew school."

"Which half?" the rabbi said.

"What?"

"Which half is Jewish?"

"My mom."

"Then you're all Jewish. By law."

"Oh."

The rabbi picked up an autographed baseball that sat on a small mahogany block on his desk. He passed it lightly from hand to hand, clearly a habit. "The 2004 world champions. I got it from the Bostoner Rebbe himself." The rabbi shrugged, sheepishly, endearingly. "I shouldn't do this, because the ink rubs off. But for some reason, whenever I'm sitting here talking to someone, I can't help picking it up. I feel like it's my lucky baseball."

Adam looked at the baseball, wondering what, exactly, it had to do with him wanting a bar mitzvah.

"Do you know how the Jews are like the Red Sox?" Rabbi Mendel asked.

Adam shook his head.

"The Jews are the oldest monotheistic religion. The Red Sox have the oldest park in Major League baseball. Joseph's brothers sold him into slavery. The Sox sold Ruth. They both wandered through the desert for years and years, but what got them through it was faith. Being a Jew is like living in New England winter after winter. Sure, it would be easier to live in Florida. But we're a people whose character has been forged in adversity."

Adam waited.

"What I'm saying," the rabbi continued, "is that you're signing up for a New England winter. Your mom's Jewish, your dad is Christian. Am I correct?"

"Yes."

"And so you probably celebrate Christmas and Chanukah. You have a great big Christmas tree in your living room every winter, decorated with lights, and lots of presents under it. Am I right?"

Adam gulped.

"Are you willing to give that up? And why? Why now? Why the bar mitzvah? Why do you want to become a Jew?"

Adam cracked the knuckles on his right hand as he thought about the answer. Was it really for the money? Or about Lisa Epstein? Was he just trying to drive his mother crazy? And what should he tell this man? He felt like he had the few times he'd been allowed, as a little kid, to wait in the long line at a shopping mall to sit on Santa's lap. Here was the guy with the keys to the kingdom, the one who dispensed the loot. But he could see inside you, too, see if you were naughty or nice. And if you asked for too much, maybe you'd get a lump of coal instead.

Adam suddenly had a flash of inspiration. "The chair! I want to be lifted up in a chair. I want people to dance around me."

Rabbi Mendel put down the baseball and leaned back. He put his fingers together into a little church steeple and tapped them together a few times. "Okay," he said. "The chair. Family. Community. Belongingness. That's not a terrible reason to want a bar mitzvah. We can work with that."

Adam felt like a dog that had just been patted. "We can?"

"Sure, why not?"

"Well the Reform synagogue said I should have started Hebrew school in third grade."

"And if you don't start Hebrew in third grade you can't be a Jew?" The rabbi's voice was disdainful. "That's not our shtick. We'll take any Jew, at any stage or level of Judaism, and help them find more meaning in their Judaism. We don't judge. And we don't charge dues."

"My mom will like that," Adam blurted. He added silently, *That's the only part she'll like.*

"I'd like to meet your mom. In fact I'd like to meet your whole family. Here's the first step." Rabbi Mendel grabbed a pen, wrote something down, and handed it to Adam. "My address. Tomorrow's Friday night. Shabbat. I want you and your family to come for Shabbat dinner at my home. You know what Shabbat is, don't you?"

"The Jewish Sabbath?" Adam said uncertainly.

"Good boy."

"Can I bring my grandparents? The Jewish ones? They're visiting."

"Even more of a mitzvah," the rabbi said. He looked up at a calendar next to his desk. "Candle lighting tomorrow night is at 6:02 P.M. So try to be there by five-thirty, okay?"

"Should we bring anything?"

"Not a thing." The rabbi looked amused. "And if you did, I couldn't even bring it in my house."

Belle was in the bathroom when the phone rang again. She quickly pulled up her panties and ran out, without even washing her hands. This time it had to be Max. Her poor Max!

But it wasn't. Instead, it was a gum-cracking woman asking for Michael. She sounded like she was calling from a nightclub, though it was barely midafternoon.

"I'm sorry," Belle said stiffly, "but Michael's not here. Can I take a message?"

"Yeah. Tell him it's Xenon from the Vixen Den, okay? He left his credit card."

"Zee-non? *Z-e-e-n-o-n?*"

"Close enough, honey," Xenon said. "It's with an *X* not a *Z*. Don't worry, he'll remember me."

I'll bet he will, Belle thought. *That son of a bitch didn't pick me up at the airport yesterday because he was hanging out in some club with a bimbo named Xenon.* She knew there was something up with her son-in-law.

It couldn't have been more than seven or eight minutes, tops. Michael sprinted to the parking lot, started the ignition, maneuvered the spaghetti tangle of airport service roads, and pulled neatly into the arrival area in front of Terminal C. The only trouble he anticipated was herding Max into the Prius fast enough for the security guys who, in this paranoid post-9/11 era, didn't like any cars idling for more than a few seconds. Well, once he spotted the old man, he'd just have to put his emergency blinkers on, hop out, and corral him as fast as he could.

Michael slowed the car to a roll, looking between the SUVs and car-rental courtesy vans for the bench where he'd left Max. He'd marked the spot in his mind, the way you'd mentally mark a wall where you were planning to hang a painting. It was easy enough to find—the bench where he'd left Max—except that Max wasn't there. Michael pulled the car up a few more feet, craning his neck to see around a Hilton courtesy van that had just pulled up. Maybe he'd remembered the wrong spot. Maybe it was the next bench down. But no. No sign of Max anywhere. He'd either have to drive around the whole airport again and come back, or park the car and hop out.

Damn.

Hadn't he sat Max down and told him to wait? How hard was it to sit on a bench and keep an eye out for someone? Michael pulled his keys out and put on his emergency blinkers, annoyed that he had to squander his brief opportunity to idle, when he should have been packing Max into the car. He got out, stood next to the car, and scanned the entire length of the sidewalk for his father-in-law. Still, nothing.

Michael was reminded suddenly of all the times Adam had wandered off when he was three or four. Times he'd found him hiding under a clothing rack at Kmart, or wandering down the cookie aisle in the A&P. Michael remembered that creeping fear that would start to overtake him, the urban legends about kidnappers whisking children into store bathrooms and dyeing their hair, the wild, disorganized thoughts about finding a store manager and demanding a lockdown—and the mixture of relief and irritation when Adam would jump out from under a big rack of women's slacks and yell, "Boo!" You were never supposed to take your eyes off your kid in a public place, not even for an instant, or leave an unsupervised toddler strapped into a car. In the second it took you to run into a 7-Eleven to get a cup of coffee, a carjacker could swoop in, steal your car with your kid in it, and turn you into one of those hysterical pleading parents on the news.

Michael began to wonder if he'd made a mistake leaving Max on his own, and how big a price he—or Max—would have to pay for it.

Looking around anxiously, Michael took a chance and sprinted down the sidewalk. Maybe Max was just in a blind spot, hidden from view by a big pillar. He passed the empty bench, cursed the old man for not being there, cursed himself for leaving Max alone. He'd failed to recognize that Max was, after whatever happened up in Boston, a child again. Or at least childlike.

And then, in a forehead-slapping moment of recognition, the simple answer came to him. Max had just gotten cold. Old people got cold all the time, even in October, especially if they'd been living the past eight years in Florida. Michael ran into the terminal, hopeful he'd find his father-in-law right next to the door. But there were hundreds of people all lugging suitcases in different directions, an endlessly moving haystack in which to find his needle. He found the luggage carousel for the flight they'd just gotten off, thinking maybe Max would be there, but even though he recognized a few passengers from the flight they'd just come in on, none of them were Max. His heart pumping with the awareness that each second away from the car increased his risk of trouble exponentially, Michael hopped the escalator leading up to the main terminal. But once he got to the top, he realized the choices were even more endless, the chances of finding his father-in-law even more remote.

He decided to turn around and go to the car. Maybe he'd be lucky. Maybe Max would be waiting there.

Instead, he found a SWAT team of blue-uniformed men

and his car alarm blaring at the indignity of having its driver-side window smashed in. All the doors of the Prius were wide open. The cops had popped the trunk, were searching the glove compartment, the ashtrays, under seat cushions. A German shepherd wearing a K-9 bib was up on its hind legs, sniffing at the trunk.

Michael spoke before he thought. Before it had dawned on him that he should just walk away, silently blend into the cab line, or seek anonymity inside an airport news kiosk. But when he saw a guy in a uniform pull out a knife and plunge it into the plush of the passenger seat, looking for drugs or explosives or God knew what, Michael made his second big tactical mistake of the afternoon. "What the hell?" he blurted.

Three words. That was all it took. A second later, he was grabbed by a man in a navy blue Windbreaker, who had both hands behind his back and clamped into something metal and cold.

"Motherfucker," said Patrick McCarthy. "Did you think I was joking when I told you to stay away from this place?" He shoved Michael against the car with a ferocity that made yesterday's body slam look tender. The K-9 unit leapt toward Michael's crotch with bared teeth, pulling against its leash so hard that Michael almost began to believe he was guilty. He tried to shrink back, to make space between his groin and the beast, but there wasn't much he could do with his arms behind him and his wrists handcuffed together.

Belle had given up struggling with the TV and was back to cleaning the pigsty that was Nina's house. She was working now on the clutter in Nina's entryway, trying to rid it of the totes, shoes, backpacks, and shopping bags, hoping at least to redistribute some of the disorder, to take some things upstairs, so at least you didn't have to encounter chaos the minute you walked in. She thought about her old foyer in Great Neck, of the tight ship she'd run despite three kids—and Nina had only one!—and wondered why it was that women these days seemed so befuddled by the simple task of running a household.

Once some of the clutter was clear, Belle spotted a shopping bag next to the front door and, bending down to pick it up, debated whether to look inside. Just a little peek, she thought, wouldn't hurt anybody. Something about a nice crisp shopping bag almost demanded inspection; besides, how would she know whose room to put it in if she didn't check to see what was in it? Belle ruffled through the white tissue paper with a slight thrill, as if opening a present—maybe it was a present!—and discovered a brown suede Prada bag inside. She picked it up, turned it over, inspecting, frowning. *Not my taste,* she thought critically. And then, more uncharitably: *Interesting how she can afford a Prada. She's always complaining about money.*

Belle was about to rewrap the suede bag in tissue when she noticed it had a certain heft, more than what you'd expect from the paper stuffed inside a purse to give it shape in the store. She unzipped it. And there, like in one of those nesting Russian dolls, was a smaller shopping bag containing yet another secret. Belle hesitated just a second this time, then opened it to find an odd little octagonal mirror. It was a strange little piece, with some Chinese or Japanese characters on it, Belle wasn't sure which. She was holding it up and turning it over to inspect the back side, when the phone rang. Hastily, she propped the mirror against a wall, then walked back into the living room, where she'd put down the phone after the unfortunate call from Xenon.

"Hello?" she said.

"Collect to anyone from Max Gettleman."

SIXTEEN

Nina called the garage and asked for Garvey. She was hoping the job was done and maybe she could talk him into picking her up. Sometimes, if they weren't too busy, the mechanics would do that. And it would save Nina the trouble of calling in a favor from one of her friends.

"This is Nina Gettleman-Summer," she said. "Michael's wife? With the Honda? I was just wondering if you were finished with the brakes?"

"Brakes?"

"Yes," she said, tapping her fingers on her desk. "We dropped it off this morning."

"Sure, the Honda," Garvey said. "But Mr. Summer didn't say anything about brakes. He asked me to change the oil and rotate the tires for winter."

"Of course he said something about brakes! That's why . . ." Nina stopped. She thought about yesterday, about Michael's sudden disappearance, his mysterious cell phone drop-out, his failure to pick up Belle. She completed the sentence in her own head. . . . *that's why he took the Prius.* But why? What was he hiding?

"Right," she said to Garvey. "I forgot. Look, is there any chance you could come by with the Honda and pick me up?"

She pulled onto Berkeley Place forty-five minutes later, hoping to see the Prius already parked in the driveway. Michael and her dad should be there by now—it was almost five—and she'd take a few minutes before dinner to pull him upstairs to their bedroom for a little marital tête-à-tête. Away from the prying ears of Belle, of course. Just what the fuck was going on? She intended to find out.

But the driveway was empty.

Nina walked in and immediately noticed a flicker of movement that didn't belong. She felt an involuntary speeding of her heart, an impulse toward alertness. An animal must have gotten in, a squirrel or a bird, maybe something rabid. She took one wary step, and detected motion again. And then, she realized suddenly, it was her own motion. In a mirror—a mirror that hadn't been there in the morning when she left.

She felt foolish, like someone who'd been frightened of her own shadow. And then she recognized it, the bagua mirror that she'd bought in New York; for some reason, it was out of the Prada bag she'd left it in, and was leaning against the wall in her entryway. Suddenly, her nervousness gave way to something subtler, deeper, and more confusing. Dread, she realized. The Yin Bagua, she remembered reading, should never be left inside the house. It was way too powerful. She'd bought the mirror to capture the menacing energy of the poison arrow— the street that faced her front door—and send it back. But she hadn't followed through, just as she hadn't followed through on purifying her studio. And now, despite precautions and against all advice, the powerful bad luck reflector had been turned right toward her house, her family, everything in life she held dear.

Nina remembered, suddenly, the Disney animation of *The Sorcerer's Apprentice* with Mickey Mouse, and how things had spun wildly out of control, the brooms splitting, buckets emptying, water rising. She shivered, remembering the flood in her studio that had started everything, and felt as feckless as poor Mickey. See what happened when you tried to play with magic? She grabbed the mirror, turned it over, and wrapped it with her jacket as if trying to muffle a ticking time bomb.

"Mom!" she shouted.

But Belle was already there, hands on hips, her mouth a tight button of indignation.

"Mom," Nina said. "Why did you take that mirror out of my bag? It's a special mirror." She stopped. Her mom would never understand feng shui. But it wasn't just that. Belle had that expression on her face, that wilting one that she'd used on all three kids growing up, the one that made you want to find the nearest manhole cover and duck under it.

"What?" Nina said. "What? What did I do now?"

"Max called. Collect. A little while ago," Belle said. "It seems Michael just disappeared. Left him sitting on a bench at Newark Airport and never came back."

"Oy," Nina said.

"And oh, by the way, Michael got a call from someone named Xenon at the Vixen Den. Seems he left his credit card there yesterday."

"Shit." So Michael was hiding something. Not just one lie—the brakes in the Honda—but now two. He'd spent yesterday afternoon at a place called the Vixen Den, which apparently was the reason for his failure to pick up Belle. Was that the end of the lies? Or were there more? Why had he deserted Max? Had he even lost his job?

"And one more message," Belle said. "A Principal Drabyak called today from Adam's school. He has detention on Saturday."

It appeared that the bagua mirror had done its work.

"Where's Dad?" Nina asked.

"He's waiting at a Starbucks at Newark Airport," Belle said. "And I told him not to move a muscle until you get there."

"And Adam?"

"I have no idea."

Nina picked up her cell phone and looked to make sure it still had a charge. "Okay," she said. "I'll go to the airport. If you hear from Adam, tell him to call me on my cell."

A Starbucks at Newark Airport, Nina thought. How many friggin' Starbucks could there be at Newark Airport? She opened the front door, but before she could go down the steps and cross to the driveway, she was confronted by a young man with rimless glasses and a patchy beard, approaching her with a clipboard. He looked like a canvasser for PIRG or Clean Water NJ.

"Nina Gettleman?" he asked.

Normally, she'd be the first to support clean water or fresh air, but the guy's timing was terrible. "Yes," Nina said. "But I'm sorry. I can't sign your petition now."

"Quite all right, Ms. Gettleman. I just needed to give you this." He smiled a little maliciously, then handed her a small official-looking packet.

Nina looked at the official-looking type on the creamy envelope. Very formal. All caps.

CIVIL SUIT. HENDRICKS V. GETTLEMAN.

Nina looked up to see the process server slam the door of a VW Beetle and speed off. Oh, yes. Her day was now complete.

At nine o'clock they were all sitting around Nina's kitchen table. All, that is, except for Michael, who was still unaccounted for and not answering his phone. They'd had pizza for the second night straight, and despite the late hour, only Max ate with any appetite. Belle was now dumping paper plates and napkins into the trash.

"Adam," Belle said. "Stamp on that box and fold it up, so we can put that in the trash, too."

"We recycle," Nina said.

Mother and daughter locked eyes.

"Fine," Belle said. "I've always said no kitchen was big enough for two women. You clean up. I'll go in the living room. Adam, can you turn on the TV for Grandma?"

Max got up slowly, following Adam and Belle into the living room. Nina cleaned up quietly, relishing the brief interlude without anyone around. Nina threw the pizza box into the recycling pile on the back porch and stood outside for a moment, trying to call Michael on his cell again. Still nothing. Surely, she should report his disappearance to the police—even though she'd heard that people had to be gone twenty-four hours before police took a missing persons report. She picked up the phone book and looked up the nonemergency number for the police department. She had all but the last digit dialed when she hung up. What would she say? My husband is two hours late for dinner? He didn't pick up my mother at Newark Airport yesterday and he stranded my dad at the airport today? He lied about the brakes on his car? No, he just sounded like a jerk. And it was too early for the cops to take her seriously.

A heaviness began to settle on Nina's chest, a feeling, actually, of doom. It was different from the myriad annoyances that routinely cropped up in her life, different from her exasperation at restaurants that failed to offer vegetarian entrées or packed doggy bags in ozone-destroying Styrofoam, different from the prickly defensiveness she felt around her mom, different, especially, from her normal impatience at the eight million little annoying things that Michael did, like snoring or putting a red shirt in a white wash. She tried feeling angry at Michael, angry at him for fucking up, for stranding each of her parents, separately, at the airport, two days running. But her heart and imagination skipped right past irritation into something unfamiliar.

She'd lost him. Maybe he'd been abducted. Or maybe he'd run off with a bimbo named Xenon. She'd nagged him repeatedly to stay out of the house—she'd been so embarrassed he was out of work, and worried her mom would find out, she hadn't even considered his feelings—and he had, finally, obliged her. It was like the sudden disappearance of the sun, or oxygen, something that she both relied on and took absolutely for granted, and which she now belatedly realized she couldn't live without.

Finally, Nina walked wearily into the living room. "Adam," she said, sighing heavily. "Why don't you come into the kitchen and take out the garbage?" She hadn't had an opportunity yet to find out what the trouble had been about in school. As if she didn't have enough problems already.

She found all three of them staring at the Weather Channel.

"It's coming here," Belle said.

"What's coming here?"

"The hurricane. Ida."

"It *might* be coming here," Max corrected. "They're saying it reorganized itself over South Carolina and is heading north. You can count on some rain, anyway, this weekend."

"Is that possible?" Nina asked. Of course the person who knew whether it was possible or impossible happened to be missing. But at least her father, who'd seemed so shaky when she'd finally found him at Newark Airport, seemed to have regained his faculties.

"Unusual, but not impossible," Adam said. "They've been talking about Hurricane Hazel in '54."

"It's just . . ." Nina dropped down onto the sofa next to Adam. "Yesterday, it was down in Florida, and now it's coming here? What is it, following you guys?"

"I told you we would have been better off in Florida," Max said.

Belle folded her arms tightly across her chest. It was the closest she ever got to contrition.

Max leaned over and kissed her on the cheek. "I was *kidding*."

"But you know," said Adam. "It could have something to do with Dad being gone. Maybe they called him in to work the hurricane."

Belle rolled her eyes. "And he doesn't have a phone?"

But Nina saw the possibility like a tiny feather floating ahead of her, just out of reach. A long shot, maybe—like a hurricane chasing her parents all the way from Florida to New Jersey—but it was possible. A hurricane was coming. Or possibly coming. A freak of nature. Maybe Michael heard about it when he went to get his car at the airport. Maybe they needed him in the tower, needed him to predict the storm, to prevent airplanes from crashing. Yes, a matter of life and death. Of course, it didn't explain the brakes, or Xenon, or why he'd failed to pick up Belle yesterday. And it didn't even explain the lack of a phone call. But as it was the only whisper of hope Nina had, she concentrated on the fact that Michael did get terribly focused once he started plugging numbers into his weather models, especially when a big storm was coming.

The storm, Adam added, was supposed to hit the New York area sometime Saturday.

The one good thing about having your dad missing and a hurricane coming was that it tended to put other things in perspective. Like, for example, a little school detention. Adam knew that, under different circumstances, his ass would be in the frying pan. But whatever he'd done to fuck up, his dad apparently had fucked up worse. And so the call from Principal

Drabyak had miraculously retreated into the backdrop, like scenery in a play.

Adam was worried about his dad, but appreciative of the small favor he'd been granted. So it seemed a bit, well, greedy to be looking for something else in the favor department. Say, asking the whole family—including his Godless mom, to go to Shabbat dinner at a Chabad rabbi's house.

The problem was, Adam had already promised Rabbi Mendel he'd bring his parents, and even his grandparents, to dinner on Friday night. And in a strange way, he'd actually begun to look forward to it, and not just for mercenary reasons, like having a bar mitzvah and getting a ton of money. Maybe it was what had happened in the principal's office today. Maybe he wanted to be, like the rabbi said, a "good boy."

But his mom. That was going to be tough.

Adam could read his mother's moods the way his father could read the clouds, and this one was as threatening as a summer thunderstorm. She jumped whenever the phone rang, even though it just turned out to be a couple of telemarketers and Josh Leavitt asking him to fax over the math homework. She picked up books and magazines, held them in her lap, and didn't open them, but clicked between different news stations—CNN, CNBC, even Fox—to check on the progress of the storm. Then she walked into the kitchen, washed dishes noisily, slamming cupboards. Finally she went upstairs to her bedroom and started making calls. Adam couldn't hear what she was saying, but he could hear her pacing up there and could tell how stressed out she was by the way her voice spiraled into the higher registers.

The last thing she wanted to hear about now was an invitation for some nice old-fashioned Judaism.

Adam pulled the paper the rabbi had given him out of his pocket, unfolded it, and went to the sunroom to look it up in MapQuest. It turned out to be just a few blocks from the

Chabad office. He'd gotten to the office under his own power and, worst case, he could get to Shabbat dinner on his own, too. Still, the rabbi had specifically asked to meet his mom.

Adam returned to the living room, sat down, and stared at the TV. Then he looked over at his grandparents huddled together on the sofa, holding hands and watching the storm news together with grim expressions. Suddenly, he had an inspiration. If there was anyone in the family who'd be in favor of Adam getting a bar mitzvah, it would be Belle and Max. Maybe they wouldn't be crazy about this Rabbi Mendel with his black coat and his black hat. But they'd see it as a first step in bringing some Judaism into their daughter's house, and they'd jump on it.

"So, Grandpa," Adam began.

Nina at last came downstairs and, in a small gesture of hospitality, asked her parents if they needed anything else before she went to bed.

"We're fine," Max said. "In fact, we're just going to sleep down here tonight. The sofa is fine for me, and your mom can snuggle up on the love seat. And we'll be able to keep an eye on the storm."

"You're sleeping downstairs?" Nina felt both insulted and relieved. Maybe she'd get her meditation room back after all.

"Dad's knees," Belle said. "And we really need a bathroom on the same floor."

It was a complaint; that's what it was. They weren't being accommodating. They were being critical.

"Okay," Nina said stiffly. "If that's how you feel."

"But listen," said Max. "There's something we'd like to talk to you about."

Something we'd like to talk to you about. Her least favorite phrase in the English language. When she was growing up, it almost always meant she was in trouble. Sometimes it meant something else bad, like one of her parents going in the next day for a biopsy. Nina could imagine a lot of things they might want to talk about, and of course Michael was at the top of the list. But she didn't want to talk about Michael. She couldn't bear it. Not with them.

"What?"

"It's about Adam."

Nina exhaled, relieved. "Oh, the thing in school. I know. I'm on it."

"We're sure you're on it," Max said. "But it's not what we wanted to talk about."

Nina was confused. "What, then?"

"He wants a bar mitzvah."

"What?"

"Your son, Adam, wants to be a Jew."

"He told you that?" Nina said. "Tonight? With everything going on?"

"Well," Belle said. "Would you like it if he picked a more convenient time to rediscover his Judaism?"

"Belle, shhh," Max said. "Don't upset her. She's had a rough day."

Oh, was that what you called it when your husband dropped off the face of the earth, your son got in trouble for writing obscenities on the Spanish teacher's blackboard, and you were served legal papers for a lawsuit?

"Look." Max used the kind of voice that cops used when they were talking to jumpers on bridges. "We know what you're going through. But Adam, just today, biked up to this Chabad center and talked to a rabbi. And the guy invited him, well, us—all of us—to his house for Shabbat dinner tomorrow night."

"And we think it would be a very good influence on your family," Belle added.

Good influence. Like Ronnie Minkoff had been a good influence when Nina was in eighth grade. And temple youth group and all those losers had been a good influence. *Good influence.* The words made Nina seethe. Her mother's idea of good influence was always somebody or something that Nina loathed. Almost as much as she loathed the idea that she needed a good influence.

"Mom." It was Adam, halfway down the stairs.

Nina turned around and looked up at Adam. Adam looked just like his dad, she noticed suddenly, even though people always said he looked like her. Why did it take Michael's disappearance to realize this? Was Adam all that she was going to have left of him?

"Yes?"

"It's true. I did meet this rabbi today, and I'd really, really like it if we could go to his house tomorrow night for dinner."

Nina turned back to her parents, who were looking up at Adam with their *nachas* smiles, the kind she'd seen when they were called up to light candles at their other grandchildren's bar and bat mitzvahs. They were all ganging up on her: Adam, Belle, and Max. And Nina didn't even have Michael on her side.

"Mom," Nina said. "Dad. Adam. This is a Chabad rabbi you're talking about, right?"

"Yes."

"Do you know what kind of nuts they are? They're the guys who go around in those mitzvah wagons at Christmastime, with the loudspeakers and menorahs."

"You mean Chanukah. Right, darling?" Belle corrected.

Nina ignored her. "They're black-hatters. They have those weird sideburns. They don't answer their phones on Saturday. They're a . . . a . . . cult." She turned to her mother. "You'll *hate* them."

Adam came down the stairs and stood behind the sofa and his grandparents. "You know, Mom, you hang out with some pretty weird people yourself sometimes."

"What do you mean?"

"You know when you go to one of those yoga places, and

there are those people with those tags pinned on them saying they've taken a vow of silence?"

It was true. The vow-of-silence types were pretty weird.

"And how about all those people there who take Sanskrit names?"

"Look, dear, we know how you feel about Judaism," said Belle. "But sometimes you just have to be a little open-minded."

That took the cake—Belle talking about being open-minded!

"And you know," Max said. "It couldn't hurt to ask for a little miracle right about now, could it?"

She knew, of course, what he was talking about. Michael. Her disappearing husband. And maybe they were right. Maybe it couldn't hurt. It was just one night. And in all likelihood, after one dinner with these *yiddishe* nutbags, Adam would give up all this bar mitzvah nonsense and come to his senses.

"Okay, I can't fight all of you." Nina picked up a few glasses on the coffee table to take into the kitchen. "I'm going to bed."

Michael had been taken to a small room, a place with a plain table and a bare lightbulb over it, and a small window affording a glimpse of the control tower where he'd spent most of his working career. He'd been strip-searched and forced to change into overalls. They'd taken his wallet, his watch, and his cell phone. The Prius, McCarthy said—his mouth curling into a sneer, as if the very idea of the car both amused and disgusted him—had been impounded.

But at least they'd taken off Michael's handcuffs. McCarthy was sitting across the table with a tape recorder, trying to break him down, asking the same questions over and over.

"What were you doing at the airport yesterday?"

"I was taking pictures of the clouds." He'd been saying the same thing for hours.

"Clouds?" McCarthy spit the word out like a bad taste in his mouth. "Yes, you're a big fan of clouds. And today, when you left the car unattended? You were looking at the clouds again?"

"No, I told you. I'd just picked up my father-in-law from Logan."

"Where he'd been held in security," McCarthy said. "So it's a whole family operation. I can't believe we let the old guy get away."

"The 'old guy,'" Michael sighed, "is a Jewish dentist from Great Neck, who retired eight years ago and went to live in Delray Beach. His idea of a crime against humanity is eating three Krispy Kreme doughnuts in one sitting. Not exactly *America's Most Wanted.*"

"And what was your car doing sitting in the arrivals lane for ten minutes? Despite all the signs about not even standing, let alone parking? And what were you doing getting on a flight today without luggage, and returning the same day?"

"I doubt it was ten minutes," Michael said. "I keep telling you the same thing. I was bringing my father-in-law back from Boston. He has bad knees. I sat him on a bench and said I'd go get the car. And when I came back he was gone. So I tried to find him."

"Perfect son-in-law."

"I try," Michael said. "Look, please. Can I have my one call home? My wife is probably worried sick."

"Listen, bozo. This isn't your local police precinct. This is Homeland Security. The Major Leagues. You don't get phone calls. Do you understand? You get zip. Ever hear of Guantanamo? If we worried about every asshat's little crying wife, we'd have planes blowing up left and right over the Atlantic."

Michael rubbed his eyes. "I have to pee," he said.

McCarthy looked in the wastebasket, pulled out an empty two-liter bottle of Coca-Cola, and thrust it at him. "Here."

Michael looked at the bottle in disbelief. Was he understanding this right? McCarthy was suggesting he empty his bladder into a Coke bottle?

"I was kind of hoping for a bathroom."

"I was kind of hoping for a bathroom," McCarthy mimicked. "Listen, asshat. Just pee in the fucking bottle. If you want privacy, turn around."

Friday

Nina looked over to Michael's side of the bed, and for half an instant imagined him up, already in the shower. She listened for water, the radio, the electric razor, and then remembered. He wasn't there. He hadn't come home. He hadn't called.

Today she would have to do something. She would have to file a missing persons report, or maybe—she remembered her mother's message about the woman named Xenon and the Vixen Den—maybe she would go there and ask some very pointed questions.

She wanted to indulge a well-deserved sulk, to turn over, pull the covers up, and fall back asleep, but she was way too agitated. And she had to get to her classes. If she was going to be a single mom—her mind had leapt to a Michael-less future, the very idea of which made her stomach sink—she would have to make a real living.

She dressed, woke Adam up, and then started downstairs, where she heard her parents whispering conspiratorially. When she walked into the kitchen, they looked up, bright, false optimistic smiles plastered on their faces.

"Good morning, darling, did you sleep well?" Belle asked.

Nina looked up suspiciously. Why was her mother being so solicitous?

Nina walked into the pantry and took out a box of granola. "As well as can be expected." She was reaching for a cereal bowl in the cupboard when she noticed Max and Belle look at each other, exchanging some kind of signal.

"Your mom and I—" Max hesitated. "Your mom and I would like to help you out with your current, um, situation."

Nina waited.

"We'd like to pay for a private detective."

Nina dropped the bowl, which broke neatly into two pieces. She stared at her parents, as if they'd just recommended electroshock, or a quick little outing to Mars. Then she bent down, picked up the broken bowl. It looked like a child's rendition of a broken heart.

"I really don't think that's necessary," she said.

"But, Nina—"

"Mom, not now. Look, you have my cell phone number if you need me. Or if you hear anything. Okay?"

Luckily the cell had survived the impact with Charlotte Hendricks's mouth. Ironic that this small hunk of Japanese electronics was the only thing that seemed to be holding up these days. If things ever got back to normal, Nina told herself, she'd buy some stock in Nokia.

Adam's father hadn't been there to make his lunch, and his mother seemed to have forgotten it altogether. Luckily, Adam had a five-dollar bill tucked in his locker for such emergencies. He waited glumly in the cafeteria line, mulling the choice between tasteless chop suey and soggy fish sticks, and tried not to think about all the trouble he'd gotten into yesterday.

It wasn't until he came out of the line with his tray—he'd opted for fish sticks, which could be drenched in ketchup—that he remembered he was still furious at Philip. He surveyed the cafeteria, looking for a different table to sit at. Everybody, it seemed, was staring back. He saw pity, curiosity, suppressed hilarity.

Everybody knew.

He considered, briefly, looking for the mighty goddess, Lisa Epstein herself, who, after all, owed him. Big-time. But she wasn't sitting at her usual table. Her normal posse was still there, but they seemed a little lackluster and more than usually clueless without her.

Philip, who continued to eat his bagged lunch with his usual stiff-backed dignity, was the only one not staring at him.

Adam's need to get out of the glare of public scrutiny trumped his desire to avoid Philip. He slid his tray down, jostling his friend's chocolate milk. Then he sat down and frowned at his lunch, stabbing a fish stick without lifting it.

"So," Adam said finally.

"So."

They ate in silence, staring straight ahead.

"So," Philip repeated. "Have you heard about Lisa Epstein?"

"What? I noticed she wasn't sitting at her usual table."

"Our Lady of Instant Rehabilitation."

"What?"

"Catholic school."

"You're kidding! After her bat mitzvah? Just last weekend?"

"Remember who her dad works for, right?" Philip said knowingly. "And they told him there was nothing that would straighten a kid out faster than a bunch of sadistic nuns."

"Holy shit," Adam said.

"Exactly."

They both looked over at Lisa's entourage, which looked hopelessly disorganized and aimless, like an ant colony after a kid had stepped on it. Adam wondered briefly who would emerge as the new Lisa Epstein, the alpha female of junior high.

"Can you imagine her wearing one of those little plaid Catholic schoolgirl uniforms?" Philip asked, getting up to dump his lunch scraps.

"Actually, I can." Adam pictured the plaid uniform hitting Lisa Epstein at midthigh.

Once Philip left, Adam tested his emotions to see if he had sudden interest in converting to Catholicism, now that Lisa Epstein was in Catholic school. What did he know about Catholicism? Even less than he knew about Judaism. There was a pope, confession, incense, kneeling, nuns with rulers. The Father, the Son, the Holy Ghost. What was the Holy Ghost anyway? It sounded a little Stephen King.

Adam thought about Rabbi Mendel, with his strange outfit and his full beard, tossing the baseball from hand to hand, talking about Jews and the Red Sox. He reflected momentarily on Philip's synagogue, where all the kids, carefully tutored in Hebrew from third grade on, hung out in the bathroom during services. Finally, he considered his own Unitarian Church, with its blue jeans–wearing, guitar-strumming minister, Gary. Just Gary. Or was Gary even called a minister? Maybe he was just a leader. Gary liked to joke that Unitarians believed in one God—at most. The grown-ups always laughed, but Adam wasn't sure what it meant. So many religions to choose from, like all the different cell phone plans. After a while, you got tired of trying to tell them apart.

Her parents had already called twice on Nina's drive to work, once to ask if she had flashlights, and another time to check on batteries, candles, matches, and bottled water.

"Okay," she said, trying not to sound shrill. "I know. All right? I hear the news myself. I'll pick up everything before I come home."

"You better not wait until the last minute," Belle warned. "We know a thing or two about hurricanes. People run to the stores early and buy everything out."

"Mom," Nina protested. "They're not even sure it's going to be a hurricane. If it gets here at all."

She'd just come back from picking up a sandwich and was walking into her building when the third call came.

"And toilet paper. You'd better buy extra. We're out of it in the powder room, and I didn't see any under your bathroom sink. I'm using tissue."

"Thanks for sharing that, Mom. Okay. I'll get toilet paper, too."

Nina was just putting her cell phone back in her purse when she literally bumped into Coriander, who was heading out with a large stack of mail. Coriander bobbled the pile, and three padded envelopes bumped to the floor. Nina bent down to retrieve them.

"Sorry," Nina said. "I'm a little stressed."

"That's pretty obvious."

Nina gulped. Was Coriander reading her aura? Could she tell that Michael had left her? Was heartsickness written across her face?

"You can tell?"

"Oh, yes," Coriander said. "Pain in your heart, plain as day."

Nina's shoulders started to shake. She wanted to cry, to let herself go, but somehow all that watery stuff seemed to have evaporated. She shook silently, hoping that none of her students happened to walk in. Coriander carefully placed her packages on the floor and held Nina, wordlessly, until the shaking subsided.

"I'm going to the post office," Coriander said finally. "Do you want to walk with me? And maybe go to Starbucks?"

Nina sniffed. "Okay, but let me put a sign on the door first." And for the second time that week she canceled class for a family emergency. Only this time, there really was one.

McCarthy had gone home the previous night and left Michael under the supervision of another Homeland Security goon (it was surprising how fast one could start sympathizing with the other side), a black guy named Harrison with a shaved head and a scar that ran from his right eye to the left side of his jaw. Where McCarthy was a tightly coiled little plug of a man, Harrison was tall and cool. He leaned back in his chair, looking more like a stoned-out jazz musician than a cop, and studied Michael with a laconic smirk. Harrison kept Michael up all night, asking the same questions McCarthy had. He had one favorite sadistic twist on the whole interrogation routine. Whenever Michael's eyes started to flutter, Harrison would suddenly lean forward, pound his fist on the table, and then laugh maniacally as Michael struggled to wake up.

Apparently the strategy was to wear him down through sleep deprivation and endless questioning. They couldn't, or wouldn't, believe that he was who he said he was, just an ordinary guy who'd been laid off and was bored and who, because of a professional interest in cloud formations, had come to the airport with his camera two days in a row to take pictures. And they sure as hell couldn't believe—as McCarthy said when he came back Friday morning rested, showered, and ready to break Michael's resistance—that only one day after Michael had been slammed up against his car with explicit instructions to stay away from Newark Airport, he'd chosen to show up again. This time parked illegally in a no-standing zone, no less, with a cockamamie story about having gone up to Boston, without luggage, to pick up a father-in-law, who was nowhere in evidence.

Already, the effects of being held in an airless room, under a single incandescent bulb, without sleep, were beginning to make Michael feel severely jet-lagged. He felt his eyelids fighting gravity, his brain growing fuzzy, his judgment faltering. Time had become a wobbly miasma of semiconsciousness. Only the scant morning light from the tiny window indicated that it was indeed day when Harrison left and McCarthy returned. He'd begun to dread the indignity of the Coke bottle, and the very thought of having to submit to it one more time made him abnormally conscious of his bladder. And through all this discomfort and bleariness, he wondered what Nina must be thinking, and the hell he was going to catch when he got home.

But McCarthy didn't show any inclination toward letting Michael go home. If anything, he was growing more sadistic by the hour. He was shouting more, and from closer range. When he spoke without shouting, it was through gritted teeth, and six inches from Michael's face. And, most ominously, he was starting to hint at physical violence. He snapped pencils, tapped his fingers impatiently against his holster, and—in a fit of rage—slammed a pitcher of water across the table onto the floor.

"See what you did?" he hissed, as if Michael had been the one who'd lost his temper and knocked over the pitcher.

Michael looked down at his hands, hoping to evade trouble the way he had since childhood, by trying to become invisible. But McCarthy wasn't letting him be invisible.

"Down on your hands and knees!" McCarthy shouted. "Clean it up."

"How?" Michael asked.

"I said *down*." In a sudden, unexpected gesture, McCarthy knocked Michael to the floor. Then he flicked a few paper napkins onto the floor.

Panting, Michael thought he felt his knee bleeding, but maybe it was just the water. He stared at the napkins, already waterlogged, inadequate to the flood McCarthy had made, and was reminded of the school cafeteria bullies of child-hood.

"*Don't. Make. Me. Ask. Twice,*" McCarthy barked.

Michael felt the hard nose of the gun against his back. He put his head down, picked up a soggy napkin, and swabbed.

Despite evidence to the contrary, notably the absence of the Prius in the driveway, Nina allowed herself a shred of hope when she got home. Her heart fluttered at the slight possibility that Michael had just arrived, somehow. Maybe the car had broken down and someone had given him a ride. Maybe he'd just walked in seconds earlier, and that's why nobody had called to let her know.

But no, Michael was not home. She was still sleepwalking in the same nightmare she'd woken to that morning. Yet the rest of her family seemed oblivious. Adam was on the Internet, and Max and Belle were glued to the Weather Channel.

Nina unloaded the provisions she'd picked up during the A&P pre-hurricane stampede: bottled water, flashlights, toilet paper. She'd tried to concentrate on the weather forecasts on her drive home, but found her mind blanking out whenever they came on. She caught a phrase here and there. "Heavy rains" . . . "after midnight" . . . "near miss." Near miss? Was there going to be a hurricane or not? So far, to her eye at least, the weather didn't seem too ominous. It was overcast, yes, and there'd been evidence of some sprinkles during the afternoon, but nothing that seemed to justify the apocalyptic lines at the A&P.

Nina quietly went upstairs and closed the bedroom door, against the unlikely possibility that either her parents or her son might leave their command posts. She reached into a little paper gift bag and pulled out an almost weightless package wrapped in aubergine tissue paper. Inside were the crystals Coriander had told her to place under the marital bed—a feng shui cure for a wandering husband. Sheepishly, Nina tossed them onto the floor under the box spring, as she'd been instructed, making a mental note to warn the housekeepers before they came to clean.

She picked up the phone and checked her messages. Still nothing from Michael.

Earlier, Nina had splurged on a pumpkin spice latte at the Starbucks, choosing to overlook the thousands of empty calories it contained. It was all well and good to drink plain spring water and munch on raw carrots when times were good, but there was nothing like sugar to get you through a crisis. She'd leaned across the table and whispered her whole story to Coriander, confessing even the trip to Chinatown to buy the bagua mirror, and at the end she felt not only purged but also strangely calm. When Nina finished, Coriander had reached over and placed her hand on Nina's. It was the exact right gesture, communicating everything Nina needed at that moment: *I heard you. You're in pain. Help is coming.* Not once, Nina realized, had her mother ever comforted her like that.

Coriander advised Nina not to call the police. Not yet. Michael was a grown man, capable of taking care of himself, and it sounded to Coriander as if his ego had been wounded by his loss of work and Nina's insistence that he stay out of the house all week. The call from the "other woman"—this Xenon character—only made Coriander more sure. But Michael and Nina had been married eighteen years, and that weighed heavier in the scheme of things than one lousy week. Besides, Coriander said, she still detected a lovely gold and lavender aura around Nina's heart. Michael was coming back. Coriander was almost certain. In the meantime, Nina could hasten his return with a little active feng shui.

Still, despite the fact that this was coming from Coriander, Nina felt a little silly about the crystals—silly and somewhat pathetic. She sat on her knees for a little while, looking at them, lost among the dust bunnies, and wondered how in the world such magic worked. She liked the idea, symbolically, but it did seem a little hocus-pocus. When she stood up, she reached under Michael's pillow and took out the T-shirt he usually slept in. She lifted it to her face, buried her nose in it and inhaled deeply, folded the T-shirt tenderly and put it back.

And then, despite Coriander's advice, she reached into her night table and found the slip of paper on which she'd written down the nonemergency number for the police.

Coriander was probably right, Nina thought. Michael would come back. An eighteen-year marriage wasn't something you discarded like a used tissue. And there were the crystals. . . .

She picked up the phone.

She didn't like going against Coriander's advice. But waiting wasn't her strong suit. She pictured her husband tied up in the trunk of a car, his mouth duct-taped, his hands cuffed behind his back, and wondered how long the oxygen would last. Or was it already too late?

Heart racing, her hands shaking, Nina punched in the phone number. "Hello," she began. "My husband's been missing for twenty-four hours—"

Michael was beginning to feel as if he'd always been a prisoner and always would be. No matter what he said, McCarthy wouldn't believe him. He wasn't granted a phone call, and McCarthy just laughed at his requests for a lawyer. Nobody knew where he was, or had any way of finding him. It was like Guantanamo or Abu Ghraib—the humiliation without provocation, being cut off from the world. He knew that when he got out—*if* he got out—he'd take the story to the press. Like everyone else, he'd lived through the horror of 9/11 and knew what a serious business terrorism was, especially at airports. But there were a couple dozen guys just yards away in the control tower who could vouch for him. And it seemed like it should be obvious that there was nobody more mild-mannered, and less likely to cause an international incident, than himself.

The idea that this had all started because he liked to look at clouds—cumulonimbus clouds that had, on Wednesday, floated like bloated marshmallows across an innocent sky—seemed preposterous. And that was when he realized that he hadn't even thought of the weather since he'd been hand-cuffed and taken to this dreary room, where angry men got angrier at him by the minute.

Outside the window, the sky was oppressively gray and growing darker, matching Michael's mood. In fact, he could barely make out the outlines of the control tower. They were in for some heavy rain. Michael tried to remember if he'd re-membered to take in the grill, as Nina had asked.

Nina, driving up the big hill to the rabbi's house, was noting the clouds as well. The sky, which had started off that morning as light and innocent as a nursery mural, had turned the color of oysters by the time she'd gone with Coriander to Starbucks, and was now brackish, menacing. Kansas, Nina thought. Right when Dorothy runs away and meets the fortune-teller. But that was a tornado, she reminded herself, and they were predicting a hurricane, a different thing altogether. Hurricanes give plenty of warning. If there turned out to be one at all.

Nina still couldn't understand why they were heading out for a Shabbat dinner. It seemed ridiculous under any circum-stances, but now—with Michael missing and a storm coming on? She'd allowed herself to be bullied by her parents, who were so excited by Adam's potential return to the fold, you might have thought he'd spotted a burning bush.

Belle, sitting in the passenger seat next to her, stared out the window, frowning.

"Do you think it's okay we're out? With the storm coming?"

Nina had wondered why her normally fretful parents weren't hiding in the basement, or flying off to another city for safety. But they'd been watching the Weather Channel all day, and had assured her over and over that the storm wasn't supposed to hit the New York area until after midnight. Of course, she'd much rather be home, hoping and waiting for Michael, but Adam had set the house phone up to forward to her cell, and set it to vibrate so it wouldn't ring and offend the nuts they were visiting. And of course, Nina had left a note on the kitchen table, in case Michael did return home, with a full explanation of what they were doing and MapQuest directions.

"A little late to think of that now, isn't it?" Nina snapped.

She reached for the radio, hoping for a weather forecast, but found herself instead in the middle of an NPR story about a Palestinian barber who'd lost his right arm in an unprovoked attack by the Israeli army. Since then, he'd been unable to cut hair. Religion, Nina thought sullenly. How much suffering had been inflicted on the world in the name of religion? The Israelis and the Palestinians, the Sunnis and the Shiites, the Protestants and the Catholics. What was it that made everybody think their religion was right, and want to kill everyone who didn't agree?

"Turn it off," yelled Max from the backseat.

Nina tuned to an all-news station down the dial.

"National Palestinian Radio," Max muttered.

"I changed it."

"I don't know how Susan Stamberg can live with herself."

"Chill," Nina said. "I'm just trying to hear the weather."

Belle sniffed. "We'd know about the weather. If you-know-who was here."

You-know-who? That's what her mother was going to call Michael from now on, you-know-who? Like Voldemort in the

Harry Potter books? He who couldn't be named? Was that supposed to be subtle? Nina gunned her engine and passed a slow-moving car.

"Enough," said Max. "You two behave."

There was silence, a truce, for the next couple of minutes. Then Belle reached into her pocketbook and pulled something out.

"No! Not perfume!" Nina shrieked. The last time Nina had been in a car with her mother, Belle had "spritzed" herself, and the car had stunk of disintegrating flowers, rotting fruit, and Bloomingdale's for the next week. Now, with the Prius gone, Nina was stuck with the Honda. "You know I'm fragrance sensitive."

"Don't pee yourself," Belle said. "I was just getting out some gum." She held out a stick to Nina.

The peace pipe of Jewish women, Nina thought, accepting it.

Adam slunk down in the backseat, trying to keep out of the line of fire. He felt, strangely, like the only adult in the car. His mother and his grandparents were acting like small children bickering on a long car ride. And this was just a ten-minute drive. How would he get them to behave when they got to Rabbi Mendel's?

He'd spent some time on the Internet after school, looking up the customs of observant Jews. There were all kinds of rules, not just no milk together with meat. You couldn't answer phones on Shabbat, or turn lights on or off. You couldn't write. He'd even read that some religious Jews tore their toilet paper ahead of time to avoid the labor of tearing it on the Sabbath.

He might as well be asking his mother to eat ground glass.

Maybe he'd miscalculated. What if the rabbi had some kind of supermystical rabbi powers and could see Adam for the money-grubbing fraud he was. What if Adam forgot and turned off the bathroom light? Or if his mom did? Would the rabbi's family and guests have to go to the bathroom in the dark until the next morning?

"Look, guys," he said. "There's a couple of rules you should know about before we get there."

"He's a Jew for fifteen minutes and he's already an expert," Belle snorted.

"I'm not an *expert*. But I did go on the Internet after school."

"Go ahead," said Max. "Tell us."

"First of all, they're *shomar shabbas*. Which means you can't turn lights on or off or answer the phone or anything like that."

"Duh," said Nina.

"And it's not just like we sit down and eat and then we're out of there in half an hour. There's all sorts of praying and singing. They call it *benching*, I don't know why. And there's special hand-washing rituals and stuff like that. And, I'm not sure, but they might have pieces of toilet paper already torn so you don't have to do the work of tearing it on Shabbat, and I'm not sure if you're allowed to flush the toilet after the sun sets."

Nina sighed and rolled her eyes.

"Of course," Belle turned toward Nina, "if you'd joined a normal synagogue, instead of a church, we wouldn't have to be going to dinner with religious fanatics the minute your son got interested in Judaism."

"Belle!" Max said.

"Define normal," Nina replied calmly. "A place where you have to pay three hundred dollars a ticket to show up for the High Holidays?"

Michael could feel the stubble on his jaw, and he knew how bad his mouth smelled after hours without brushing his teeth. He'd had nothing to eat, although he had been given a couple of cups of coffee. It was just one indignity after another, starting with the moment he'd received his pink slip. He'd been kicked out of his office, his airport, his house. He'd been thrown against a car, mistaken for a terrorist, handcuffed, arrested, held overnight without a phone call, a lawyer, or even a trip to the men's room. He'd been made to clean a wet floor with a paper napkin and urinate in a Coke bottle.

Michael had suffered all this with the patience of Job, but where had his patience gotten him?

Now there was a knock at the door, and a uniformed security guard came in with a bag from McDonald's, tossing it on the table.

"For the prisoner," he said.

Prisoner, Michael thought. Not suspect. Not "person of interest." *Prisoner.*

McCarthy slid the bag across the table at Michael, who stared down at it with a mixture of hunger and repulsion. He folded his arms tightly and clenched his teeth.

"I don't eat meat."

"Well, maybe our friend got you some french fries," McCarthy snarled.

"And I don't eat anything cooked in trans-fats, either."

"So the prisoner's pulling a hunger strike?"

Maybe, Michael thought, that would be a good idea. He looked out the window and noticed that the clouds had gotten even darker.

The house corresponding to Nina's MapQuest directions was an utterly unremarkable brick ranch with colorful chalk drawings on the sidewalk and a basketball hoop in the driveway. The only sign that a rabbi might live there was a small brass mezuzah to the side of the front door. Adam hesitated ringing the bell, but it didn't matter. They'd been seen coming. A little girl, holding a Barbie doll, slowly opened the door and led them into a living room already filled with other guests.

The girl knelt down on the floor to play with a big pile of Barbies—all of them dressed immodestly and some of them naked and headless, Nina noticed—while two boys a little older, wearing yarmulkes, sat on the floor playing *Battleship*. There was no rabbi in sight, no *rebbetzin*, no crackers or wine on the coffee table, although some intriguing smells emanated from the kitchen. Too bad, Nina thought, they didn't allow dinner guests to bring a little nosh.

Adam hovered wordlessly over the boys, waiting to be acknowledged, and Belle and Max stood shyly to the side. In the absence of any host, Nina did what she had to. She hadn't known there would be other guests. But as long as there were, she smiled, reached her hand out, and introduced herself. Even as she brooded inwardly about her missing husband.

A brunette named Fran, with long pale blue fingernails and stiletto heels, turned out to be the *rebbetzin*'s manicurist. A black woman named Pearl had a son in California who'd just become engaged to a Jewish girl; Pearl wanted to learn more about the Jewish faith. A man wearing an Israeli army uniform, whose unibrow was knitted into a fierce scowl, identified himself as Ari but didn't elaborate. Others offered names, hands, "good Shabbas" greetings. Nina softened slightly. Maybe it wouldn't be so terrible.

She excused herself to go to the bathroom, thinking it might be safer to go before sunset, when she was sure she could still tear off toilet paper and flush the toilet. She found it down the hall, pink-tiled in a 1960s fashion, a messy room with mismatched towels, overflowing packages of toiletries, and, Nina noticed with relief, a night-light with an automatic sensor. So that was how they dealt with the electricity problem after sunset.

Nina took out her cell phone. Good, she had a signal. Under

normal circumstances—if there were normal circumstances for attending Shabbat dinner at a Chabad rabbi's house—she wouldn't have brought it at all. But with Michael possibly in a ditch somewhere, bleeding, unconscious, she couldn't take the chance. And besides, the cops might call.

When she returned to the living room, it felt like a different place. A man wearing a long silk coat and a fur-trimmed hat commanded the center of the room, greeting all his guests and laughing heartily. He wasn't tall, but he seemed tall. Maybe it was an optical illusion because of the hat. Everybody suddenly seemed relaxed, as if they'd all been holding their breath for hours and had just been given permission to exhale. The rabbi's sons had put away their game, other children had emerged from bedrooms, and they were now all talking to Adam. Max and the Israeli soldier were arguing, amiably, about American policy in the Middle East, and Belle had an arm around Pearl and was explaining to her all about Reform Jews. It was as if a magic wand had been waved, turning a funeral parlor into a circus. Or at least a friendly dinner party. Despite his beard and his odd dress, the rabbi seemed modern, even handsome, Nina thought, a bear of a man with hairy hands, and twinkling eyes peering out from under bushy eyebrows. Beards, she suddenly realized, could be sexy.

"So you're the one who's raised little Lance Armstrong here," the man said to Nina, knowing her immediately as Adam's mother. "I'm Rabbi Mendel. And I've already met your parents, who seem to bring hurricanes wherever they go."

Nina chuckled, politely, and stretched out her hand. "Nice to meet you, too."

Her hand sliced the air, ready to join a stranger's hand in a brief pulse of greeting. But there was nothing waiting for her. The rabbi, like a recalcitrant trapeze partner, had tucked his hands behind his back. Was it a joke, like those trick birthday candles?

"Sorry," he said. "I'm just not allowed to touch a woman not my wife."

Nina's hand dropped, and blood rushed to her cheeks. She looked around the room. Did everybody else know this except her? She felt rebuffed, mortified, and quickly brushed her hand against her pants as if it had been covered with slime. "Oh," she said weakly. "I'm sorry."

"Don't worry." The rabbi chortled like a Jewish Santa Claus. "No big deal. Happens all the time. Come into the dining room, it's time for Shabbas." He gestured to the rest of the room. "Come! Shabbas!" He touched the little girl gently on the shoulder. "Come, Rifkala, time to help Mama light candles."

It didn't take Michael's full concentration to answer McCarthy's questions, which had become as banal and repetitive as 1960s television theme songs. What was capturing Michael's attention now—aside from the grumbling of his stomach, that is, and the tantalizing smell of grease from the untouched McDonald's bag—was what was happening outside. Over the past hour the sky had blackened. Then it had begun to rain. Now the wind suddenly picked up, and the rain was pelting the window noisily, insistently.

Even McCarthy had turned around to look. He scowled— as if the weather had been personally cooked up to ruin his evening. Maybe he'd left the windows down in his car, or he was going on a Boy Scout camping trip with his son. It was, if Michael still had his days straight, a Friday. Did interrogators take off for the weekend?

Michael tried to make out the outline of the control tower, thinking what his day might have been like if he hadn't been laid off the week before, what might be happening with flights trying to land in Newark. He tried to remember the last time he'd heard a weather forecast. Was it yesterday, before his trip up to Boston? He doubted it; he'd been concentrating too hard on getting the Prius away from Nina. So it must have been Wednesday. A lot could happen in a couple of days. This looked big. Probably the tail end of Hurricane Ida.

A flash of lightning suddenly illuminated the sky.

It was frustrating to be sitting here, just feet from the control tower, knowing that there could be planes in danger.

Michael composed his face into an expression of sober respect, the same face you'd show a cop who'd just pulled you over for speeding. "You know, I'm a meteorologist," he said, gesturing toward the window. "There's some weather going on. I was thinking the tower, maybe, could use my help."

The thunder, a few seconds behind the lightning, arrived like an exclamation point, and with it the sky really opened up.

McCarthy laughed. "'Some weather,'" he mimicked. "Very scientific. What's that noise we just heard? Thunder? Is that the technical term? And the wet stuff? What's that called?"

The bare lightbulb over their heads flickered, but McCarthy didn't seem to notice. Nor did he seem to notice the prodigious volume of rain that had suddenly been unleashed. He was too busy smirking at his own hilarity.

Nina's second gaffe came during the ritual hand-washing. Candles had been lit, prayers recited, and then without any apparent explanation people were standing up, pulling out chairs from the impossibly cramped tables, and snaking into the kitchen, where they waited patiently for a chance at the sink.

Nina watched the ritual from her place in line. There was a small pitcher. You filled it and splashed the water three times on your left hand, then filled it again and splashed it three times on your right.

Nina watched Adam, then her parents, each perform the

ritual flawlessly. When it came her turn, she knew exactly what to do. And yet, taking the pitcher that had been passed from hand to hand, Nina felt a revulsion at all the germs she knew remained on the handle. Nobody used any kind of soap. What kind of hand-washing left your hands dirtier than when you'd started? Nina wasn't a cleanliness freak, normally. Maybe it was just the rebel in her. Or maybe she was still mad at the rabbi, who'd acted as if her hands were covered with deadly skin-eating microbes.

All she did was pick up the dishwasher soap and squeeze a drop—one single drop—into her right hand. But suddenly the pitcher filled with glistening bubbles, and the people still in line gasped as if she'd taken the tablets from Sinai and smashed them on the ground.

"What's the big deal?" Nina said. "It's just *soap.*"

"Ssshhhh," a voice whispered sternly. "There's no talking until we've all sat down."

Nina felt her face heat up. If there was anything she hated, it was being admonished. And here, during the biggest crisis in her life, she was wasting her time with pointless ritual. Angrily, she rinsed the soap off her hands the best she could, ignoring the pitcher, then reached for a dish towel to dry up. "This is bullshit," she muttered under her breath as she returned to the table.

Just as Nina pulled out her seat, a bolt of lightning illuminated the sky. A thunderclap of biblical proportions followed seconds later, and with it, the swollen clouds began unburdening themselves. Everybody at the table looked at Nina, as if she were personally responsible for God's apparent fury. Everybody, that is, except for Adam, Max, and Belle, who were all looking down at their silverware and trying to pretend they didn't know the crazy woman sitting next to them.

"What's the matter?" Nina said. "Nobody's ever seen rain before?"

Adam felt a buzzing in his ears, which he recognized as the physical manifestation of extreme embarrassment. One of the rabbi's elder daughters, an ethereal creature named Esther who looked like she belonged in a fairy-tale castle, looked at him with concern. Pity. Adam imagined her pitying him for his mother, who must have seemed, to her, like a monster. It wasn't just the mistakes his mother had made—anybody could make mistakes when it came to rituals they weren't familiar with—it was her barely disguised rage. And her profanity, especially on Shabbat.

At least, Adam thought with relief, she hadn't yet said the F-word.

Rabbi Mendel, continuing the singsong service, shot Adam a weak smile from the head of the table, but Adam knew it was over. Just looking at Esther he knew it. There was nothing here for him, nothing here that promised an inkling of whatever he had found last week at Lisa Epstein's magnificent, outrageous, and (he understood now) ultimately profane bat mitzvah. The Judaism he'd witnessed last weekend and the Judaism he was seeing right now at this table were as different as ham and brisket, as different as Lisa Epstein and Esther Abraham. And the truth was, he didn't belong with either.

Lightning flashed, and thunder crashed again, like God was playing laser bowling right outside the Abrahams' dining room. The rabbi and his family sang louder, as if the weather were just a little friendly competition from a neighboring band of Chasids. Then the chandelier over the table flickered twice and the lights went out and there was only a soft glow coming from the Shabbat candles in the middle of the table, candles—Adam noticed—that had only about an inch of wax left.

Now there was a real commotion, and Adam wasn't surprised that his grandparents were making most of the noise. "Where's a flashlight?" he heard Belle say. "Or extra candles?"

One of the rabbi's children explained that they were not allowed to turn on a flashlight or light a candle after Shabbat had started.

"But it's an emergency!" Max protested. "It's a power failure!"

"If you're too religious to turn on a flashlight, I'll do it," Belle offered.

"Nobody will turn on a flashlight," the rabbi said.

"This is meshuggah," Max blustered. "What if . . . what if . . ."

"What if what?" said Rabbi Mendel. "We're sitting here, together with family and friends. There's plenty to eat. The rain is outside. God in his mercy has put a roof over our heads and wine in our glasses. And the lightning is even providing illumination for us to see."

"What if the hurricane's come early! We should turn on the TV."

"We can't turn on the TV," Adam said quietly. "There's no electricity."

"At least the radio! They must have a transistor radio."

"God will protect us," the rabbi said. "Just as he did our forefathers. Let's return to our prayers."

"Bullshit," Nina said. "Can't you see my parents are scared to death? I can't shake your hand. I can't use soap when I wash up. And now, the lights go off and we can't even turn on a fucking flashlight?"

There, Adam thought. *She said it.*

"Adam." Nina rose, her irritation clearly having galvanized into a mission. She was the mighty foe of superstition and backwardness, of rabbinical authority and outdated ritual, and now she was ready to let her people go—straight out of the rabbi's dining room. "Mom, Dad. Let's get out of here."

There was barely any time for McCarthy to enjoy his own merriment when the lightning flashed again, followed by an almost instantaneous boom. God, Michael thought, this storm was moving fast. He wished he'd counted the seconds between the last flash and its accompanying thunderclap so he'd know how far and fast the storm had traveled. If only he had some instruments, a barometer, a computer, some radar.

With the next crack, the light above Michael's head flickered again. And then, like a miracle, it went out.

Michael had just a second to decide.

He knew there were backup generators at the airport. There was no way a major U.S. transportation hub could stay pitched in darkness for more than a minute or two. Lightning flashed again, briefly illuminating the outline of the control tower in the distance, and Michael could see the lights were out there, too. Once again, he winced at the thought of planes trying to land in this mess.

But he had more urgent things to think about.

Michael had never been anything but an obedient child and a law-obeying model citizen. Every molecule in his body, every lesson of his upbringing, every ounce of his personality was telling him to sit perfectly still, to be a model prisoner, to wait patiently for the system to release him.

Then he heard the sound of something hard crash to the floor. McCarthy's gun! It had been sitting on the table. When the lights went out, McCarthy must have reached for it, and accidentally knocked it down.

It wasn't much of an opening, but Michael took it. He jumped up and ran toward the door, making sure to swipe the crouching cop as he made his escape. It wasn't much, nothing more than a nudge really, but it did the trick. Michael heard McCarthy's head bump against the metal table, followed by an angry "Son of a bitch!"

But by then he was already out the door and racing down the corridor.

———

Nina couldn't wait to leave the shtetl, couldn't wait to breathe the fresh air of religious freedom, but when she pulled the front door open to make her exit, water exploded in like the ocean through a porthole. It wasn't a rainstorm, it was an onslaught, it was all the water that had ever been created in the history of the world; and it wasn't wind, it was the anger of a vengeful God, the thrust of a space shuttle breaking free of earth's gravity.

Nina walked straight out into it, as sure as Moses stepping into the Red Sea.

In half a second, she was completely drenched. Her blouse, her bra, her shoes, her hair, everything. "Jesus!" she screamed, turning around to check on her parents and Adam. She was stunned to discover they were still inside.

They stood there, a safe distance inside the rabbi's living room, and stared at her as if she'd just volunteered to be shot out of a cannon.

She gestured wildly for them to hurry. They continued staring.

So she would do this alone.

Nina ran to the Honda, fumbled for her keys, got in, and laid the cell phone on the seat next to her, where she could lay her hands on it in a hurry. Shivering, she turned on the ignition, the lights, the heat, and the windshield wipers. The wipers were a joke; they slashed at the onslaught like disposable chopsticks. It was ridiculous to try to drive anywhere, suicidal even. But then Nina imagined them all inside the house, the rabbi and his whole brood, staring at her and judging. Out of habit, she checked the rearview mirror, but there was nothing to see but night and rain. Well, she thought, screeching into reverse with zero visibility, nobody else would be out on the roads. At least she couldn't kill anybody else.

There was only one thing on her mind, one goal, and that was Newark Airport. The last place anybody had seen Michael.

It was terrifying running into the dark hallway, and Michael just kept praying that he wouldn't smash into a wall. Then suddenly, he was in a wide open space. A concourse. It sounded like a disaster movie: a cacophony of screaming children, panicking passengers, and airline functionaries all struggling to be heard above the raging storm. The chaos worked to his advantage, but he knew he wouldn't have that advantage for long. The lights would come back any second, and McCarthy would be on top of him.

He had only one move, and that was to make a call. That's what had been missing in all the hours of interrogation: the knowledge that somebody in the outside world was working the system to get him out.

But of course they'd taken away his cell phone. He had to grab the first one he could find.

Michael had seen plenty of TV shows and movies where undercover cops, racing on foot down city streets, had to commandeer someone's car in order to catch a bad guy. Of course, it helped, in the movies, when the person doing the commandeering had a gun. All Michael had was the cover of darkness and the commotion. But then he didn't have to kick someone out from behind a steering wheel. He just had to snatch two inches of metal from the first available person. And he saw cell phones everywhere, their illuminated keypads the only thing visible in the darkness.

The closest one belonged to a kid. A boy, it looked like, smaller even than Adam.

Michael hesitated. It was such a brutish thing to do, like taking candy from a baby. It was a mugging, basically, and it could screw up the kid for years—give him phobias about power blackouts, airports, maybe even talking on the phone. He couldn't help but imagine Adam at that age, traumatized by some idiot running through an airport during a power blackout and snatching his cell phone. What kind of man would do that to a ten-year-old?

A man who'd been peeing into a Coke bottle for the past twenty-four hours. Michael grabbed the phone, punching in the number even as he ran.

He heard it ring once, twice, three times. The space between each ring felt like an eternity.

It hadn't even occurred to Michael that she might not answer. He needed her, needed her more than he'd ever needed anyone in his entire life. Of course she would answer. But what if she was in the bathroom? Or in the middle of an argument with Belle? Or mad? He'd stranded both her parents, after all. And lied about the Honda. And now he didn't even have a job. What a screwup! She had every right to be mad!

And then, as suddenly as they'd gone out, the lights in the airport blinked back on.

There was a collective sigh from the crowd, relief that the forces of civilization and order had successfully overcome those of nature. The airport was back in business! They were safe! And that's when Michael, running, panting, his face contorted by sweat and desperation, realized that he stood out like the fugitive he was.

On the fourth ring, Michael heard a scared, frail voice coming from what sounded like a wind tunnel. "Hello?"

"Nina!" Michael shouted. "It's me, Michael."

"Michael!" The wail that came out of the phone was more animal than human. He could picture Nina's shoulders shaking, the snot pouring from her nose, and with effort, he was able to pick the words out from the sobs. "I . . . thought . . . you . . . were . . . dead."

Michael spotted the navy Windbreaker first, and then the gun.

Nina didn't get like this often. Maybe once or twice every ten years. But when she did, when something cracked the steel of her personality, the storm usually went on for a while. Twenty minutes, half an hour. Time Michael didn't have.

He had to be forceful. To break through the hysteria. To get through to his wife. Later, there would be time for tears, for consolation, for apologies. Now, there were only seconds, and each one counted.

Michael mustered all the authority he could. He wasn't used to raising his voice to Nina. He wasn't used to raising his voice to anybody. But there was an angry man running toward him, pointing a .45. He had one chance.

"Nina!" Michael shouted. "I'm at Newark Airport and they think I'm a terrorist."

And then McCarthy tackled him.

EIGHTEEN

Spring

There had been no way to get Michael out of serving time, but his lawyer had been brilliant, and the four-month sentence was mercifully short. At least the lawyer seemed to think he'd been brilliant and that the sentence was mercifully short; he often said so. It could have been ten years, he reminded Nina, handing her a bill for twenty-two thousand dollars. True, Michael was no terrorist. But you couldn't sneeze at charges of escaping custody and assaulting a federal officer, let alone petty larceny and assault on a juvenile.

She'd covered the legal bill (and the ten-thousand-dollar settlement with Charlotte Hendricks) the way anybody covered a large and unexpected bill in the affluent suburbs. She'd taken out a home equity line of credit. Nina's earth luck and mankind luck may have been crappy, but certain things—like rising house values and lower interest rates—were still in her favor. Luckily, their congressman had pulled strings and managed to get Michael into a low-security prison in Allenwood, Pennsylvania. It was still prison, but he could take long walks, and they even had a meditation and yoga group.

There was help from the predictable sources. The left-leaning Unitarians, livid about the way Michael had been bullied by Homeland Security, had organized two months' worth of covered-dish suppers delivered to their home. Too bad so many people never got the message that the Gettleman-Summer family didn't eat meat. And there was help from unpredictable sources, too. Envelopes filled with big wads of cash started showing up mysteriously, shoved through the space under the front door that they'd never, ironically, gotten around to weather-stripping. It was Philip who figured out that the money was coming from Lisa Epstein, or her parents, at any rate, when he noticed a girl in a plaid skirt running down Adam's sidewalk one day. And after the first night it snowed, Nina woke in the morning to find her sidewalk neatly shoveled and her driveway cleared. Michael's poker buddies took turns clearing snow, unclogging toilets, and doing the other manly tasks that cropped up in Michael's absence.

Adam never trekked up the hill to see the Chabad rabbi again. Eventually, the fantasy of having a bar mitzvah had evaporated, along with fantasies of buying a Segway scooter and the butterfly dreams with Lisa Epstein. He did, however, become a man—stepping in to take care of his mother in unexpected ways. Taking out the trash without being asked, for example, and waking up ten minutes early to make coffee before he left for school, so it would be brewing in the kitchen when Nina woke up. Even more beneficial, however, was how well he handled his grandparents when they called.

Adam had, for example, fielded Belle's call back in February when she invited them to fly down for Passover—"Come! You'll go to the beach! We'll pay for tickets!"—by adroitly offering their apologies while mustering up an imaginary chess tournament that prevented their travel. He wouldn't have minded a trip to Florida, but he knew that it would be hell for his mother.

There was a special trip they had planned for the spring, though it didn't have anything to do with Passover, or Easter. Adam and Nina were planning to visit Michael on the vernal equinox. The first day of spring, when the earth stood straight on its axis and day and night were equal. It had been Michael's favorite day of the year as a boy—he'd loved the ritual of balancing an egg on its end—and Adam and Nina were hoping to be able to bring an egg for him to balance. Yes, it was all hopelessly sentimental, and the whole egg-balancing thing had long been debunked as a wives' tale, and bringing any food into Allenwood was explicitly against the rules. But just as some things had come to lose their importance over the months, others had gained significance. Balancing an egg was one of them. .

Michael, in a strange way, was thriving in the estrogen-free atmosphere of the prison. Nobody complained when his clothes stank with secondhand smoke after a poker game. In fact, his proclivity for assessing probabilities was working well for him in prison poker, and the fact he always won a commodity he didn't need—cigarettes—made him the richest man in Allenwood. But in the end, it wasn't his mathematical ability that had turned him into an excellent poker player. It was the way he'd broken free from McCarthy. After all, once you'd body-slammed a Homeland Security officer bending down to retrieve his gun, taking half a pack of Camels off Louie the Fish with just a pair of sixes was child's play.

Nina was holding it together as a temporarily single mom, and her yoga classes were fully subscribed. But all the great ideas of the fall had withered away. She gave up feng shui after the crystals under her bed ruined a practically new Oreck vacuum cleaner. (She'd forgotten to tell the cleaning ladies.) Feng shui, she ultimately decided, was just another collection of superstitions. She couldn't remember why she'd allowed herself to obsess over the white cloths she should use to purify her studio. She disposed of all her feng shui cures, donating her bagua mirror and feng shui books to a rummage sale at the Unitarian Church.

It was there that she accidentally came upon her newest passion in the form of someone's discarded bongo drum. She bought it with Adam in mind, but a few weeks later, she noticed an item in the church newsletter for a monthly Sunday-night drumming circle and went herself. Though self-conscious at first, Nina ultimately lost herself in the steady timbre of palms pounding against stretched skins. When she closed her eyes, she could imagine herself transported to a primordial jungle. There was magic in this. Or no—something even better than magic. A genuine mind/body/spirit connection.

Too bad, though, it was mostly men. After a few months, Nina did some research on the Internet and decided what their community really needed was a women's drumming circle. Now she was looking for a place where she and her same-gendered co-rhythmists could usher in each new moon. The Unitarian Church was available, of course, but Nina was looking for some place more cosmic, less prosaic. This wasn't, after all, some humdrum potluck dinner. This was the very heartbeat of the universe.

F
GAL

Galant, Debra.

Fear and yoga in New
Jersey.

MAR 0 8

$23.95

DATE			